the *Locket*

STACEY JAY

The Locket

RAZORBILL

Published by the Penguin Group
Penguin Young Readers Group
345 Hudson Street, New York, New York 10014, U.S.A.
Penguin Group (USA) Inc., 375 Hudson Street, New York, New York 10014, U.S.A.
Penguin Group (Canada), 90 Eglinton Avenue East, Suite 700, Toronto, Ontario,
Canada M4P 2Y3 (a division of Pearson Penguin Canada Inc.)
Penguin Books Ltd, 80 Strand, London WC2R 0RL, England
Penguin Ireland, 25 St Stephen's Green, Dublin 2, Ireland (a division of Penguin
Books Ltd)
Penguin Group (Australia), 250 Camberwell Road, Camberwell, Victoria 3124,
Australia (a division of Pearson Australia Group Pty Ltd)
Penguin Books India Pvt Ltd, 11 Community Centre, Panchsheel Park,
New Delhi –110 017, India
Penguin Group (NZ), 67 Apollo Drive, Mairangi Bay, Auckland 1311, New Zealand
(a division of Pearson New Zealand Ltd)
Penguin Books (South Africa) (Pty) Ltd, 24 Sturdee Avenue, Rosebank, Johannesburg
2196, South Africa

Penguin Books Ltd, Registered Offices: 80 Strand, London WC2R 0RL, England

10 9 8 7 6 5 4 3 2 1

ISBN: 978-1-59514-335-8

Library of Congress Cataloging-in-Publication Data is available

Printed in the United States of America

To the resilient people of Nashville.

Prologue

It was raining so hard I could barely see my hands as I wrapped my fingers around the tree house step and started to climb. Even the shelter of the leaves still clinging to the branches didn't offer much relief from the downpour. I was climbing blind, the lack of visual cues making the swaying of the massive trunk and the groans lurching from deep inside the tree even more disturbing.

It was a horrible storm, worse than it had been the first time around. Freezing wind whipped through the valley behind my house, cutting through the tightly woven fabric of my fleece v-neck, plastering it to my skin with another layer of cold and wet.

But still I climbed, shouting his name as I went. I had no choice but to go to him. He hadn't heard me the first or second or *third* time I'd called from the ground.

Or maybe he was just ignoring me.

"I'm coming up!" I screamed again, the act of forcing my stiff lips to form words helping keep my mind off the fact that I was six . . . seven . . . ten . . . *twelve* feet in the air. I shivered, fingers clawing into the damp wood, fear of heights throbbing through my body in new and powerful ways.

I could feel the empty space behind me growling, a hungry void that wanted my slick hands to slip, wanted to watch me fall and gobble up my fear as I dropped. I licked my lips, tasting salt and sticky, and thought for a second I must have bitten myself.

Cramped fingers dared a brush up and down my face, swiping away water and something hotter that rolled down into my mouth. The blood was coming from my nose, from the place where the locket's chain had scraped away my skin.

The locket . . . . It had drawn blood.

Bringing both hands to cling onto the ladder once more, I turned and brushed my face against my shoulder, leaving a spot of black on the gray fabric.

"Go away," he yelled above me, his voice slurred and thick.

"I'm not going away. You shouldn't be drinking up here," I said, shouting to be heard over a sudden gust of wind. The tree rocked back and forth, moaning, while my pulse raced and my hands gripped the ladder step so tightly my knuckles snapped and cracked.

For the first time since that night in Isaac's truck, I felt the obscene weight of holding the future in my own hands. I had to get us both out of this tree before something bad happened, before someone was seriously hurt, before anything else was lost or broken . . . .

Chapter One

Lavender and rotted peaches and old-lady face cream. *Ugh.* The smell was enough to make me cringe even if it hadn't been underscored by VapoRub and the fruit-flavored Tums Gran ate like candy. My bathroom had been hijacked, right when I needed sanctuary more than ever.

Since the day my family moved into my great-grandmother's old house, my big room with the window seat and private bath had been my safe place. It was where I felt peaceful, in control, no matter what was going on in the outside world.

Unfortunately, my sanctuary had been violated by Gran's arrival for her first visit in years. She was sleeping in the guest room, but sharing my bath. The counter was covered in pillboxes, the vanity buried in jewelry and face cream, and the entire room reeked of sweet and flowery old person.

I loved Gran to death, but really . . . her nose must have ceased to function or there was no way she'd be able to live with her own odor.

As I rushed through drying my hair and brushed blush on my cheeks, I wondered if the scent would linger on my clothes. Would Isaac smell it and think I'd used that body spray he hated? The one my mom had given me for my sweet sixteen that Rachel Pruitt had said made her nauseous and Isaac had made me promise never to wear again?

My forehead bunched, making the penciling in of my light red brows more challenging than usual. More than anything, I wanted this night to be perfect. I *needed* it to be perfect. It had only been two weeks, but it felt like I'd been living with this horrible ache in my chest for years. I couldn't remember what it felt like to be at home in my own skin.

Even before my screwup, there were times when I'd felt out of place. In the lunchroom, at parties, even just hanging out at Ramon's or Jukebox Java after school, I was just . . . awkward with Isaac's crowd, the girl who never said the right thing, who never knew when to laugh or toss her hair. Despite the fact that I'd been dating the star of the basketball team my entire dateable life, I'd never fit in with the perfect people. I was pretty, but not *that* pretty, smart, but not *that* smart, and I didn't possess a single athletic bone in my body, so volleyball or cheerleading—the approved platinum sports—were out of the question.

I wasn't even a good drama geek. The closest I'd come to landing a starring role was being cast as first understudy in *Our Town*.

That's why *it* had happened. Because I'd felt uncomfortable, and frustrated with Isaac because of it. I had to do better. *Be* better. I had to make sure nothing like *that* happened ever again. Our anniversary had to be perfect, romantic, unforgettable.

I didn't even care that today was also my birthday. Seventeen was a weird number anyway, and celebrating three years with Isaac was what really mattered.

I'd spent the better part of the morning choosing the perfect anniversary outfit—a silver-and-black-striped tissue tee with a clingy black cotton skirt—and for once was happy with the way I looked. I felt sexy, but casual, and my pale skin actually looked dramatic rather than sickly. My red hair had cooperated and dried in smooth waves down to my shoulders and—slightly crooked eyebrows aside—my makeup had turned out better than usual. I looked as pretty as I ever did . . . but something still seemed to be missing.

I was stabbing around in my jewelry drawer, looking for my oversized hoop earrings, when I spotted the locket in the tangle of necklaces on top of the vanity. It was silver, engraved with intricate swirls and a cursive *G* on one side. It looked old. And expensive. And it was *sooo* pretty. My inner cat perked up and demanded I bat my paw at the shiny object.

I knew I shouldn't invade Gran's privacy, but I couldn't seem to help myself. I reached for the locket, flipping it over, running my fingers over the cursive-scratched silver. There, in delicate scrawl, an inscription read, *Some mistakes weren't meant to last.*

My chest tightened and a shiver ran across my skin, raising all the little blond hairs. The message was eerie, *disturbing* almost.

Lifting the locket from the pile of jewelry, I thumbed open the latch holding it closed. Inside, two faded pictures smiled at each other. The woman I recognized as a very young version of my gran, so I assumed the man with the dimple popping in his left cheek and eyes sparkling with mischief must be my grandfather. I hadn't seen many pictures of him—he'd died when I was a baby—but I'd heard Gran's stories. They'd met when they were fifteen, married when they were seventeen, and divorced a few months later under pressure from Gran's parents.

Grandpa had gone away to war soon after and they hadn't seen each other for five years, until the day they'd run into each other on the street, gone for coffee, and eloped to Nashville a few hours later, proving that—

"Some mistakes weren't meant to last." Now I understood the inscription. *Aw.* So sweet. It made me smile.

Gran and Grandpa had been together for almost forty years before he'd passed away. Their happiness proved that young love didn't always have to end. Sometimes young love became old love, *forever* love. I still believed it would be like that for Isaac and me. We were going to be together until we were old and gray.

I snapped the locket closed, my fingers wrapping around the metal. I loved the feel of it, the comforting weight and warmth. I couldn't imagine a more romantic piece of jewelry. Almost before I'd made a conscious decision, I had a delicate chain in each hand, lifting them around my neck. The clasp was smaller than most necklaces', but I finally managed to slip one link into the tiny fastener and slide it closed.

I'd only meant to try it on, but when I looked up at my

reflection, I knew the locket had to stay. It was beautiful. It pulled together my silver and black outfit, brought out the green in my eyes, and made me look older, more sophisticated. And the inscription . . . Well, that couldn't be more perfect. For the first time in weeks, the shame and guilt that had underscored my every waking moment faded to background noise. I felt confident, hopeful.

Everything was going to be all right. Isaac and I were going to have our happily ever after, just like Gran and—

The grandfather clock downstairs began its hourly melody. It was six already. Isaac would be here any minute!

I hurried through my room and down the stairs, grateful that my parents and Gran had already left for their movie. Gran was known for being super-generous, and probably wouldn't have minded me borrowing her necklace, but it was nice not to have to ask. I really didn't want to take it off.

This way, I could have the locket back in her pile before morning and no one would know I'd touched it. It would be between me, Isaac, and my new good-luck charm. My fingers smoothed along the cool silver, and a bit of that peace I'd been missing seeped through me, bringing a real smile to my face.

Isaac's perpetually muddy red truck pulled into the driveway twenty-five minutes late. It wouldn't have been a big deal—traffic being what it is on Saturday night—but there was no pleading traffic delay when you live five houses down.

Still, I decided not to make a big deal out of it. This wasn't a night to pick a fight. Besides, his lateness had given me plenty of time to double-check my hair and run through a few sprays of Febreze—ensuring I smelled like laundry freshness instead of flowers and medicine.

I watched through the narrow window by the door as he ambled up the front walk with that lazy stride he always had when he was off the court. I'd recognize that walk from a mile away. Even more than his signature jagged haircut that left strips of dark blond hair hanging down into his blue eyes, his stocky, bulldog build, or his obsession with orange shirts, that walk *was* Isaac.

I'd learned to adjust my pace to fit his when we first started holding hands in seventh grade. I imagined I'd still be doing the same when we were walking our kids in their strollers years from now.

Isaac and I had talked about kids—how many we wanted, what we might name them, whether they'd have blue eyes or green. We weren't like the rest of our friends. We didn't pretend our relationship would end after high school, or college, or . . . ever. We were in this for the long haul.

And we *really were* going to be together forever. Our lives were going to play out exactly the way we'd planned. I was sure of that now, in spite of my mistake.

The thought made electricity shoot across my skin. I was suddenly hyper-aware of the locket, feeling it seem to grow heavier, hotter, like a curling iron warming its way up to scalding. It was a disturbing sensation and—for a split second—I thought about taking it off and leaving it in the bowl of keys near the door.

But what if Gran saw it when she came home? Maybe I should just slip it into my pocket or run it back to my room or—

Isaac's footsteps sounded on the brick steps. The locket and everything else was forgotten.

"Hey!" I opened the door before he could knock, throwing my arms around his neck. I aimed a kiss at his mouth, but ended up getting his jaw instead when he turned his head at the last second.

Beneath my lips, I felt the scratch of unshaven whiskers and a tremor snaked through my newfound confidence, leaving fractures in its wake. Why hadn't he shaved? He knew whisker burn made my skin splotchy, and surely I was going to be at threat-level-orange risk of burn tonight. We hadn't been together for two and a half weeks. It was a long time, probably the longest we'd gone since we started having sex a year ago.

But I'd been too stressed out and Isaac had been too busy. Basketball practice had started, and I'd become the second love in his life until the season ended in the spring. It was the way it had always been. I was used to it by now.

Still, it was our anniversary. It was a night for being together. Surely he felt the same way?

"Hey, girl. Happy birthday." His arms closed around me, pulling me in for a tight hug. A breath I hadn't realized I'd been holding rushed from between my lips.

"Happy anniversary." I nuzzled my face into his neck and kissed him again. He smelled so good. So familiar. I breathed in his scent, not minding that he hadn't shaved anymore. He'd obviously showered. He smelled of soap and boy. *My* boy.

"Yeah. You too." He pulled away and took my hand, not looking me in the eye before he led the way back to his truck.

Hmm . . . something was definitely wrong. I wondered what was bothering him. The Bearcats hadn't played any games so far this season, so there was no way his dad could be giving him hell about basketball stuff yet. Maybe he was just tired. They'd been practicing hard this week. I'd barely seen him since Tuesday.

"You look nice," he said as he opened the passenger's door and helped me into the truck, but for some reason I felt uglier for the compliment.

As he circled around the front, I wished I'd opted for jeans with the T-shirt and locket instead of a skirt. Isaac liked me best in jeans. He always wore jeans. Tonight it was black jeans and an orange and white polo shirt. Nice, but not dressy. I looked too dressed up next to him. For a second, I thought about running in to change, but before I could ask if he'd mind waiting, Isaac had started the truck and pulled down the driveway.

It seemed like he was in a hurry.

"Are we late? Do you have reservations?"

"No. No reservations," he said, staring straight ahead as he braked at the stop sign. He turned right without another word, steering down Skylar Street, away from the highway, back toward the park and the farm country beyond.

Guess we weren't going to Nashville, which was . . . surprising. Isaac loved going into the city. He had a fake ID and they let him into all the clubs on Broadway. They let me in too, without an ID, despite the fact that I looked about twelve years old even with major makeup intervention and a padded bra. The bouncers probably would have kicked me out if I'd tried to order a beer, but I never drank anything except Coke.

Alcohol and I weren't a good mix.

An image flashed on my mental screen. The cast party. Me.

Three shots of spiced rum. Mitch. His hands at the bottom of my shirt, his mouth on my bare stomach, lips hot against my skin.

I took a deep breath and pushed the image away, but it wasn't easy. Especially considering we were passing Mitch's house on the right. It was closed up, dark and quiet. His dad had rounds every other Saturday at the children's hospital and Mitch and his band played at a lot of coffee shops and bar mitzvahs on weekends. Maybe he'd had a gig after the Belle Meade plantation fall festival where we'd both volunteered this afternoon.

Or maybe he had a date. It would be *good* if he had a date. Mitch needed to find someone. Then maybe he and I would really be able to put our mistake behind us and be friends again. We'd barely spoken at the festival, both of us strained and awkward in our historic servants' uniforms, as uncomfortable as strangers.

Just thinking about it made my stomach ache.

"Mitch hasn't been around much," Isaac observed, speeding up as we passed the Birnbaums' and headed out of the subdivision where we'd all grown up playing together. Three best friends. Even when Isaac and I had paired off, we'd all stayed friends. It was only in the past year that Isaac and Mitch had grown apart.

I shrugged, trying to look casual though the sound of Mitch's name on Isaac's lips made me want to fidget. "He must be busy with his band."

"His band sucks."

I laughed. "They do, kind of. But they have fun, and they've gotten a lot better lately."

"You've heard them play? When?"

"I caught one of their practices in his garage. Mom had me

bring over the rest of the cake she made for Dad's birthday so she and Dad wouldn't eat it all." My voice was thin and strained. I might as well take a Magic Marker and write *guilty as sin* on my forehead. I had to pull it together, steer the conversation to safer topics. "Speaking of eating, have you had dinner?"

"No. I wasn't hungry."

"Good. I'm starving. I didn't get a chance to eat at the festival. The volunteers didn't even get a snack break." I reached over to play with the hair at the nape of Isaac's neck. He'd always said my touch gave him chills—in the good way—but his muscles didn't relax beneath my fingers the way they usually did. "We could get some corn dogs at Lovelace's and take them to the park near Bellevue."

"We could." His eyes stayed on the road.

I bit my lip, torn between asking him what was wrong and trying to make the best of his bad mood. Isaac didn't like to talk about things that were bothering him. He kept quiet and worked through his feelings on his own. Mitch joked that Isaac went into his "man cave" when he was upset.

No. Not going to think about Mitch. Any. More.

I turned to look out the window, watching as we flew past the historic park and the 1800s schoolhouse we'd all been forced to tour a dozen times in elementary school, and the houses began to get farther and farther apart. Fenced yards gave way to fields and pastures lit by soft sunset light. Lovelace's, the country drive-in with the best corn dogs and thick malted shakes in the Nashville area, was still a good five miles away.

Five miles of tense, cranky-Isaac-pouting-in-his-man-cave silence.

I cracked the window, suddenly needing some air. The smell of fresh-cut hay swept inside, sharp like baked sunshine. "The old mill is still open until November. We could climb up to the roof and have a picnic."

Isaac loved picnics. It was the kind of thing he wouldn't want me telling his basketball friends, but he loved packing up my mom's old Victorian lunch box and taking it to a park. For my last birthday, he'd snuck some wine into the basket along with our ham-and-cheese sandwiches and barbecue-flavored chips. The wine was pink and sticky sweet and awful, but we'd drunk it all, giggling by the end. Then, after two years of waiting, we'd finally slept together.

It had been good, so good, and gotten even better. I loved being with Isaac, loved feeling him so close to me, knowing he was all mine for a half hour or more. I didn't want to be with anyone else, I didn't want to remember—

"Practice has been interesting this week," Isaac said.

"Yeah?" I struggled to focus. "Good interesting or bad interesting?"

"The new equipment manager is really funny." He was in non sequitur mode. Typical Isaac, especially when he was in a mood. "Hunter Needles, he's in ninth grade. You know him, right?"

"I know his big sister, Sarah. She's one of my drama friends." Well, I *supposed* she was still one of my friends. She'd slipped me a birthday card at school yesterday. It had surprised the heck out of me, and I'd stuttered through my thank-you. I hadn't remembered her birthday a few months before and felt awful.

But then, we'd grown apart in the last year too, just like Isaac

13

and Mitch. We were both so busy—her with the young artists' program at Nashville Rep, the professional theater in the city, and me with Isaac. Maybe Isaac and I needed to make more time for friends. Maybe we'd been spending too much time together. After all, we had our entire lives to be a couple; shouldn't we make some space for other people?

Do you really *want Mitch and Isaac becoming BFFs again? Really?*

No. I didn't. Not at all. "Sarah's really cool," I said, forcing a smile, struggling to put all Mitch-flavored thoughts out of my mind.

"Yeah. Hunter said she talks about you sometimes." The sentence hung in the air, heavy and threatening, an ax that could swing in my direction any second. The atmosphere in the truck crackled and pricked and in that moment, I knew . . .

He knew.

I hadn't dated the boy for three years for nothing. I knew Isaac's angry voice, I knew his *really* angry voice, and I knew how he sounded when he talked about wanting to punch his dad in the face for embarrassing him at another game, for screaming Isaac's every mistake from the stands until Mr. Tayte had to be removed by one of the refs.

When Isaac was his angriest, his voice wasn't much more than a whisper. Soft, quiet. Like now. I'd had to strain to hear him over the hum of the wheels.

My heart raced and my tongue darted out to dampen my lips as I sent up a silent prayer that for once I was reading Isaac wrong. "Sarah's sweet. She gave me a birthday card yesterday."

"Yeah, she seems sweet. Honest, too."

His words pressed in around me, crowding, shoving the truth

in my face, but I refused to admit that I'd seen it. "She is. I really like her." The locket burned on my chest, so hot I could feel it through my T-shirt.

Maybe this was why Gran never wore the necklace, because it had some kind of weird short-circuited wires inside or something. I should have just tossed it into the key dish without worrying about her getting angry. It was *so* hot, as if a fire burned inside the silver plates.

I reached up to grasp it between my fingers. It cooled in my hand, and, strangely, I felt a little calmer with it fisted in my fingers. It had given me hope earlier.

Some mistakes weren't meant to last.

This *had* to be one of those mistakes. It was only *one* time. *One* slipup, in years of trying so hard to be everything Isaac wanted me to be.

"I was thinking about asking Sarah to come over this weekend," I said, smiling though it felt like my face would shatter. "Maybe on Sunday to—"

"Don't, Katie."

He never said my name. Isaac called me "babe" or "girl" or sometimes "shorty" when he was joking around with some of the other guys from the team. He didn't call me Katie. Ever. When he flipped on his turn signal, my stomach cramped in a way that had nothing to do with hunger.

"Where are we going? Isaac, where—"

With a frustrated sound, Isaac steered onto a gravel road and slammed the truck into park. He shut off the ignition with an angry twist and turned to face me. Finally. Horribly.

His eyes met mine: crystal blue, with darker blue stripes all around—like a tiger's-eye stone, but pale and cool. They were the most beautiful eyes I'd ever seen. It ripped at things inside me to think that I'd never see love in those eyes ever again. But there wasn't any love there now. There was only anger. And hurt. And a tiny shred of doubt that was making him crazy. He had to know for sure if I'd cheated, but he didn't really *want* to know. And he would never forgive me if I told him the truth.

"Tell me, Katie. Is it true?"

No, I couldn't. I *wouldn't*. If I tried hard enough, I could keep this from happening. "Is what true?"

"Stop it!" His face was red, his cheeks flushed the way they were at the end of a rough quarter. "Don't lie. You suck at lying."

I clutched the locket even tighter. "Isaac, please, I—"

"Just tell me." Soft now, soft voice working to convince me he was still in control. But he wasn't. I could tell. Just like he could tell I was lying through my freshly brushed teeth. We knew each other too well. "Were you with him? At the cast party?"

Oh, God. What could I say? What could I do?

"Were you. With him?"

When I finally spoke, my voice was even softer than his. "You were supposed to be there."

He sucked in a breath. It came out shaky, surprise and grief mixing in the soft sound he made as his hands gripped the steering wheel and fisted tight. "Practice ran late and then I fell asleep on the couch. I *told* you that." His eyes were shining. That was all it took to make the tears in mine spill down my cheeks. This couldn't be happening. It couldn't be.

The locket burned hot again, so hot I dropped my hands to my lap, twining my fingers together. Stupid thing! I couldn't deal with malfunctioning jewelry right now. My entire life was falling apart!

"You said you would come."

"So I didn't, so you decided to sleep with Mitch?"

"No! I didn't sleep with him." I wanted to jump out of the truck and run or reach over and pull Isaac into my arms, but knew I couldn't do either. I had to stay here—alone and condemned on my side of the truck—taking my medicine and praying for another chance. "And I didn't *decide* anything, it just—"

"It just happened?" The contempt in his voice made me flinch and the tears come faster. "You just ended up half naked with him by the Regises' pool where everybody could see you?"

My cheeks burned. "I wasn't half naked . . . and no one could see."

"Sarah saw."

"Isaac." A sob rose in my throat, but I swallowed it. I couldn't lose it completely, I had to convince Isaac it wasn't the way he imagined it. That I'd just been angry and hurt and Mitch had been there to listen and things had gone too far. "Please, I swear to you, I—"

"And Sarah told her brother, a loudmouth little freshman who I'm sure told half the school you cheated on me!" Louder now and even angrier, angrier than I'd ever seen him. "Was that even the first time?"

"It was, you *know* it was." The sob escaped, I couldn't stop it. I reached for him, needing to touch him, but he pulled away, upper lip curling like my hands were covered in cow dung from the pasture outside the window.

"I don't know anything." He shook his head, back and forth, back and forth, an eraser clearing all memory of me out of his brain, his heart. "For all I know, you and Mitch could have been hooking up for years."

"No." My voice was firm, stronger. He had the right to be angry, but he knew better. He was everything to me. Everything. "You *know* that's not true."

"Come on, Katie." His tone turned my name into a disgusting, dirty thing. "You always were great about sharing. Even when we were babies. So maybe you wanted me and Mitch to share you."

"No."

"Mitch can take a bite, then Isaac can take a bite, then Mitch, then Isaac, until the cookie is all gone." The sarcasm was so thick I could taste it, his grin as cruel as any expression I'd ever seen on his face. "Just like when we were kids."

"Yeah, and I never took a bite for myself," I sobbed, tears falling harder. "It was always about keeping *you* happy. Making sure you and Mitch got along and *you* were happy with me. That you *liked* me. I've tried so hard. For years!"

His blue eyes froze so cold I swore I could feel the temperature in the truck drop ten degrees. "Well, you won't have to try so hard anymore. You don't have to worry about me *liking* you ever again." He reached across my lap and popped the door. "Get out."

"What?" I couldn't seem to process what he was saying, even when he grabbed my purse and threw it outside. We were at least three miles outside of town and even farther from my house. Surely he wouldn't.

"Get! Out!" And then he grabbed my arm, so tight I knew there would be a bruise there tomorrow, and shoved me out the door.

I fell onto the gravel, palms catching my fall just before my face could connect with rock and dirt. Thunder crashed through the darkening sky, making me flinch, ensuring there wasn't time to get to my feet before Isaac fired up his truck and drove away, spraying dust all over me and my birthday outfit, ending three years of togetherness in a squeal of tires.

Chapter Two

Sometimes storms come out of nowhere in Nashville.

One minute, the sky is clear, the sun setting pink and purple behind a field of baled hay and sleepy cows. The next minute, black clouds sweep in from the west, full of cold rain and electricity, rumbling out a warning to all living things still unlucky enough to be outdoors.

The cows even knew something nasty was coming. One of the big mamas called from a tree near the center of the field and the rest of the herd turned away from their munching at the fence, ambling toward the sound of her moo. I paused at the edge of the road, watching them go, listening to the thunder roll, flinching as the first cold drops fell on my bare arms. As the rain began to fall in earnest, I fumbled in my purse one last time, praying I'd missed my cell the first three times I'd looked.

20

But my cell still wasn't there. I never took my phone when I went out with Isaac. He had his phone and no one ever called me except him. And Mitch.

Mitch. Why had he kissed me? Why? After all the years we'd been friends?

I hadn't even expected to see him at the cast party—he wasn't into drama-club events any more than Isaac. But there he was, just inside the Regises' door, one of the first things I'd seen when I'd arrived, flushed and giggling, high on my first and only performance as Emily in *Our Town*.

I'd been an understudy for three plays, but that was the first time I'd ever had to fill in for someone. The first time and it had been the *lead* role in the last scheduled performance. I'd been so scared, shaking all over in the minutes before I stepped onstage, but I'd done it. I'd pulled it off and the crowd had given us a standing ovation.

The applause had lifted me up so high that it had been a long fall back down to earth. I'd hit hard once I'd realized Isaac wasn't with Mitch, that Isaac hadn't made it to the second act of the play like he'd promised, that he hadn't even bothered to come to the cast party to celebrate with me.

I'd tried calling his cell four times, but he hadn't answered.

After years of making sure I was there for every single basketball game, I'd been sick with disappointment. Literally *sick*, my stomach gurgling and pitching, even before I'd started in with the rum.

"He was probably wiped from practice. His car was still in the parking lot when I got there for the play," Mitch said, his dark brown eyes concerned as he watched me pour my second shot of spiced rum into a red plastic cup.

The alcohol was flowing freely and Becca Regis's parents were nowhere to be seen. But that's why we always had our cast parties at her house. Her parents didn't care what we did so long as nothing got broken, no one drowned in their pool, and we promised to pick designated drivers to get all the drunk teenagers home safely.

"Yeah, probably." I tossed back the drink, wincing as it burned my throat and sent clouds of toxic fumes surging into my head. It was nasty stuff, but I didn't care. I wanted to get drunk. Really drunk.

"His loss." Mitch shrugged, then leaned down to prop his elbows on the counter of the island in the center of the kitchen. He was tall—even taller than Isaac. The movement barely brought his face even with mine. "You were great tonight. You know that, right? It doesn't matter if Isaac was there or not."

I reached for the rum. "It does to me."

"Yeah. I hear you." He dropped his head and his wavy brown hair fell over one eye.

He'd been growing it out since last Christmas and it was nearly down to his chin. It looked surprisingly good on him. I'd never thought Mitch could pull off the whole rocker look, but he did. Black jeans and long hair worked for him. The funny shirts he wore made all the difference. At the moment it was a dark gray A CITY BUILT ON ROCK AND ROLL WOULD BE STRUCTURALLY UNSOUND Threadless tee. It had made me laugh when I'd first seen him, before I'd realized he was at the party alone.

I took another drink, a smaller one. I could feel my head beginning to float. I'd only been drunk a handful of times, but I knew enough to slow down and wait to see how the alcohol was hitting me before I drank any more.

"I'm glad I was there. I had no idea you were so good." He chucked me on the arm with a gentle fist. "I was really surprised."

"Wow. Thanks."

"Sorry." He grinned in a way that made it clear he wasn't sorry at all. "But I really thought you were going to be awful."

I laughed in spite of myself. "Thanks, again."

"Then I would have had to find some nice way to get you to give up this drama stuff once and for all." Mitch made a grab for my cup and took a drink. He was a drink stealer from way back. I'd given up telling him to get his own. "Friends don't let friends make idiots of themselves in public."

"Really?" I snatched my cup before he could finish the last of my rum. "And here I've let you play in that band for all these years."

"Oh! Low blow there, Minnesota." When we'd first met, when he was six and I was five, he'd thought my last name was Minnesota instead of Mottola. It was one of our oldest jokes.

"Whatever, Burn Butt." Isaac had given Mitch his nickname, a play on Birnbaum. Isaac, who hadn't been there to support me the *one* time I'd asked him to be.

Mitch sighed, as if he could tell where my thoughts had drifted. "Anyway, you were really good. I don't know why you didn't get that part for real."

"I'm a horrible audition-nen-ner. Audition-nen-nen—" I

shook my head with a laugh. It was getting harder to talk and my head was even floatier than it was before. "I stink at auditioning. I freeze up every time."

"Then you should do it more often. Then you won't freeze."

"No, I think I'll always freeze." I tried to take another drink, but Mitch smoothly plucked my cup from my hand.

"I got nervous when we first started playing real gigs. I don't anymore."

"Give me my drink, please."

"I think you've had enough."

"Are you my boss?" I reached for the cup, but he tossed back the last of the rum before setting it down in front of me.

"No, I'm your friend." He grabbed my hand, pulling me away from the island and its vast array of bottles and cups. "And friends don't let friends get wasted."

"Some friends do." I cast a pointed glance to the living room, where most of the cast was sitting in a circle on the floor, playing a game of strip spin the bottle and chugging tequila. In the far corner, another clutch of people passed around a joint, while a handful of girls tried to get some dirty dancing started on the landing halfway up the stairs. Most people wouldn't think it, but the drama kids could be a wild and uninhibited crowd. I was one of the most conservative theater geeks I knew.

"Yeah, let's go outside," Mitch said, moving toward the back door. "I'm afraid they're going to make me play that game if we stay in here any longer."

"They don't pressure anyone to play."

"Katie, please. With this body, how could they resist trying to get me naked?" He gestured down his long length, making the same joke about his scrawniness that he'd been making for years. He wasn't nearly as thin as he used to be, but it was still funny. Mitch was just funny to me. Always had been, always would be.

I was smiling as he opened the back door and we stepped out onto the patio.

It was late September, but the Regises' pool still had water inside. After the cool nights we'd had, I was sure it was way too cold to swim in, but it looked pretty. Pink and blue lights glowed beneath the water, making the air around the pool ripple with pink, blue, and purple.

Everyone else was inside the house, so we had the line of white plastic deck chairs to ourselves. Mitch pulled two together and plunked himself down. I settled next to him, swinging my feet out before me with a sigh, surprised at how tired I felt. My entire body was buzzing with leftover adrenaline and alcohol, but I was still tired.

Or maybe I was just sad. Yes, that was it. I was sad.

"Katie, come on, don't cry. It's not worth it."

"I'm not crying." I sniffed and swiped at my cheeks. I *was* crying, and I hadn't even realized it. Mitch was right, I'd probably had enough to drink.

"You look like you're crying."

"Well, I'm not." Or I wouldn't be in a second. I wasn't a big baby who was going to boo hoo about my boyfriend missing some dumb play. My parents had come, Mitch had come. That was enough.

"You're stubborn, you know that?"

"I do." I sniffed again, grateful for the arm Mitch slid around my shoulders. I leaned into him, dropping my cheek onto his narrow chest.

"I do too." We were quiet for a second, watching the wind push a few early fall leaves across the surface of the pool. Mitch and I were good at being quiet together. Silences with him never felt anxious, just . . . silent, calm. "I wonder if Isaac knows."

"Knows what?"

"Knows how stubborn you are." His tone was casual, but I sensed that he was being serious for once. "I mean, you two have been together since you were fetuses."

"Fourteen is not a fetus. And he was fifteen."

Mitch grunted. "Still, I don't think he knows how stubborn you are. I don't think he knows how much he hurt your feelings tonight either."

I lifted my head from his chest, searching his face. "So you think I should forgive him? Just forget about this? Because he didn't get it?"

"I didn't say that. I said he was a clueless idiot."

I smiled. "No you didn't."

"Well, I'm saying it now." He leaned in, bumping his forehead against mine. "He's an idiot. He doesn't have a clue." He leaned in again, but this time he didn't move back, but left his forehead pressed to mine. "How special you are."

Apprehension slithered along my spine, finding its way into my stomach to spin around with the alcohol in my belly. I swallowed and thought about moving away from Mitch, but I didn't.

"Special?" I asked.

"Yeah."

"Are you making fun of me?"

"Do I look like I'm making fun of you?" His breath was warm on my lips and the air between us thick with possibilities. Bad possibilities. Wrong possibilities.

"No." *Move.* I should move. Run back inside before this moment got any stranger.

"I think you're special." His hand was warm as it smoothed across my back, down to rest on my hip, touching me in a way Mitch had never touched me before. In a way no one but Isaac had *ever* touched me. "To me, anyway."

Get up, Katie. Move.

"Mitch, I—"

"I would never have missed something that was so important to you. Not for anything." His intensity was almost scary and completely captivating. I couldn't seem to move a muscle, no matter what the voice at the back of my head was saying. "Not for a gig, not for some stupid basketball practice, not for anything."

Then he kissed me. Soft at first—his lips the barest brush of heat and skin against mine. But then his hands pulled me closer, his tongue teasing between my lips. Before I really understood what I was doing, I was kissing him back.

Really kissing him back, legs tangling with his as we fell back on the deck chair, him half on top of me, my fingers in his hair. His hands were on my hips, at the small of my back, at my waist, pushing up my shirt, warm on my trembling stomach. Then his mouth was where his hands had been, mumbling my name, kissing the bare skin near my belly button, making me shiver.

The world was spinning, but it wasn't because I was drunk. It was because he felt *so* good, because he made me feel so . . . alive, so completely inside my body and outside of it at the same time. Being with Mitch was safety and rebellion, celebration and revenge, familiarity and exploration, all mixed up together. It was intoxicating. Wonderful.

And so very, *very* bad.

Mitch's hand was halfway up my shirt when I grabbed his wrist. "I can't do this. Stop."

Instantly he pulled away, hands flying to his hair, raking the wild strands out of his face. He sucked in a deep breath, wide eyes meeting mine, looking as shocked as I felt. "I'm sorry. I'm so sorry. I didn't—"

"It's okay." I sat up, shoving my shirt down, swallowing hard. "It's—"

"It's not okay." He laughed, a sharp, miserable sound. "It's *really* not okay."

"No, it's not." I crossed my arms at my stomach, wondering if I was going to be sick.

"I'm sorry, Minnesota. I know you and Isaac . . . and I . . . I'm just . . . sorry."

We sat in silence. For the first time, I felt the absence of words between me and Mitch—a giant hand squeezing us until we couldn't breathe.

"We can pretend it never happened," I finally whispered, my voice small and frightened. If Mitch told Isaac, everything would be ruined, my entire life, every little piece of future I'd stitched together. I was too out of it to think it through completely, but I knew the results of discovery would be awful. Horrible. Unimaginable.

"We can't. I can't, anyway." His hands dropped to his knees. He shook his head, and his hair fell forward again, hiding his face. "But we don't have to tell anyone else. I won't tell anyone."

My relief was so profound I thought I would choke on it. "I won't tell anyone either."

We both knew who "anyone" was. Anyone was Isaac. We weren't going to tell Isaac. We were going to keep this between the two of us, our secret mistake that would never, ever happen again.

And it wouldn't have happened again, I'd proved that to myself the past two weeks, when I'd stubbornly refused Mitch's every attempt to get me alone and "talk."

Everything would have been fine if Sarah hadn't seen whatever she'd seen or said whatever she'd said to her little brother. I should have been angry with her, but I wasn't. Sarah wasn't cruel or a gossip. She'd probably said something in private to Hunter, something she'd never expected him to tell anyone, let alone Isaac.

Even when the rain fell harder—soaking my clothes, making me shiver and my jaw ache from clenching my teeth together so they wouldn't chatter—I couldn't get up the energy to hate her. I was on this road, miles from home, darkness and rain falling all around me, drenched and miserable and alone, abandoned on my birthday, dumped on my anniversary, because of me.

I'd done this all on my own. Committed an unforgivable sin.

Stupid locket. Stupid hope. Stupid, stupid Katie.

I reached up to my neck, grabbing the locket in my fist again, half intending to rip it off and throw it into the mud beneath my freezing feet. Instead, I found myself squeezing it, grateful for its strange warmth.

I was so cold. It was almost dark and the temperature was falling fast. I was still miles from home and didn't dare hitch a ride with one of the few people driving past. Brantley Hills was a safe town, but not *that* safe. Bad things still happened. Kids disappeared, girls were raped, people were killed. Not often, almost never, but terrible things happened here, just like in any other town. People made horrible mistakes and other people paid the price for them.

Just like Isaac was paying the price now. He was out there somewhere, hating me, loathing me even more than his jerk of a dad. Our dreams for our future together were ruined, everything we'd counted on since we were barely more than kids destroyed, all because of me.

I wasn't special. I'd been told I was since I was a little girl—by my parents, teachers, Saturday morning cartoons, Disney songs, even milk commercials—but that was a lie. Not everyone is a unique individual capable of living an extraordinary dream. Some of us are just ordinary. Some of us are medium people with lukewarm futures who are lucky to stand next to someone destined for great things.

Someone like Isaac, the boy who'd loved me, the boy I'd betrayed with my stupid mistake. My mistake that was clearly "meant to last."

Lightning flashed through the sky and the locket grew hotter in my hand, so hot it almost burned, but I didn't let it go. I deserved pain. If pain could take away what had just happened, I'd take any amount of it. I'd suffer anything, I would—

Fire. Suddenly my hand was on fire. Burning, scalding, like I was holding a live coal instead of a piece of jewelry. I yelped and dropped the locket, but only exchanged one hurt for another. It fell against my shirt, burning away the thin cotton and starting in on my skin.

I cried out as I fell to the ground, hands fumbling in the puddles, splashing rain and mud onto my chest, frantic for anything to put out the fire. But the pain didn't stop. It only burned brighter, paralyzing me with its intensity. Within seconds, I was frozen on my hands and knees on the side of the road. I couldn't move, couldn't think, could only squeeze my eyes shut and scream.

I was still screaming when the rain shut off like a faucet and the ground beneath my hands shifted and squirmed—wet mud drying, soft earth firming up—becoming a cool, smooth surface that soothed away the stinging on my palm.

The burning at my chest ceased as abruptly as it began.

With a cry of relief, I reached for the clasp at the back of my neck. I had to get the locket off before it hurt me again. My hands were shaking, my breath coming in swift gasps that made me dizzy. When I opened my eyes, I thought maybe the dizziness was the reason the scenery had changed. I was hyperventilating and my eyes were playing tricks on me. That *had* to be it, because there was *no way* I could be seeing what I was seeing.

My hands slipped from my neck, down to brace against the concrete once more.

A few feet away, the Regises' pool shimmered and waved, the pinks and purples and blues mixing in the air, turning the white deck chairs a dozen subtle shades of color. Beyond the pool, picture windows glowed with warm yellow light. Inside, people poured drinks and danced to a throbbing beat I could just catch if I strained my ears.

It looked like . . . but it couldn't be . . . there was no way—

Lips parting in a silent "oh," I watched Kayla Spruel run giggling through the Regises' living room with a tequila bottle, peeling off her jacket as she went, kicking off a game of strip spin the bottle.

I remembered watching her do the exact same thing from the kitchen two weeks ago and wondering how many people she was going to convince to play.

Two weeks ago. The cast party.

It was impossible, but somehow, some way, I'd gone back in time, back to the moment when I'd made my mistake. The mistake that maybe . . . *wasn't* meant to last.

Chapter Three

My brain imploded, each little wrinkle folding in on itself like a cartoon hole on the ground wrapped up and slipped inside a briefcase.

There was no way this was happening. This was *impossible*.

I was hallucinating. That was the only explanation. Or maybe I was unconscious. Maybe I'd been hit by a car on my rainy walk back to Brantley Hills and was lying in a ditch somewhere, concussed, dreaming about the night I'd just been dwelling on before headlights came out of nowhere and some careless driver knocked me into the air.

That made sense. At least some *small* kind of sense.

But still . . . everything was so crisp and clear. I'd never experienced anything like this in a dream, even my most vivid nightmares. The ground beneath my hands was cold and rough and the jeans covering my legs were damp at the knee, right where I'd dropped makeup remover on them in my hurry to take off my stage makeup after the performance. I'd forgotten I'd done that until I reached down and felt the wet spot with my fingers.

The faded softness of the jeans felt so real. As real as the concrete. As real as the slick satin of my favorite emerald shirt, as real as the locket lying cool against my skin.

The locket.

It had burned me, it really had. I explored my new wound with trembling fingers. The skin beneath the locket was ever so slightly ridged and bumpy, slick like a scar that had mended a dozen years ago. There was no way it could have healed so fast—a burn so fresh would be raw and painful—but there was no other explanation.

Just like there was no other explanation for how I'd come to be back at this party. It was the locket. It had to be.

That is insane! I've lost my mind.

"Or I'm in a coma. I've lost my mind or I'm in a coma." I reached behind my neck, this time managing to catch hold of the locket's tiny clasp. Crazy or not, it seemed like a really good idea to take the locket off. Immediately.

Metal caught beneath my fingernail and I pulled, waiting for the clasp to give beneath the pressure, to open so I could slip the loop free. I pulled and pulled, until the metal nub tore through the tip of my nail, but the clasp didn't budge.

"Ow!" The finger with the torn nail went into my mouth, and I tasted blood and . . . hair spray. I *never* wore hair spray, but I'd sprayed it on thick the night of the play. Bright red wispies are distracting in real life, let alone onstage. I'd washed my hands several times after smoothing my hair, but the stickiness had lingered.

But not for two weeks. This was impossible, it was—

"Hey, Katie. Are you okay?"

I turned to see Sarah easing out the back door. Her long, kinky black hair was pulled into a braid and her baggy black T-shirt and cargo pants hung loose on her tiny frame. She looked like she worked backstage—which she did, most of the time. For almost two years, Sarah had ruled the theater from her stage manager's headset and kept many a production running smoothly. No one messed with her when she was in charge.

Strangely, however, not many people noticed her when she wasn't.

Despite her perfect golden brown skin, striking hazel eyes, general adorable petiteness, and diva-sized attitude, Sarah had a way of fading into the background. Being one of the only African American kids—or half African American, anyway—at our school probably had something to do with it. We were one of the "whitest" districts in the state of Tennessee. When you attracted attention for the color of your skin, I imagined fading was a desirable skill. Not to mention that in most situations, Sarah was as shy as I was. It was how we'd become friends in the first place. We'd both been sent to the counselor in third grade for refusing to answer questions in class. We'd bonded over weird flash cards and cheesy books about "coming out of our shell" and had been friends ever since.

At least until this past year, when things with Isaac and me had gotten more intense.

The first time around, I hadn't even registered the fact that Sarah was at the party. I hadn't noticed her, I hadn't said "hi," I hadn't asked her why she wasn't managing *Our Town* this semester. I'd been wrapped up in my own little world and let Sarah fade away, even though she was my best—my *only*—female friend.

I was a huge jerk. And probably deserved to have her tell everyone I'd been making out with Mitch.

Except that I *hadn't* made out with Mitch. Yet. Had I?

"Hello in there?" Sarah waved a slender hand in front of my face as she knelt down beside me on the pool deck. "Can you hear me? You okay?"

"Yeah. I'm just . . ."

I'm just in the middle of an internal debate on the possibility of time travel and think I might be totally out of my mind. Or maybe concussed. Or maybe dead.

"I felt a little dizzy."

She nodded, her eyebrows drawing together as she reached out to rub my back in slow, comforting circles. "I was standing by the window and saw you fall down. I was worried."

"Is that all you saw?" I realized how weird I sounded and hurried on. "I mean, did something . . . hit me on the head . . . or something?"

"Not that I saw."

"And there was no one else out here?"

"Um . . . no." She narrowed her eyes, and the hand on my back moved to point accusingly at my face. "Have you been drinking?"

Had I? Had I had a drink yet? I smacked my lips, not tasting any rum on my tongue. "No. I haven't. I'm just . . . it was a big night. I'm a little overwhelmed."

And the award for understatement of the year goes to . . . Katie Mottola!

Sarah smiled, thankfully buying my load of crap. "I heard you were great. I'm so sorry I couldn't be there tonight. I really wanted to see you do Emily. I bet everyone cried at the end when you died! Tell all, was the mascara running all over the place?"

I laughed in spite of myself. Sarah was shy with new people, but she was a talker once she got going. "Some people did cry. My mom cried."

"Oh, good! I love making people cry." She laughed with me, a sound of such pure joy it made me look at her more closely. She was *really* happy, happier than I'd seen her in . . . ever.

"What's up with you?"

"What's up with *me*?" She grinned a grin full of secrets. Something was definitely up. "Nothing. *You're* the one who fainted."

"I didn't faint. I had a dizzy spell."

"Oh, a dizzy spell?" she asked, mimicking my twang. "You're so cute when you get all southern."

"You're as southern as I am."

"But I don't sound it." Sarah settled beside me, stretching her legs out, leaning back on her hands. "I have mastered the art of speaking in Standard American English."

"You have." I was a little surprised, but it was true. She'd been working on getting rid of her accent for years. Now she'd finally done it, sometime during the months that I'd had my head up my butt being a very bad friend. "But now what will you learn at acting school? You might have to pick another major at Julliard."

"I might not get accepted. I haven't auditioned yet."

"You'll get accepted. You're great," I said, meaning every word. She was a great actress. That's why she was in the young artists' acting academy at Nashville Rep. She was amazing, too good to even bother auditioning for our school plays.

"Even if I do get in, I might not go."

"What? But you've always wanted to—"

"I might just start working. I got my Equity card last week," she said, her excitement at spilling the news catching, making my breath come faster. "They cast me in the Nashville Rep's production of *Romeo and Juliet*."

"You're kidding! Which part?" Like I had to ask. I knew it had to be a lead role for her to qualify for her actors' union card, so it had to be—

"Juliet!"

I grabbed her hands and much excited squee-ing ensued. We were loud, *really* loud, I guess, because Mitch stuck his head out the back door a second later.

My heart lurched and my smile slipped as my eyes met his—the memory of his kiss making my lips burn. But then . . . it wasn't a memory anymore. Was it? It was something that hadn't happened, that would *never* happen. I could tell by the look in his eyes that we hadn't kissed.

Now we never would. I wasn't going to make the same mistake again.

"There you are," he said, spotting me on the ground. "I lost you."

"I was getting some air."

"Cool. So, is this an all-girl squeal fest or can anyone join?"

"You can join," Sarah said, motioning him over.

"Oh, goodie!" Mitch squealed in true girlie fashion and pranced over to join us, doing an excellent impression of a four-year-old girl who had just found out there were pink ponies at her birthday party.

Sarah and I laughed and made room for him between us. This was the real Mitch, my *friend* Mitch who I'd thought I'd lost forever. But there was no tension between us now, no secrets, no shame. It was . . . amazing. Impossible. Wonderful.

I was smiling so hard my cheeks hurt by the time Sarah finished telling Mitch about her starring roll, her Equity card, and the really cool girl who would be playing Romeo.

"So they're having Romeo and Juliet be gay? Edgy." Mitchell nodded approvingly.

"Interracial, too. Even edgier," Sarah said. "I'm really excited about it. It's something my mom and dad have had to deal with ever since—"

"Being gay?" Mitch asked, going for the joke.

Sarah slapped his arm. "No, doofus. Being interracial."

"I hear you," Mitch said, suddenly serious. And a little . . . sad, if I was reading him correctly. "My mom wasn't Jewish. It's not the same thing, but it was a big deal for my dad's family."

Over the years, Mitch had come to be able to talk about his mom without getting down, but I knew it still made him sad to think about her. Right now he reminded me of the lost little boy I'd met when my family first moved into the neighborhood. He'd been six and his mom had died about a year before. He'd been devastated, and his dad not much better off.

If it hadn't been for my mom, I don't know that Mitch would have had supper on the table every night, let alone a healthy, homemade supper. It had taken his dad a couple of years to pull it together. In the meantime, my family had been happy to pick up the slack. We'd all loved Mitch from the first time we met him. He was just that type of person, the kind who made everyone feel comfortable.

"My mom and dad's families never made a big deal out of it." Sarah shrugged. "But my dad's the whitest black man in the world. He's from Connecticut. I don't think he even realizes Brantley Hills is a weird place."

Mitch laughed. "Doesn't he wonder why our basketball teams always lose?"

Sarah snorted. "Um, it is a *total* stereotype that black people are better at basketball," she said, waving an accusing finger in his face.

"A *true* stereotype." Mitch laughed again as he lay back on the concrete, stretching out like he was basking in sunshine, not moonlight. There was something sensual in the movement, something that made me look away. Quickly. "Isaac's the only one on the team who has a chance at a scholarship."

"Isaac's amazing," Sarah said, a sincerity in her tone that tripped something inside me. She sounded so in awe, so ... crushy, almost. Did she have a thing for Isaac? Was that why she'd told her big-mouthed little brother about what she'd seen?

For a second the thought made me angry. How dare she? I was her friend, her *best* friend. Or at least I had been for years.

"You and Isaac are the cutest couple, Katie." She sighed, innocently, and I felt awful. "You're so lucky."

"Thanks," I said, pushing away my anger. There was nothing to be angry about. Sarah hadn't done anything, and . . . neither had I.

God, this was confusing. *Mind melting.*

But if it was really two weeks ago . . . then Isaac was at home in his basement, where he'd fallen asleep on the couch. If I hurried, maybe I could make it over to his house in time to see him, to talk to him face-to-face and find out for sure if I'd really rewound the clock. If Isaac still loved me, then this had to be real.

He might still love me! I might really have a second chance to keep everything Isaac and I had built and dreamed about from being destroyed. The possibility left me breathless.

"Hey, do either of you know what time it is?" I asked.

Sarah pulled her cell from her pocket and flipped it open, casting her face in a light blue glow for a second before she snapped it shut. "It's almost midnight. Why? Do you have a curfew? You never have a curfew!"

"No, no curfew."

Sarah sighed again. "Your mom and dad are so cool. Can I have them? I was supposed to be home half an hour ago. I'm going to tell my parents that you felt sick and I had to drive you home, okay?"

"Yeah, no problem." I wiped my hands on my jeans and stood up. "I should really get going, though, I—"

"It's too late to go hunt down Isaac," Mitch said from his place on the ground. "His dad will kill you if you show up after midnight. Isaac has to get his super-athlete sleep."

"His dad won't kill me," I said, though the thought of knocking on the Taytes' door this late at night didn't seem like a good idea. His mom might answer and it would be fine—she loved me and wouldn't care if I showed up at four o'clock in the morning—but Mr. Tayte . . . He really *was* crazy when it came to Isaac getting his rest, especially during basketball season.

"Let me drive you home and you can go yell at him tomorrow," Mitch said.

"I'm not going to yell at him."

"You *should* yell at him. He shouldn't have missed the play. Or the party."

"It's fine. It's not a big deal." My voice was harsher than I intended, but I couldn't help myself. I kept remembering the way this conversation had played out the first time.

"Okay. Fine." Mitch shrugged, but I could tell I'd hurt his feelings. When he stood, he let his hair flop forward, hiding his face. "You're right. It's not a big deal. So, do you want a ride home or not? I'm heading out."

My eyes fell on the deck chair. *The* deck chair, the one from the first time I'd lived this night. Not a good idea to be alone with Mitch. Not a good idea at all. "No, I've got my car here, so—"

He brushed his hair from his face and cocked his head. "No you don't, your parents dropped you off. Remember?"

"No they didn't."

"Um . . . Katie . . . they did." He looked concerned. "Remember, I talked to them in the driveway. I told them I'd make sure you got home safe since you left your cell at home."

"Oh. Right." Was that right? I had no idea. It hadn't been right the first time around, but maybe now . . .

But why would things be different? Hadn't the play happened the same way?

I was so confused, overwhelmed by the immensity of it all. This still seemed impossible, but there was no doubt that it was really happening. No dream could ever be so real. I'd *actually* traveled back in time. The locket had brought me back here for a second chance. A chance to make sure this mistake wasn't meant to last.

"So . . . are we going or not?" Mitch asked, his tone leading me to believe I'd been quiet longer than I thought.

"Yeah, I just . . . could you help me with something first, Sarah?" I pulled my hair over one shoulder, grateful that it was too dark for Mitch and Sarah to see my new scar. "I've been trying to get this locket off all night, but I can't get the clasp to work."

"Sure." She hopped to her feet and reached for the clasp. I felt her cool fingers on my skin, then the trembling of her muscles. Once, twice, three times. She sighed. "Sorry, I can't get it. It must be stuck or something."

"That's okay. No biggie," I said, but it was a biggie. Why couldn't I get it off?

My head spun again. Going home suddenly seemed like a very good idea. Home, where things were familiar and safe, and nothing had changed in the past two years, let alone the past two weeks. Home, where I could find Gran's phone number in Dad's BlackBerry and hopefully get some answers. She was still in Singapore—at the end of the "Asian tour" she'd completed just before coming to our house—but she always left Dad a number where he could reach her.

Maybe she knew that the locket had power . . . magic.

"Let's go," I said. "See you Monday. Congratulations." I gave Sarah a quick hug and turned back to Mitch. "You ready?"

"Ready." While we circled the house and walked down the crowded drive to Mitch's family van, I did my best to talk myself back from the brink of a crippling anxiety attack.

This *was* crazy, but it could also be that miracle I'd been praying for. I settled into the passenger seat of Mitch's car and buckled in. As we pulled away into the darkness, I let my fingertips brush against my new scar. It wasn't that big, or that noticeable, and it would be a small price to pay for a second chance.

Mitch and I didn't say a word in the ten minutes it took to cross town, but that was fine. The silence between us was comfortable again. Easy. At least until we pulled into my driveway.

"See you Monday."

"Yep. Monday," he said. "It was fun hanging out with you tonight."

"You too." I smiled at him, but he didn't smile back. He looked sad again, sadder than I'd seen him in years.

I knew a good friend would ask him what was wrong and ask him if he wanted to talk. Mitch wasn't like Isaac; he liked to talk through things that were bothering him.

But unfortunately, I had too much of my own angst to deal with.

"Let's do it again soon?" I asked, promising myself I'd make time for Mitch as soon as I figured out what was going on in my own crazy life.

"Sounds good." He still looked like someone had killed his pet bunny, but I tried not to worry too much as I climbed out of the car and hurried up the front steps. Mitch would be fine, heck, he'd be *better* than fine. We were all going to be better off if tonight was real. Me, Mitch, and Isaac.

Chapter Four

SUNDAY, SEPTEMBER 27, 11:32 A.M.

*I*t was Sunday morning in Nashville but after eleven o'clock at night in Singapore and my grandmother hadn't come back to her hotel room or checked her messages. I still couldn't get the locket off—after trying for nearly two hours—and I was no closer to figuring out how I'd come to be two weeks in the past than I was before.

But I *almost* didn't care.

I hadn't been able to get Isaac on his cell last night, but he'd called this morning a little after seven. He'd apologized for thirty minutes and sworn he would make it up to me for missing the play. For once, he seemed to get that he'd let me down. He was going to take me somewhere special to celebrate my performance as soon as he and his family got out of church.

Squee! I couldn't wait to see him! To hug him, and kiss him, and see his smile and know for certain that everything was really going to be all right.

Never in my life had I resented the fact that Baptists don't have services on Saturday nights as much as I did this morning. Isaac was going to have to convert to Catholicism when we got married. Confession and occasionally creepy priests aside, being Catholic was just so much more convenient to Sunday morning relaxing.

Not that I could relax. At. All.

"You're pacing again," Mom shouted over the clatter of mixing dishes landing in the sink.

"Sorry." I stopped at the edge of the counter, absently flipping through yesterday's mail. September postmarks, all of it, including the college information I'd requested and already sorted through. Two weeks ago.

I was going to have to redo all the work I'd done, but that was fine. I was happy to do everything over, *anything* to have a second chance with Isaac. Of course, this time two weeks ago, I'd been moping in my room—angsting out about my infidelity and general wretchedness—so I didn't quite know what to do with myself right now. It was making me nervous, twitchy.

"That's okay." Mom laughed as she reached around me, grabbing the pot holders from their hook.

Sunday was her baking day. She made all our bread and muffins for the week from scratch. She was *that* mom and I loved her for it. There was nothing like the smell of fresh bread cooking. I'd always thought I'd like to do the same thing for my family when I was a mom. For the family Isaac and I would have. That we were *still* going to have because of the locket.

The locket. I tapped the cool metal, once, twice.

Three hours of research on the Internet hadn't led me to any information on magic necklaces, but I was sure the locket was responsible. It *had* to be. There was no other explanation. I had no idea how it worked, but it hadn't changed temperature since the do over started, which made me think that it had completed its mission. I was in the past, reliving two weeks of my life, my wish for my mistake "not to last" granted.

Still . . . I couldn't relax. If only I'd been able to talk to Gran, to see if she knew that the locket had supernatural powers and, if so, how they worked. It would be so nice to be certain that this was real, that I wasn't going to be hurled back to the present at any moment.

Once I saw Isaac, I would feel better. Once I saw for sure that—

"Pacing. Again." Mom grabbed the mail from my hands and dropped it back into the mail dish. "Why don't you go help Dad in the backyard?"

"But Isaac could be here any second."

"Church let out less than ten minutes ago." Mom cracked the stove, checking on her muffins, causing a burst of blueberry and sugar to waft through the kitchen. "He won't be here for at least another ten. Go help your dad."

"But Mom, I—"

"Go help Dad or you can vacuum the downstairs."

I hurried to the sliding glass door and out into the cool fall day before Mom could put me to foul, vacuuming-type work. Sunday was also her cleaning day—a tradition I was *not* going to continue when I was grown. Cleaning the entire house, top to bottom, including baseboards and ceiling fans, *every week*, was excessive. *Crazy*, some might say.

Maybe insanity ran in my family and this time-travel-inducing jewelry episode was just a schizophrenic delusion. But then, Gran was Dad's grandmother, not Mom's.

Hmm . . . maybe Dad would know something about the locket if I got up the courage to ask. I stepped out to the edge of the patio, scanning the leaf-strewn yard.

"Dad? Are you—ah!" My words ended in a scream as fingers danced up my ribs, finding every ticklish place along the way.

Mitch laughed as I spun around, slapping his hands together. "Got you. Again. That's three times this month." He smiled. "Your dad went around front to get an extra rake."

"You are disturbed," I said, my heart still racing.

Mitch loved to lurk just outside our sliding door and scare the crap out of me when I came outside. He'd been doing it since we were ten. I should have learned to watch my back by now, but I hadn't. I hadn't expected to see him so soon. Especially today. It seemed . . . wrong for him to be in my backyard.

I reminded myself for the zillionth time that we had never kissed, never crossed the line that separated friends from more-than-friends. This was fine, normal even. Everything was good. Great.

"I *am* disturbed," Mitch said, a shadow creeping across his face.

Okay, maybe everything was *not* so great.

"You serious?" I asked, voice low.

"Kind of." He shrugged. "That's actually why I came—"

"Babe? Are you back there?" Isaac's voice sounded from around the side of the house. My stomach jumped into my throat and sucker-punched my brain stem, making the world tilt on its axis.

He was here. He was really here!

"Back here!" My breath caught as I turned to watch the door to the fence open.

For a moment, my mind flashed on an image of Isaac's face, seeing again the disgust twisting his features when I'd reached for him on the night of our breakup. I heard him telling me again how I wouldn't have to worry about him "liking" me anymore, let alone loving me, and everything inside me cringed.

This was it, the true test of the entire do over. Would Isaac be like he had been on the phone—sweet and apologetic? Or would he be the boy who'd kicked me out of his truck onto the side of the road and left me to walk miles in a thunderstorm?

I was terrified, frozen in place, certain this dream of a second chance was going to crumble like the brown sugar topping on the blueberry muffins Mom was baking. But then Isaac pushed through the gate, hair shining gold in the sun, big grin on his face, wearing his favorite orange shirt with the sketches of brown feathers on the front. He stopped to give Mitch a quick, easy high five, then pulled me into his arms. He hugged me tight, his cheek smooth against mine, his smell as perfectly, familiarly Isaac as ever.

I squeezed him until he made a grunting sound and laughed into my hair. It was all I could do not to bawl like a baby. Isaac was here and he still loved me. I was the luckiest girl in the world.

As I pulled away, my fingers flew to press against the locket, lying cool against my skin beneath my short-sleeved, brown sweater. I sent out a silent thank-you to God and the universe and enchanted jewelry makers and Gran's leave-my-jewelry-lying-in-a-big-messy-pile nature for this chance, this miracle.

It really *was* a miracle. Isaac's eyes held not a single shred of hate or doubt. This was the Isaac of two weeks ago, the Isaac who still loved me. Who called me babe and thought I was beautiful and wanted to marry me and be together forever.

Oh man, I really was going to get sniffly if I didn't watch out. I was just so thankful.

"I'm sorry, babe," he said, mistaking the reason for my obvious emotional instability. "I suck."

"You don't suck!"

"You do suck, but she's already forgiven you," Mitch said. "You are a lucky bastard."

"I am a lucky bastard." Isaac turned to punch Mitch on the arm, then the stomach, and then they were doing that weird not-quite-fighting thing boys do to bond. They were halfway across the lawn, falling into a pile of leaves, when my dad showed up with the rake.

"You two are ruining my piles!" Dad yelled, but I could tell he didn't mind. Now it would take him even longer to clear the yard and he'd be spared that vacuuming I'd so narrowly avoided.

"Love you, Dad. We're going to go," I said, leaning in for a hug.

"You all have fun. Don't get into any trouble."

"We won't," Mitch said. "Later, Mr. M."

I shot Isaac a look, but he was already heading for the gate be-hind Mitch, not at all surprised or annoyed that Mitch had invited himself on our date. But then, Mitch had invited himself on our dates lots of times. Especially when he was the only one of us with a vehicle. Mitch was six months older than Isaac and had gotten his license early because his dad was a single parent and a doctor who worked odd hours.

Still, this was supposed to be a special day. For me and Isaac. I couldn't help but wish Mitch would go home. Just this once.

"I brought bikes to take into Nashville. That sound cool?" Isaac asked when we reached the drive.

"Sounds perfect." I loved riding bikes in the city, but Isaac usually hated the hassle of loading them up.

"So your car or mine?" he asked. This time, I didn't bother to answer. I knew he was talking to Mitch. Isaac never let me drive.

It was a man thing. Or a southern thing. Or some kind of thing. It had never bothered me before, but I couldn't suppress a flash of anger as I watched the boys debate the pros and cons of Mitch's family van versus Isaac's souped-up Accord. If Isaac had let me drive on my birthday, I wouldn't have been stuck walking home in the rain on a very dangerous stretch of country road, worrying that I was about to be struck by lightning.

That. Never. Happened. Get it through your head, Katie. That was then, this is now.

Actually . . . *now* was *then* and *then* was *now*. Or . . . something. I had to quit thinking about it or I was going to lose what was left of my mind.

"Katie? Is my van cool with you?" Mitch asked, waiting for my approval. "Or do you want to drive? We could put the bike rack on your car."

"No, I'm fine. Let's go." I smiled and followed the boys to Mitch's old family van, helping load my and Isaac's bike inside.

From here on out, there was no more angst, only awesome. I was going to make sure these two weeks were the best of my and Isaac's life, starting right now.

"I'm not wearing a wig, man!" Isaac laughed until his cheeks turned red as he watched Mitch struggle into the long blond wig the costume lady at the Broadway end of the Shelby Street Bridge had given him to wear.

"It's cross-*dress*-ing the bridge," Mitch insisted. "There's no other way across."

"I put on the dress. That's enough," Isaac said, gesturing at the bright red prom dress that hung down over his jeans. Somehow, he managed to look even more masculine in sequins. Maybe it was the barrel chest straining the seams at the sides.

Mitch, on the other hand, was weirdly pretty. With his big brown eyes and full lips, he really could have been mistaken for a girl. Except for the size-fourteen shoes, weirdly wide shoulders, and the hint of stubble on his chin, of course.

"Isaac, you need hair, you have to *complete* your look. Besides, it's for charity," Mitch said, keeping a straight face when the giggling costume woman handed him two round pillows to use to stuff the front of his blue polka-dotted dress. "Thanks!" He genuinely looked excited to be sporting fake boobs, the nut. "Do these make me look fat?"

I laughed. "No, you can totally pull off a D cup," I assured him. "You just look a little top heavy."

"Pamela Anderson top heavy or Bubbe Birnbaum top heavy?"

I snorted, nearly dislodging my newly affixed mustache. Girls had to cross-dress to get across the bridge too. My brown sweater was now covered by a ratty old man's suit jacket, my hair was shoved under a bowler cap, and my upper lip sported a thick mustache. The lady had even dug through her makeup kit to find a red one to match my hair. I was sure I looked like a little boy with a testosterone problem, but I didn't care. It was exciting to be part of the charity event. I wanted to work for a nonprofit organization when I got out of college and loved seeing how creative people could get in the name of getting other people involved.

The Shelby Street Bridge—the easiest bike route from downtown to the larger city parks—had been taken over by Nashville's Society for Breast Cancer Awareness for a cross-dressing-the-bridge fund-raiser. They were charging five dollars to bike or walk across the bridge and supplying everyone with opposite gender "costumes" that smelled like they'd come straight from the Salvation Army donation box.

We were probably all going to get lice or bedbugs or something, but at least everyone was having fun doing it.

"How about a tiara?" the costume lady asked, grabbing one from the corner of her table and holding it out to Isaac. "We're running low on wigs, and it would be a shame to cover that pretty blond hair."

Isaac blushed and took the tiara. The woman had him. The manners ingrained in him by his southern mama wouldn't allow him to say "no" after he'd received a compliment. He was going to have to wear the tiara.

"Thanks, ma'am." He plunked it down on his head and jumped back on his bike. "Are you two coming? Or what?" Oh, he was annoyed, but the tiara was hysterical. The funniest thing I'd seen in months.

Mitch and I managed to hold our laughter for about thirty seconds before we both lost it. I giggled so hard I nearly fell off my bike.

"What pretty blond hair you have, Isaac," Mitch said, in an exaggerated southern drawl. "You were just born to wear a tiara."

"Shut up, jackass." Isaac flipped Mitch off, but I could tell he wasn't really mad.

"Mitch is right. If I'd known, I would have given you my crown at homecoming last year," I said, still laughing so hard I could barely form the words.

"I'll get you later, girl. You just wait." Isaac's threat was accompanied by a heated look that made my pulse pick up. I sincerely hoped he'd "get me" later, preferably as soon as Mitch dropped us off at my house and we could sneak up to my room while my parents were watching TiVoed episodes of *Iron Chef*.

"Homecoming's only a couple of weeks away," Mitch said. "You know you two are going to be king and queen again. It's not too late for Isaac to show the rest of the senior class how to sparkle."

"I think Katie does a better job of sparkling," Isaac said with a sincerity that made me blush. "You looked awesome last year."

"She was awesome in the play last night," Mitch said. "You

should have seen her. I was shocked. I thought she was going to suck."

"Thanks, Mitch." I forced a laugh, shrugging off the apprehension clutching at the back of my throat. The conversation was similar to the one Mitch and I had at the original cast party. So what? It didn't have to mean anything.

"No, you were good. You really were."

"Thanks."

"I'm not going to miss another one," Isaac said. "Next time you get to go onstage, I'll be there, I promise." His smile made me smile, but I couldn't help but think that there wouldn't be a "next time."

I'd been at the understudy stuff since freshman year and only had to fill in one time. The spring musical was the last play left before Isaac graduated, and I highly doubted he'd have time to come home from college to see me perform even if I managed to land a full-fledged speaking part of my own my senior year.

But, whatever. It didn't matter. Isaac and I were together. That was the most important thing, the *only* important thing.

"What a beautiful day," I said, turning my attention to brighter thoughts.

The view from the bridge was one of my favorites. Nashville's skyline stood out in crisp relief against a perfect blue sky while the Cumberland River rolled slowly by, reflecting the antenna of the Sommet Center, where Isaac had taken me to a Predators game last February. He loved hockey. I loved popcorn and giant hot dogs and the excitement of screaming along with the crowd, so it all worked out.

"We should come back and do this again," Mitch said. "I forgot how much I love riding bikes."

"Remember when we rode our bikes across the highway to get McDonald's ice cream in third grade?" I asked, the memory sending a shiver across my skin even now. Our parents had nearly killed us. Dead. I'd never seen my dad so mad. "I thought we were going to be grounded forever."

"That was all you, Minnesota." Mitch shook his head at me. "That was your big idea."

"It was not, it was Isaac! It was always Isaac," I protested. Isaac had gone out of his way to get us in trouble as kids, his daredevil nature inspiring Mitch and me to heights of bravery and stupidity we never would have achieved on our own.

Isaac was the one who dared us to sneak into the old mill when it was still condemned, instigated a race across the deep end of the pool when all three of us could barely swim, and had to call the fire department when he'd talked me into climbing out on his roof and I'd been too scared to climb back in. Isaac had been *trouble* when we were little, but Mitch and I had loved him for it. Without him, our play adventures wouldn't have been nearly as exhilarating.

"Not that time," Mitch said. "It was *you* who had to have ice cream at ten in the morning."

"Yeah, it was totally you," Isaac agreed. "Remember, you already had your piggy bank in your backpack when you showed up at my house."

"Then we had to break the bank when we got to McDonald's to pay for the ice cream, but there wasn't enough money in there, so they called our parents." Mitch waved at a group of girls standing at the edge of the bridge, staring and pointing at his outfit. With his wig and fake boobs, he was one of the girliest men on the bridge, but he didn't seem to care. Mitch honestly didn't worry about what other people thought of him. It was one of his best, and most enviable, traits.

"Okay, fine," I said, smiling. "But you two should have known better than to listen to a nine-year-old."

"You were very persuasive, always have been," Mitch said, something in his voice making me glance over my shoulder.

Even his wig, dress, and padding couldn't detract from the intensity of his look. He was thinking about something other than little kids getting in trouble for riding their bikes too far from home.

For a second, the air between us hummed with that "not just friends" energy, but then he stuck his tongue out at me and it was over. It probably had never been there in the first place. I was just having a hard time forgetting the things I didn't need to remember anymore.

I turned around, pinning my eyes on Isaac, who had come to the end of the bridge and was turning his bike around with some kind of crazy wheelie.

"And we were only ten. Boys are dumb at ten." Isaac's front wheel plunked back to the ground. He pulled at the neck of his sparkly gown. "Dudes, I'm about done being a girl. It's too itchy. Ya'll want to take these clothes back and go get a beer? You've got a fake ID, right, Mitch?"

"Yeah, I've got one." Mitch shrugged. "I'm not up for beer yet, but I'm definitely in for some music. Legends has good stuff on Sundays and it's all ages until seven o'clock so Katie won't have any trouble getting in."

"Awesome. You in, babe?"

"Sounds perfect." And it did. The perfect end to a perfect afternoon with my two best friends.

I was so glad Mitch had invited himself on our date. He and Isaac and I hadn't had so much fun together in years. I couldn't believe we'd nearly lost this. Friendships like ours were rare, special, not the kind of thing you tossed away because you were too busy with basketball or your band or angry with your boyfriend and had a few too many shots of rum.

The three of us had too much history to let it all slip away. Thanks to the locket, we'd gotten a second chance to save our friendship. This wasn't just about me and Isaac, it was about all of us. Three lives were going to be better because of my do over.

I pumped a little harder, catching up with the boys, full of enough energy to light up every honky-tonk on Broadway.

Chapter Five

*L*unch hour is the most overrated forty-five minutes of the entire school day.

Even at a well-funded school like BHH, the cafeteria food stinks, the lines are horrible, and the choice of where to sit is fraught with dangerous social implications. Last year, Isaac and I hadn't had the same lunch, so I'd sat with Mitch, Michael— the drummer in his band—Sarah, and a couple of our drama-club friends. I'd missed seeing Isaac but enjoyed significantly lower stress levels than the year before, when I'd shared a table with Isaac and the other platinum people.

This year, however, I'd been lucky enough to get second lunch with my senior boyfriend. Or *unlucky* enough, depending on the day and whether Rachel Pruitt decided to eat lunch on campus and bless us with her shining presence.

Today was a "blessed" day.

"It's going to be amazing, Isaac." Rachel stabbed a tomato from her salad, managing to make even that simple movement elegant, perfect. Her dark brown hair caught the sunlight streaming in from the nearby windows and gleamed like the coat of a ridiculously expensive horse, attracting the attention of every male passing by our table. "You and Rader should come with us to Ziggies to pick out outfits. You'd be great models."

"I don't model." Rader took a huge bite of whatever meat was masquerading as chicken-fried steak and glared at the rest of the lunchroom. He looked cranky. But then, he always looked cranky. Ever since he and Rachel had broken up their sophomore year, Rader had been in a foul mood.

Losing Rachel inspired years of mourning. *Years.* She was *that* kind of girl.

"Me either," Isaac said around a mouthful of food. His mom had packed his lunch today—two ham sandwiches and three bananas. Isaac had a strange and unnatural love of bananas. He probably ate more in one week than your average marmoset. It was amazing he hadn't overdosed on potassium.

"It's for charity." Rachel cocked her head and pushed her bow-shaped lips into a pout. I could feel the boys wavering, wondering if it wouldn't be worth the shame of prancing around at the fashion show in the name of making Rachel Pruitt happy.

"I wore a dress for charity yesterday." Isaac's reason for refusing was different than the first time around, but I was relieved all the same.

Not everything today had gone down the same way it had

before. It was only little things that were different—the reading assignment in AP English, the cracked mirror in the girls' bathroom—but little things were enough to make me nervous. A part of me wished I could fast-forward to my birthday and be done with my do over. Or at least fast-forward to my gran's arrival in five days.

Talking to someone else about the locket would really have made me feel better. Too bad she still hadn't answered the phone at her hotel. Dad said she'd probably changed hotels without bothering to let him know—Gran was over eighty years old and forgot things all the time—but still ... her vanishing act made me worry. Just a little.

"You wore a dress?" Rader asked, scooting away as if he feared Isaac's dress-wearing cooties would jump across the table and infect him.

"Dude, I bet that was hysterical! Cross-dressing the bridge, right? I saw some pictures of that on Facebook last night." Rachel's best friend, Ally, poked Isaac on the arm. "I didn't see you, though. Did you look fabulous?"

"Of course. I was wearing a tiara," Isaac said, a hint of flirtation in his voice. Isaac was a flirt, always had been, but I knew it didn't mean anything. "So I've done my part for the less fortunate. But Katie will help. She's into charity. She organized that Full Pantry Project thing last year."

Oh, no. Here we were again, the place where Rachel sweetly infers that I'm too ugly and misshapen to model with the rest of the girls and would be better off running the light grid in the dark to spare the masses my hideousness.

I buried my face in my turkey and cheese, doing my best not to attract attention. Maybe no one had heard Isaac.

"Yeah, that's great, Katie," Rachel said.

Maybe not.

"I saw you signed up to work at the Belle Meade fall festival," Rachel continued, turning her soft brown eyes in my direction. "We'll have to try to get you assigned to work the Junior League bake sale with us."

"That would be great." I forced a smile. I could do this. I'd had a practice run, I didn't have to make a fool out of myself the second time around. "And Isaac's right, I'd love to help at the fashion show."

"Well, that's—"

"But there's no way I'd feel comfortable modeling," I said, cutting her off before she could tell me that she doubted there would be anything "that would compliment my build or coloring" at Ziggies, her mother's ultra-expensive, ultra-fashionable, ultra-snotty boutique. "I could help out some other way, though. Maybe do sound, or lights? I've had training on all the systems in the theater."

Rachel's eyes lit up. She looked . . . relieved.

A strange thought bloomed in my mind, a hothouse flower growing in the arctic tundra. Maybe Rachel hadn't meant to hurt my feelings before, maybe she'd just been trying to get me to work lights the whole time and hadn't known how to ask.

"That would be perfect. We're going to set up Friday at noon."

"I'll be there," I said.

"Cool. Thanks." She snapped her empty salad container shut and passed one of her two after-lunch mints to Ally. This time, however, she slid her own mint over to me. "I love that color on you, by the way. You are amazing in green."

"Thanks." My smile was real this time.

Seconds later, the loudspeaker squealed to life and Principal McAdams's voice boomed through the crowded cafeteria. Saved by the squeal. For the first time the entire school year, I'd had a conversation with Rachel that ended before I'd made a total idiot of myself. The realization was a little giddy-making. "Attention, senior class. The votes are in, and your homecoming-week theme has been decided."

"Dude, I hope it's not that jungle thing," Ally said, sucking her mint so hard her cheeks hollowed. "That was the dumbest idea ever."

I nodded along with everyone else at the table, agreeing when Radar added that Welcome to the Jungle was 1980s in the lame way, not the cool way, but secretly knowing we all had animal prints in our future. I'd lived through this announcement—and the disappointed aftermath—once before.

"We had a lot of great ideas this year," the principal's voice continued, "but . . . Undead Disney was the clear front-runner."

What? *Undead Disney?* That hadn't even been an option the first time around. What did that even mean?

The mint I'd just popped in my mouth soured, and my throat got so tight I could barely swallow my own saliva. Another little difference in the world as I'd known it. It was just a homecoming theme, no big deal, but still . . . it made my hands tremble as I wadded up my empty lunch bag. Why was this happening? Why was now different than then?

"Awesome!" Ally squealed as Principal McAdams droned on about the dress code being strictly enforced during spirit week and reminded us that all costumes must adhere to decency standards. "I call zombie Little Mermaid!"

"No way, Ally," Rachel said. "Katie has to be zombie Little Mermaid."

"I do?" I asked, too thrown to think of something better to say.

"Yes. You're the only one with red hair, duh." Rachel wrinkled her nose in disapproval of my stupidity, but I was saved from further commentary. The bell rang a second later, signaling the end of lunch.

Without further social ado, we shoved our chairs back and grabbed bags and purses. BHH teachers were notoriously evil about handing out tardy slips after lunch. Mitch thought it was their way of getting revenge on juniors and seniors who were allowed to go off campus while the teachers were forced to eat in the depressing, lime green faculty lounge every day.

That was still the same; I'd seen the green post-nuclear glow of the walls when I'd walked by the office this morning. Almost everything was still the same. There was no reason to freak out about a change in the homecoming theme. I mean, Undead Disney did sound like a lot more fun than Welcome to the Jungle, and I already had my character picked out and approved by the platinum set. There was nothing to worry about. I did my best to throw off time-travel-related angst as Isaac and I dumped our trash and headed toward our locker.

My locker, really, but Isaac kept all of his stuff in there. My locker was more centrally located and conducive to meeting up for kisses between classes. Public displays of affection were strongly discouraged at Brantley Hills High, but we were rebels with a need for lip locking between second and third period. If making out was wrong, we didn't want to be right.

The thought helped my grin recover. "So, I'll see you after school? At Ramon's?"

"Yeah. That's cool." Isaac sighed as he grabbed his calculus book. When I turned to glance at his profile, I was surprised to see a scowl on his face.

"I mean, it's Monday, right? You'll have time?" Basketball practice didn't start until later on Mondays. Coach Nader had parking lot duty and couldn't get to the gym until four. Isaac and I always took advantage of the extra thirty minutes together and shared a slice at the pizza place down the street before he had to head to the gym.

"Sure, I'll have time."

"Okay." He still didn't seem too happy about our mini-date, however. After our wonderful afternoon the day before, his moodiness was more troubling than usual. "Is something wrong?"

"No." He slammed the locker door shut with a little too much force.

"Isaac, you can tell me if something's wrong."

Isaac sighed again and scanned the area behind me before leaning down to whisper his next words close to my face. "I just wish you wouldn't be like that with Rachel."

"Like what?"

"So nervous. Or whatever."

"I wasn't nervous," I said, just thinking about talking to Rachel enough to make me nervous all over again. I was nervous every single lunch period, so much so that sometimes I faked the need to head to the library to do homework just to avoid the stress of not fitting in at the platinum lunch table.

Oh, *crap*, homework!

I reached out to spin the combination on the lock again. The first time around, I'd forgotten my math homework, left it in my locker because I was too busy angsting out about Mitch and Isaac and being dubbed too lumpy and redheaded for modeling. Mr. Thames, my trig teacher, had yelled at me in front of the entire class and docked me three points on my next test for having to leave his classroom to fetch my assignment after the hour had started.

This time, I was bringing that homework with me. Thank you very much, locket, once again.

Tight shoulders relaxed as I honed in on the feel of the locket's cool metal against my chest. It made a little lump beneath my tight green sweater, but I preferred to wear it close to my skin where no one else could see it. I wasn't ready to answer questions about where it had come from or why I *always* wore it, not until I talked to Gran.

"Then why did you say that?" Isaac asked, shaking his head before turning to amble down the hall. "About working the lights?"

"Because I wanted to help." I grabbed the homework and hurried after him.

"You could have been *in the show* with them," he said, still not looking at me. He could never look someone in the eye when he was annoyed. It was a tic he'd had as long as I'd known him, but for some reason it bugged me more than usual. Why couldn't he just let me enjoy my Rachel victory? "You're just as pretty as Ally and Rachel and their friends. Prettier than some of them."

Aw. Now I felt like a jerk for being annoyed. "I don't really think I'm as pretty as Rachel, but thanks."

"Babe, if you don't think you're hot, no one else is going to think you're hot," he said, turning to face me. The crowd in the hall parted around us. Everyone got out of Isaac's way. He had no idea what it was like to be the ordinary person I was when I wasn't with him, a person who had to dart and weave not to get crushed. "It's all a head game. It's like basketball. If you think you're going to win, you have a chance at winning. But if you think you're going to lose, you'll always lose."

"All the thinking in the world is not going to make my freckles go away." I laughed, but my joke fell flat.

"Well . . . you could wear makeup or something."

"I was running late this morning." My tone was sharp. "Someone wanted to stay in Nashville until ten o'clock on a Sunday night and I didn't get in bed until almost midnight."

"So now you're mad at me?"

"No, I'm not mad at you." But I was, a little. Where did he get off telling me to wear makeup? This from the boy who thought nothing of coming to school in the shirt he'd slept in if he was running late? At least I always took a shower and put on clean clothes in the morning.

"You sound mad."

"Well, I'm not." I forced a small smile. It wasn't worth arguing about. Not today, not after the wonderful day we'd had and the miracle of the entire do over. "I'm just . . . tired."

"Okay." Isaac looked confused that I'd given up so easily. But he didn't get the double standard. He never would. Explanations and arguments would be futile. "Well . . . I love you."

"I love you too." The hall was emptying fast.

"We're going to be late. See you after school?"

"See you at Ramon's," I said, ducking into my class just as the tardy bell rang. Isaac wasn't going to get to calculus in time, but it probably wouldn't matter.

Star basketball players didn't seem to get tardy slips the same way as the rest of us did. In fact, I'd bet if I turned back to look, Isaac wouldn't even be running down the hall. He'd still be working the Isaac shuffle, refusing to let anything but basketball motivate him into full-fledged activity.

For a second I hesitated, tempted to sneak a peek down the hall, but then hurried to my seat. I didn't really want to have my suspicions confirmed. Knowing the truth was one thing, having it slap you in the face was another.

"You sure you're okay?" Isaac asked, three hours later. He sat close on the bench outside Jukebox Java, clearly concerned, if a little grossed out.

He'd never seen me puke before. I wasn't the kind of person who did that sort of thing in front of her boyfriend. Isaac wasn't invited over when I had the flu, and I never drank enough to make myself sick. I hated vomiting, *really* hated it, but I hadn't been able to help myself. I'd seen the sign on the door of Jukebox Java as we were leaving Ramon's and my stomach had simply rejected my pepperoni slice and medium Coke.

The sign was *completely* different. JUKEBOX JAVA, COFFEE AND JIVE was spelled out in red letters instead of dark blue and yellow, and the logo was an espresso bean microphone instead of a coffee cup with a guitar on the side. Like the homecoming announcement, it wasn't a big deal . . . but at the same time, it was. It *really* was.

"I'm okay." But I wasn't. I was shaking and clammy beneath my sweater, hot, but with a cold sweat breaking out on my upper lip. And I was afraid, *so* afraid. The reality of *traveling through time* was starting to hit. Hard.

I was probably going into shock—over my favorite coffee shop having a different sign out in front. It seemed ridiculous, but what if it wasn't? What if these small differences meant something? What if this wasn't my life after all? What if I'd been sucked through a wormhole or found a wrinkle in time or . . . something? There was so much I didn't know about what had happened to me, about the locket.

"I can be a few minutes late if you need me to sit with you a little longer."

A few minutes late. He couldn't skip practice to tend to his sickly girlfriend. He could only be a "few minutes late." But what did I expect? This was Isaac; basketball came first.

Strangely, the thought helped calm me down. Some things might be different, but Isaac was still exactly the same. Safe. Predictable. Sweet and frustrating, perfect and flawed, all at the same time.

"No, I don't want you to be late. But could you do something for me really quick?" I turned and pulled up my hair, heart beating faster as I tugged the clasp of the locket out of my sweater. "Could you help me with my necklace? The clasp is stuck. I think maybe I'm not strong enough to pull it open."

"Sure." His warm hands brushed against the nape of my neck. Maybe this would work. Maybe Isaac would force the clasp open and I could take the locket off and put it somewhere safe until Gran arrived in a few days. I knew I'd feel better if I could just get it off.

"Is it working?"

Isaac grunted. "Nope. It's stuck, I think. It's hard to get a grip. It's so small."

"That's okay." I let my hair swish down, covering the clasp, feeling relieved and a little . . . trapped at the same time. "I'll figure it out later. Have a good practice."

"You sure you don't need me to stay for a little while? Make sure you're not going to be sick again?" he asked, but he was already standing up and swinging his backpack over his shoulder.

"No, I'm fine." I waved at him, trying to look better than I felt. "Call me."

"Right after practice." He leaned down as if to kiss my lips, but thought better of it and pecked my forehead instead before turning to dig through the front of his backpack. "Here, you want to use my practice toothbrush and toothpaste?" He pulled out the mini-kit and handed it to me. "I mean, I've used it, but—"

"That's okay, I think I have your germs." I took the kit with a smile. Isaac smiled back, looking pleased by the reminder that we'd been in lip lock less than an hour ago.

"I think you do too." He zipped up his bag and kissed me on the cheek again. "Later."

"Later." I watched him jog down the street toward school, suddenly hyper-aware of the bitter taste in my mouth. Yuck.

I pulled out the kit, squeezed toothpaste on the brush, and went to work, not even thinking about how weird it was to brush my teeth on the sidewalk until a couple of sophomore girls who were walking by shot me sideways looks as I spit into the trash can.

God, why did I have to be so normal impaired? Thank goodness Rachel or one of the other platinums hadn't seen me or I would have lost all the cool ground I'd gained during lunch.

I tossed the kit into the trash and swiped at my mouth, vowing to buy Isaac another kit later. Right now, my stomach was still too churny to think about walking the eight blocks home to get my car or make a trip to the drugstore. Despite my quick brush, I still felt icky inside, hollowed out and shaky.

There was only one solution—a peppermint mocha from Jukebox Java. I didn't want to go home and lurk inside a lonely house by myself until Mom and Dad got home. I needed to be around people, noise. Jukebox Java had both in abundance. It was a combination recording studio and coffee shop and was always filled with musicians as well as the usual caffeine-addicted crowd.

Taking a deep breath of cool, head-clearing fall air, I scooped up my purse and backpack and headed toward the newly red—not blue and yellow—door of the shop.

I could bang out my reading for AP English while sipping my mocha and maybe, if I was lucky, listening to a band lay down some country music. Monday wasn't usually a big recording day, but there was always a chance. I loved listening to live country. It was so much better than anything on the radio.

"Hey, Katie." Sarah was coming out as I was going in, her hair wrapped in a bright, multi-colored scarf that brought out the golden undertone in her skin. She glanced over my shoulder, searching for my better half, I assumed. "You alone?"

"Isaac had practice. I was going to have a mocha, want to sit with me?" I asked, excited by the possibility of girl talk.

"I'd love to, but I have to get to rehearsal by four thirty."

"Maybe tomorrow, then?"

"I've got rehearsal every day," she said, looking genuinely disappointed. "But we get out at noon on Friday for the teacher-conference things. Want to have lunch or something?"

"I can't. I have to set up the lights for the charity fashion show Rachel Pruitt is organizing."

"She asked me to work on that too!" Sarah curled her upper lip in distaste. She'd never bothered hiding her contempt for Rachel. "She wanted me to stage manage and do sound. I was going to say no, but maybe I should do it."

"That would be great," I said, sounding way too eager. But man, would it be nice to have one of "my" people backstage.

"Then we could hang out and make fun of all the rhinestone denim."

I laughed. "Surely there won't be rhinestone denim."

"Oh you *know* there will be. Mrs. Pruitt thinks she's country music royalty because she had that one-hit wonder back in the seventies," Sarah said, digging her keys out of a hobo bag nearly as big as she was. "The denim will be copious and the rhinestones plentiful."

"Well, I wouldn't want to suffer through that alone. You have to do it."

"Perfect." She smiled. "I'll tell her I'm in tomorrow. Talk soon." Sarah gave me a quick hug and started toward her car, but twirled back around almost immediately. "Oh, and I was going to tell you—Mitch is inside."

"Oh?" I hesitated for a second, my hand lingering above the door handle before I remembered I had no reason to be nervous about seeing Mitch today. "Good."

"I'm not sure. He doesn't look too good. I said 'hi,' but . . ." Sarah shrugged. "Maybe he would want to talk to a friend."

"You're his friend."

She raised one eyebrow. "Not his best friend."

Cheesy or not, the words made me feel warm all over. "Got it. I'll check on him." I waved goodbye and headed inside, grateful to still be able to call Mitch my "best friend."

The locket had done that, given me that gift. It was silly to worry about little things like a cracked mirror in the girls' bathroom or a new sign outside the coffee shop. The things that mattered were all the same, and the locket was just stuck, not "trapping" me. It was Gran's necklace. She would be able to help me take it off when she got here.

In the meantime, I was going to stop stressing. There was nothing to fear but fear itself. And denim and rhinestones.

The thought made me smile as I scanned the cozy, wood-paneled room for Mitch, but my smile vanished when I spotted him. He seemed nearly as upset as he had the first time we'd lived this day, when the tragedy of our ruined friendship had hung around him like a dark cloud, making his brown eyes look bruised.

My stomach twisted. I rethought the wisdom of dumping a peppermint mocha on my already tumultuous tummy and headed straight for Mitch's table.

Chapter Six

There's something intimate about watching someone when they don't know you're looking. Even though I was standing two feet from his table, Mitch didn't notice me, and for some reason I didn't feel the need to announce myself right away. I sort of liked watching him like this, seeing him unguarded, without the goofy faces and crazy, funny Mitchell Birnbaum persona in full effect.

He looked . . . softer, older and younger at the same time.

He was humming beneath his breath while he scratched away in a battered red notebook, the same one he'd used for his songs since tenth grade. His writing wasn't much better than the names carved hastily into the scarred table beneath his hands. I wouldn't have been able to read a word of what he'd written, even if I'd been looking at the page right side up.

As far as penmanship was concerned, Mitch was on track to becoming a doctor just like his dad. His grades were great too, and he'd already finished a handful of college courses over the summer—things like college-level chemistry and statistics that frightened me with the size of their textbooks—and received early acceptance to the pre-med program at Vanderbilt.

Mitch was brilliant, the kind of person who was meant to heal people and cure diseases. Too bad he didn't seem nearly as excited about doctoring as his dad. I knew he would have preferred to spend his last summer before graduation writing songs and playing with his band, not locked away in a Vanderbilt classroom.

Maybe that was what was bothering him.

"Coffee for your thoughts," I said.

Mitch jumped and slammed his notebook closed, blushing like he'd been caught doing something far more scandalous than writing a song. "Katie, what are you doing here?" He squinted up at me and took a deep breath, irritation marking the place between his eyes with a checkmark.

"Getting a coffee. I saw you and I thought . . ." I suddenly felt bad for intruding. Maybe Mitch didn't want company, or at least not *my* company. "But I can sit somewhere else, I don't want to bug you."

"You're not bugging me. Sit down."

"No, really, it's not a big deal." I was still getting the vibe that he would rather I hadn't shown up.

It was weird, considering how much fun we'd had yesterday, and for a second my anxiety about the locket returned in full force. What if Isaac and Mitch *weren't* the same? What if, in this new world, Mitch—who had been like me and *never* wanted to be alone—preferred to have coffee by himself?

"Whatever, dork. Sit down, already." He smiled his usual goofy grin and shoved the chair across from him out with his foot. "You can have the rest of my mocha. I shouldn't finish it, I'm hyped enough already."

"That's okay, I'll just get some water in a second," I said, easing into the chair and dropping my bags onto the floor, my nerves soothed. Mitch was happy to see me and was trying to share beverages. It was unusual only in the fact that it was *his* drink he was offering to share instead of *mine*.

"Really, I don't mind. And it's peppermint, your favorite."

"You don't want to share, trust me," I said. "I just upchucked in the trash can down the street. I brushed my teeth, but—"

His smile faded. "Are you okay?" He reached out to brush the back of his fingers against my forehead, obviously not concerned about catching my puke germs. "You don't feel hot, but do you want me to take you to my dad's office? He'd get you in right away."

"I feel fine now. I think it was just the pizza." I sat back, breaking contact. For some reason, the feel of Mitch's hand on my forehead was making me blush. "Too greasy or something."

"But you never throw up."

"I know."

"You hate throwing up."

"I know."

"So what kind of puke was it?" he asked. "The 'all of a sudden you throw up and feel better' kind or the 'sneaks up on you and—'"

"Ugh. Stop." I swallowed hard. "Can we not talk about this? Please?"

He grinned. "Sure, if you'll have my drink."

"Fine." I took the still warm mug and turned to stare at the CDs framed on the wall. They were from bands who'd recorded right here in Brantley Hills, but some of them were also names that showed up at the Country Music Awards. It was pretty inspiring, and I knew it was one of the reasons Mitch liked to come here. "So how's the writing going?"

"Good. Sort of." He laughed. "Not really. I think I stink like socks."

"You do not! 'My Menorah' is one of my favorite songs of all time," I said. "Really. It's way better than the Adam Sandler song."

"Thanks," he said, but I could tell I hadn't really made him feel better. "I should just stick to the funny stuff. That goes over better at the kind of places we play anyway. Bar mitzvahs aren't a good staging ground for angsty ballads."

"Well, ya'll could try to get more coffee shop gigs, or maybe one of the all-ages bars. You're getting really good." I took a sip of the drink, grateful for the taste of sugar and peppermint and the extra second or two to figure out if Mitch wanted me to ask him about the reasons for his angst.

"We're getting better, but Michael and Jared aren't real into angst either. They want to go more punk rock."

So he *did* want me to ask. "I'm into angst. What's angsting you?"

"Nothing."

"It's not nothing. I can tell something's bothering you," I said, pushing on when he didn't reply. "Is it the med-school stuff? Do you not want to go anymore?"

Mitch looked genuinely surprised. "No, I do. I'm excited about it. Just because I'm a doctor doesn't mean I can't still play music."

"Oh. Good." Well, there went that theory. "So what's up?"

"Nothing." He reached for his mug, but I slapped his hand.

"You can't drink out of this anymore. It has my germs."

"I don't care." He peeled my fingers off the mug with a smile. "I like your germs."

This conversation reminded me way too much of the one I'd just had with my boyfriend. Heat crept up my fingers to infect my cheeks. I was blushing again, and way too aware of Mitch's hand on mine. This was ridiculous. He was my *friend*. The memories that were making me blush had never happened. I had to get a grip.

I released the mug and shoved it in his direction. "Fine, but if you get sick, don't come crying to me."

He grunted before he took a sip. When he set the cup back down on the table, his chin stayed down and his hair flopped down into his face. "Okay, but can I come crying to you today?"

I fought the urge to reach over and take his hand. He sounded so sad. "I told you to tell me what's bothering you, doofus."

"Yeah, I know . . . It's just . . . I feel like an idiot. Like some dumb little kid who doesn't want to share his daddy."

"What do you mean?"

"Lauren and Dad set a date." He looked up, swiping his hair

behind his ear as he pushed the mocha back to my side of the table. "They're getting married in February."

Wow. Mitch's dad had only been dating Lauren a few months, and she was the first woman he'd dated since Mitch's mom died *twelve* years ago. Poor Mitch, no wonder he was upset.

"And he's planning to adopt Ricky," Mitch added with a sigh.

"Ricky?"

"Yeah . . . Ricky." He lifted his eyebrows. "You know, Lauren's little boy? The two-year-old you helped me babysit last week?"

"Oh. Right! Ricky."

Oh, no. It was happening again. Something was different, something a whole lot more serious than reading *The Scarlet Letter* instead of *The Firm*. Mitch's dad was adopting a child who hadn't even *existed* in my previous life. My mouth went dry and my tongue suddenly felt thick and numb, but somehow I managed to sound semi-normal when I spoke again. "Sorry, yeah . . . I just . . . spaced."

"It's okay. It's because it's weird, isn't it?" Mitch asked, leaning closer, his intensity making the table feel smaller. "They've only been together a few months and getting married would be crazy enough. But adoption is *huge*. I mean, Ricky is so fun and I know his dad is dead and I feel for the kid, but . . . it just seems like too much."

"Yeah. I . . . It really does seem like a big decision to make so quickly."

My stomach clenched again, but I forced down another drink of coffee. I wasn't going to be sick. This wasn't the end of the world. It was different, but it didn't have to be *bad* different. Dr.

Birnbaum and Mitch had been on their own for a long time. Dr. Birnbaum had to be lonely.

Marriage was a big step, but the few times I'd met Lauren, she'd seemed great. And now she had a little boy who needed a dad and a family. I obviously didn't remember the babysitting Mitch had said we'd done, but I knew how great he was with kids. Mitch would be the best big brother in the world and his dad wouldn't have to be all alone once his only son went away to college next fall.

This could be a good thing. A great thing, even.

"But . . . Lauren's pretty cool, right?" I asked, treading carefully.

"Yeah, she is. Especially for a lawyer."

"And your dad cares about her? And Ricky? They make him happy?"

Mitch sighed, a guilty sigh that let me know I was headed in the right direction. "Yeah, he does . . . and they do. I don't think I've ever seen Dad smile so much."

"So . . . maybe this could be okay. I mean, you won't be living in the house after next summer anyway, right?"

"No way." He shook his head, sending his hair flying. It was getting so long. It would be down to his shoulders by winter break. I really liked it and was glad the school had finally done away with the boys-must-have-short-hair part of the dress code. "I don't care if Vanderbilt is only twenty minutes away, I'm not living with Dad another year."

"Then what are you bitching about?" I flicked him on the back of the hand, keeping my tone playful, just in case he was still feeling fragile.

82

"I don't know. It's just happening too fast, I guess. And Lauren's only thirty-five." He flicked me back, but not nearly as hard.

"Your dad's only forty-something—"

"Forty-two, and I don't care." Brown eyes rolled and his lips quirked up on the left side, like they always did when he was trying not to smile. "Thirty-five is way too young for a live-in stepmom. What if I see her in her underwear or something?"

The light dawned, making me laugh. "You think she's pretty, don't you?"

"No. Gross, no way."

"You do. You totally do." I laughed again. "You want to see your stepmom in her undies!"

"Whatever." He grabbed the mug away from me, downing the last of the contents in one big gulp. "She's just too young to be a stepmom to an eighteen-year-old, that's all I'm saying. And she's so different than my real mom."

His real mom. *Of course* that was part of this. The first Mrs. Birnbaum had been pretty amazing—a med-school student who played in a country band on weekends and started teaching Mitch guitar when he was four. I felt like I'd known Mitch's mom, even though she'd died in a car accident before we'd moved into Gran's house. Mitch had never stopped talking about her.

"Well, no one's going to be like your real mom."

"I still miss her," he said, staring into our empty mug. "Almost more now than a couple of years ago. Maybe it's just because of graduation getting so close."

"Graduation is big," I said, wishing I could think of something better to say. "It's like the end of being a kid."

"I can't believe I'm eighteen and she's been gone for twelve years." He lifted his brown eyes and I felt my heart break a little bit. "It seems like forever."

At that moment, he looked eerily like the little boy I'd found crying on my swing set. The one I'd patted on his back and asked to supper at my house. I'd been five and sure my mom's cooking could solve anything. But it couldn't bring back Mitch's mom. Nothing could.

Could it?

My fingers reached for the locket, gripping it through my sweater. For the first time since Saturday night I wondered...how powerful was this little piece of jewelry? I'd *traveled back in time* two weeks. Could I go back further? Back to when Mitch was a kid and make sure his mom never got into that accident, that her car never slid into oncoming traffic and left a little boy to mourn the woman who had been his world?

If I could, would I be a nearly seventeen-year-old trapped in a five-year-old's body? Would I have to relive my entire life? No matter how stereotypically perfect my childhood had been, the thought summoned a wave of panic. I didn't want to be a little kid again. I was ready to finish high school and start my own life. With Isaac.

Going that far back seemed dangerous. Even if I *could* do it. Which . . . I wasn't sure I could. The locket was still cool in my hand. If what I was thinking about were possible, and the death of Mitch's mom was a mistake that wasn't "meant to last," wouldn't the locket start to burn the way it had before? Was that how it worked?

I didn't know. I didn't know anything.

I dropped the locket and twined my fingers together, focusing on Mitch.

"I remember the way she smelled when she'd come in to tell me a story before bed." He rubbed at his temples, like the memories were giving him a headache. "I always asked for a story about when she was little. I've forgotten most of them, but I remember she talked about this amazing tree house her dad built her when she was five. She promised we were going to build one out back in that big tree . . ."

"The one between our yards?"

"Yeah, but she died before we could start it. The wood was in the garage for like six years before Dad finally took it to the dump."

Right then and there, I vowed to build Mitch a tree house before he graduated. It didn't matter if my construction experience was limited to the bird feeder my dad and I had made at the Home Depot kids day. I was going to find a way to build him a tree house—a memorial to his mom—and we were going to sit in it every day this summer and make the most of his last few months before he left Brantley Hills. And me.

For some reason, the thought of Mitch leaving for college hurt even more than the thought of Isaac heading off to whatever school gave him the best athletic scholarship. Isaac and I had a future together, a commitment to stay the way we were. But there was nothing to keep Mitch from changing, from going off and meeting fabulous new people and forgetting everything and everyone he'd known before.

"You'll still come home, won't you?" I asked, finally giving in to the urge to take Mitch's hand. "Even if your dad and Lauren are married?"

"Of course I will. He's my dad."

"Good." I squeezed him tighter, hoping he could feel how much he meant to me. "I'd miss you if you didn't come back to visit. I'd miss you a lot."

"I'd miss you too, Minnesota." He held on to my fingers when I tried to pull away. "You know you're my best friend, right? I don't talk to other people about . . . stuff."

"You're my best friend too." And we were never going to lose that. Not now, not ever. I gently, but firmly, removed my hand. "I had so much fun with you and Isaac yesterday. We've both missed hanging out."

"Me too. We'll have to do it again. You know, when we can find some time in our busy schedules." But he didn't look like he believed we would ever find that time.

"How about Friday?" I asked, determined to show him I was serious about our friendship. "We get out at noon for the conferences. Isaac has early practice, and I'll be done with the fashion-show thing before too late. We could all go downtown again."

"Or apple picking," he said, eyes lighting up.

"Or apple picking. Yes! That's perfect!" We'd loved apple picking when we were kids and begged our parents to take us every year. But between Mitch's Hebrew school on the weekend and Isaac's junior basketball league, we'd only made it there together twice. Now we were old enough to drive ourselves. I couldn't believe we'd let so many years go by without taking advantage of that fact. "You're a genius."

"I am, actually. I am a bona fide genius." He laughed. "My dad made me take the Mensa test this summer."

"You're kidding." Dr. Birnbaum had threatened Mitch with the Mensa test before, but Mitch had always managed to be too busy to fit it in.

"He tricked me into taking it one Saturday before lunch with Bubbe." He grabbed his notebook and shoved it into his backpack, but didn't seem in any hurry to leave. "He and Lauren took the test too. We're *all* frackin' geniuses." Mitch's eyes rolled. "I've never seen Dad so happy. He said he's going to make Ricky take the test as soon as he's old enough to hold a pencil."

"I love your dad, but he has problems."

"He totally does. I think it's because he didn't learn to read until he was ten. Everyone thought he was stupid when he was a kid and he's never lived it down."

"Isn't that strange? The things that mess with us for the rest of our lives? I mean, he's a big, successful—" My cell rang, interrupting my deep thoughts. It was Isaac. I flipped the phone open. "Hey, I was just talking about you. Are you on break?"

"No, we're done. It's five thirty."

I glanced at the clock on the wall above the barista station. He was right, it was already half past. Where had the time gone? It seemed like I'd just sat down.

"I was calling to see if you felt better," he said.

"I'm feeling much better." Aw, my boyfriend was sweeter than I gave him credit for sometimes. "I came and had a coffee at Jukebox. Mitch is here and we were talking about how much fun we had yesterday. We were thinking the three of us should go apple picking Friday afternoon. After you get off practice."

"At the old place outside of town? The one we used to go to when we were little?"

"Yeah, that one."

"That would be awesome." I could tell Isaac was already plotting what to pack in Mom's picnic basket. We were all totally on the same becoming-best-friends-again page. Yay! "We should definitely go. That place was cool."

"I know. I'd forgotten about it. So what time do you think you'll be out on Friday?" I tried to catch Mitch's eye as Isaac told me he could do three o'clock and suggested we meet up at the west parking lot, but Mitch was suddenly busy organizing the sugar packets by color. "Perfect. Love you."

"Love you too," Isaac said. "See you in ten."

I snapped my phone shut and shoved it back into my purse. "So we're on for three o'clock on Friday at the west parking lot. Isaac was really excited about it too."

"Great," Mitch said, but he didn't seem as happy as I'd thought he'd be. "That will be fun."

"It will be. We'll have a great time. Just like when we were little."

"Just like." He abandoned his work with the sugar, grabbed his bag, and pushed to his feet. "You need a ride home?"

"No, Isaac's coming to get me."

"Of course he is." It wasn't a mean thing to say, but for a second it seemed like Mitch meant the words as an insult. But then he smiled and ruffled my hair. "Hey, thanks for the talk. I feel better."

"No problem." I smoothed my hair and dodged his hand when he tried to get me again. "Anytime."

"See you later."

"Later." I watched him walk out of the new red door, strangely discontent. On the surface, everything seemed to be going perfectly. Isaac and I were together, Mitch, Isaac, and I were bonding, Sarah and I were reconnecting, and I had avoided making a fool out of myself in front of Rachel Pruitt for once in my life. I should be feeling good.

And I was. Mostly. If only I knew for sure the little differences I'd been noticing were no big deal.

Mitch's dad getting married and *adopting a kid is a very big deal, no matter what.*

That marriage would change Mitch's life, his dad's life, Lauren's life, and now her son, Ricky's, life—four people were going to be powerfully affected by my second chance. Maybe all of this was going to happen eventually anyway, and I just somehow sped things up. I could only pray that speediness would be a good thing.

I hugged my purse, wishing Isaac would hurry.

Chapter Seven

The week had been strange and, at times, awful—little changes everywhere and the continued stuck-around-my-neck state of the locket adding up to big anxiety and plenty of sleepless nights— but all my worries seemed trivial as soon as I reached the top of the stairs and eased out onto the catwalk leading to the grid high above the stage.

The fashion show run-through was finished and the light board programmed. I was done serving Rachel Pruitt for the day . . . except for one pesky spotlight that wasn't working the way it was supposed to be. One little light that I was going to have to *crawl out above the stage* and replace.

God. Help. Me.

There's nothing that will take your mind off your troubles like being seconds away from falling to your death.

"I can't do this. I have to come down," I whispered into my headset, my hands fisting around the iron railing of the catwalk.

"Did you forget the safety harness for the light?" Sarah asked, her voice echoing through my pounding head. "I can have the stagehand run one up before he leaves."

"No, I've got the harness. I just . . ."

I looked down again. Big mistake. I suddenly couldn't move. All I could do was stare out onto the iron grid where the theater lights hung—black and dusty—from their C-clamps and imagine falling fifty feet to splatter all over the stage. It didn't matter that the spaces in the grid were way too small for a grown person to fit through or that I knew members of the drama club wouldn't be allowed to hang the lights if it weren't completely safe.

All rational thoughts vanished in the face of the pure terror pumping through my veins. The air was too hot to breathe. My vision swam. "I'm coming down."

"No, you're not," Sarah said firmly, in stage manager mode. "It's fine. You're going to be fine. Just replace the spot and be done with it."

"I can't. I'm afraid of heights."

There was a moment of static on the other end of the headset and for a second I could have sworn I heard Sarah laugh. "Then why did you volunteer to work lights?"

"I forgot how scary it was up here." I sounded about three years old. What a baby. The dorkiness of it all helped me draw a slightly deeper breath.

"It's totally safe, Katie, I promise. You're going to be fine." Sarah's calm voice soothed me even further. I managed to pull one hand away from the railing to wipe my sweating palm on my jeans. "Do you want me to come up there? I've still got a few things to do at the soundboard, but—"

"No, it's okay. You'll be late for your rehearsal if you help me." Not to mention I'd be late to meet Isaac and Mitch if I kept stalling. "Just . . . keep talking, okay? It helps."

"No problem. I can talk and program sound at the same time." The beep of the computer saving settings confirmed her words as truth. "I am a multi-tasker. So how's the secret project going?"

"What secret project?" I asked, easing out onto the grid on my hands and knees. My heart jumped into my throat and did a back handspring that would have made many on the BHH cheerleading team extremely jealous.

"You know, the tree house? The one you grilled my dad about for an hour on Tuesday?"

Sarah's dad was an architect and had been cool enough to draw me a simple set of plans for a tree house platform. I'd spent all afternoon Wednesday and Thursday building it in my garage, enduring the stuffy air in the name of keeping my construction secret from Mitch—who had been known to wander into my backyard without announcing his presence.

"Right. The tree house. I'm sorry." I grabbed the spotlight from the catwalk and inched a little closer to my final destination. I could do this, as long as I didn't think about it too much. "It's going great. I already finished the platform and cut the wood for the steps."

"Awesome. You did it all yourself?"

"I did." I didn't mind her surprised tone. I'd been equally shocked that I could build something so big all on my own. It was a simple plan, but still . . . I was pretty proud of myself. "I used my dad's nail gun and power saw and sander."

"Ooh! That is so sexy." She laughed. "Don't let Isaac see you with power tools. He'd probably quit basketball to sit around and watch you whip things out of your tool belt."

Ugh, Isaac.

Thinking about him made me happy and sad all at the same time. Happy, because things were the same as they'd ever been. Sad, because . . . things were the same as they'd ever been. He was so cute and sweet and fun, but he was also *so* obsessed with basketball and *himself*. More and more, I noticed that Isaac never asked me how my day was or what my plans were. Our conversations always revolved around him, as if he took for granted the fact that he was the more interesting half of our couple.

Which he *was* . . . but still . . . it would be nice if he'd at least pretend I was interesting. Mitch seemed to find me interesting. But Mitch wasn't my boyfriend.

Mitch *wasn't* the person I should be thinking about last thing before I went to bed, Mitch *wasn't* the person I should hope to see sitting alone at a table in Jukebox Java when I walked by after school, and Mitch *certainly wasn't* the person I should be think-ing about while I was making out with my boyfriend on my back porch. I shouldn't be thinking about Mitch at all, let alone com-paring Isaac's kisses to a kiss that had never happened.

I was as horrible a girlfriend in my do over as I had been the first time around, and I needed to get a grip in a major way.

The only reason I was thinking about Mitch's kiss was because Isaac and I had been together forever. I'd never kissed anyone but Isaac and I'd kissed him for *three years*. Mitch was intriguing because I'd only kissed him once, but I knew better than to be sucked in by the lure of the new and ruin the good things I had.

Mitch was my friend and Isaac was my boyfriend. That was the way it was supposed to be. I just had to find a way to put some of the spark back into my romantic relationship.

Maybe Sarah had something. Maybe I should show Isaac how handy I'd become with power tools.

"Isaac might have to learn to deal. I'm considering a career in construction," I said, lifting the old light up to the grid and settling the new one in its place.

"Well, you'll have to work on one-story houses, Ms. Skeered of Heights."

"Ha ha. Speaking of heights, you should come see the tree house this weekend. After it's up in the tree."

"You going to climb it with me?"

"Sure. Dad's putting the platform on a low limb. He's securing it and nailing the steps on the tree this afternoon while Mitch and Isaac and I are apple picking. That way it will be a surprise."

"Very cool." She was quiet for a second, and I heard the soundboard computer shutting off. "You done yet?"

"Almost," I said, tongue slipping out to wet my lips. "I've got the old light out and the new light in. Just need to put on the safety harness."

"Perfect! See, that wasn't so bad, was it?"

"I'll let you know. I'm not back on the ground yet." She was right, though, it hadn't been that bad. My heart still raced like I'd downed three All-nighters at Jukebox, but I'd replaced the light and was on my way back to the catwalk without having a full-blown heart attack. "Thanks for talking to me."

"Oh please, Katie. You don't have to say thank you."

"Yes, I do." I left the old light sitting on the catwalk where Mr. Geery, the drama-club sponsor, had said he would pick it up later, and started down the winding circular stairs leading back to the stage. "The manners are deeply ingrained. My mom and dad wouldn't even change my diaper when I was a baby unless I said please."

"You don't need manners with friends." Sarah's voice hit me twice, once in my earbud and once from just ahead of me, at the base of the stairs.

I pulled my headset off and handed it over. "I think you do. Especially with friends. I'd rather be unmannerly with people I don't like than people I do."

Sarah shot me a sideways look before hustling back toward the equipment lockbox. "But aren't you always meaner to the people you love? I'm way meaner to my dad and mom than I am normal people. And Hunter . . . Well, I love my sweet little brother so much I punched him in the face on the way to school this morning."

I laughed and grabbed my backpack from the floor as Sarah locked up the headsets. "I'm sure that really messed him up, you being so buff and all."

"It did. He cried." She jogged the ten feet to the dressing room and knocked on the door. "Ya'll almost done in there? I need to lock up."

"Almost done, a couple more minutes," came a muffled voice from inside. Who knew it took so long to hang up clothes? Not I. But then, I usually left mine draped over the chair at the desk in my room and did my homework on the bed when the pile got too high.

Sarah sighed, crossing her thin arms and checking her watch before turning back to me. "Hey, did you hear that Hunter's the new equipment manager for the basketball team?"

Did I? In my old life, I certainly had. I'd heard about five minutes before I learned Hunter was the one who'd told Isaac about me and Mitch. "Yeah, I think Isaac told me. I think . . ."

Vague. Best to be vague when you were a time-traveling freak.

"He's so excited. He thinks it will give him an in for making varsity next year, even though he'll only be a sophomore."

"Big dreams, little Hunter."

"Especially considering he's an average player. At *best*."

"Maybe he'll get better this year. Isaac improved a lot between freshman and sophomore years." Isaac, who was probably already waiting for me in the parking lot.

I considered ducking into the dressing room to change into the clean shirt I'd brought but thought better of it. Better to stay dusty and free of embarrassing interaction for the day. So far, Rachel hadn't found a way to put me in my place this afternoon and I meant to keep it that way. "Listen, I'd better—"

"Me too." Sarah sighed. "Come on, you guys, I'm going to be late for rehearsal." She banged on the heavy metal door . . . the heavy metal door that was on the *opposite* side of the theater than it had been.

My heart rate spiked, shooting back into crawling-out-on-the-catwalk territory. I couldn't believe I hadn't noticed this before. The boys' dressing room and the girls' dressing room were flip-flopped, like I'd crossed through a mirror and was seeing backstage from the other side.

And maybe I was, maybe this was all a crazy, looking glass world, just like Alice in Wonderland.

The thought made me shuffle backward, fingers digging into the canvas of my backpack. I hadn't read the Alice books in years, but I remembered what a bad feeling they'd given me. Even as a kid, I'd hated the idea that nothing was as it seemed, that normally cute little animals were scary and disturbed, that a card queen could order a little girl's head chopped from her body, that—

"Hey, watch out!" Sarah grabbed my sleeve and pulled me forward seconds before a great metallic clattering filled the air. I spun to see one of the heavy stage ladders lying right where I'd been standing and a red-faced freshman boy a few feet away, his arms overflowing with a giant prop box.

"What the hell, Shawn?" Sarah yelled, pushing in front of me, gesturing to the fallen ladder with one angry finger. "You could have fucking hurt someone. Watch where the fuck you're going."

"I'm sorry, Sarah, I—"

"You better fucking be sorry. Now tell Katie you're sorry."

Shawn turned even redder, until he looked almost purple in the dim backstage light. "I'm so sorry, Katie. I didn't even see it."

"It's . . . fine. No worries," I said, trying to smile despite the fact that I was still pretty freaked out.

Whether it was the fact that I'd nearly been crushed or that Sarah was cussing like a sailor, however, I couldn't really say. In my real life, Sarah wouldn't say shit if she'd had a mouth full of it. Now she apparently threw the "eff" word around like it was going out of style.

This is your real life now. Get used to it.

I shivered, suddenly cold. I couldn't wait to see Gran tomorrow and learn what she knew about the locket. I couldn't wait until Saturday after next, when this do over would finally be over and I could start fresh with no conflicting memories to mess with my mind.

"Everything okay out here?" Rachel appeared at the dressing room door behind us.

"Yeah, Shawn just needs to try to suck less," Sarah said, dismissing her freshman stagehand with one final glare before she turned back to Rachel. "Are y'all ready? I need to head out."

"Just a couple more seconds," Rachel said in her talking-to-someone-who-matters voice. Ever since the fashion show girls found out Sarah was a "professional" actress, they'd been a lot friendlier. "Sorry, we're almost finished. We're just deciding on the dresses for the finale. I think I've picked mine." She gestured down at the skintight red dress she wore. It looked like something my gran would have worn to a 1960s cocktail party. It was really different. Interesting.

And not *at all* what she'd worn before.

I peeked into the room, swallowing hard as I took in the rhinestone pins and cat-eye glasses, the taffeta and chiffon and strings of pearls. All ten girls were decked out in period costume. It was like they'd stepped out of *Leave It to Beaver*. Or maybe *Stepford Wives* would be a better analogy.

More changes. More and more and more until I felt like I was going to lose what was left of my mind.

"Is something wrong, Katie?" Rachel asked.

"Um. No." I shook my head a little too long. I could feel myself shaking like an idiot, but I couldn't seem to stop. It was starting to feel like this wasn't even my life anymore.

Who had dreamed mundane details were so important? That the color of a door or the arrangement of a classroom or the expected Wednesday chili dog buffet line could mean so much?

Rachel reached out, plucking a dust ball from the end of my hair and flicking it onto the ground. "Listen, Isaac and I talked." She made the word "talked" sound like a bona fide betrayal. "I know you were upset that I didn't ask you to be part of the show."

I was going to *kill* him. How dare he talk to Rachel about me behind my back? And tell her things I'd never even said, no less? I tried to smile. "No, I wasn't upset at all. I mean, I'm *not* upset. Now, or ever."

"It's okay. I really would have asked you if it wasn't a conflict of interest."

A conflict of interest? What was she talking about?

She swiped an invisible bit of lipstick off the corner of her lips. "I mean, I really wanted this show to have all the hottest senior girls at BHH in it. I told Isaac that, but he still didn't get it. He just can't see clearly where you're concerned. But you understand, right?"

"Oh, yeah. No worries." I understood completely. She'd thrown the "senior" part in there so it wouldn't seem like she was being mean, but she was. She knew it, and I knew it. Once again, she was making it clear I wasn't good enough for Isaac and that he was the only one who hadn't gotten the memo.

Sarah took a deep breath and discreetly grabbed the strap of my backpack. "Okay, Rachel, I have to go. You can have the keys." She tossed the keys in a wide arc. For the first time in my life I witnessed Rachel Pruitt suffering from awkward as she snatched them from the air. It was only a second, but it was enough to make me silently pledge my eternal friendship to Sarah Needles. "Lock up the dressing room and the front and back doors to the theater. I'm telling Mr. Geery you're in charge, so if anything gets stolen, it's your fault."

"Thanks, Sarah," Rachel said, so sweet she'd make sugar taste artificial. "You've been a big help. You're such a good friend to our little Katie. And her boyfriend."

"Whatever, Rachel." Sarah spun away, pulling me with her. When she was in stage manager mode, Sarah was confident enough to treat a senior goddess like an equal.

I, however, turned over my shoulder and gave a little wave.

I wasn't confident enough to snub Rachel. For some stupid reason, I couldn't bring myself to be rude to the girl who had inferred I was an ugly troll more times than I could remember.

"Don't let her get to you. You're gorgeous, way prettier than she is. People would skin their babies for hair your color." Sarah flung open the back door. We both winced in the bright sunlight. It was easy to forget it was still daylight in the blackness of the theater. "I've got to run, but call me la—"

"I will!" On impulse, I lunged for Sarah, hugging her tight. "Thanks for saving me from the ladder. I'm so glad we're friends again."

"Me too." She hugged me back, tentatively at first, but then a real, strong squeeze. "It sucked not seeing you. You . . . really mean a lot to me. You know that, right?"

"I do," I said, touched by the emotion in her voice. "I hated that we were growing apart."

"Me too. Let's not let it happen again. No matter what." Sarah's green, yellow, and brown eyes practically glowed with intensity. I'd never seen her so serious. And it was because of me. Because she'd missed me. It was almost enough to make me hug her again, but I didn't. I knew she wasn't a huge fan of the touchy-feely.

"No matter what," I promised instead, waving as she turned to run to her car.

Moments like these were what I needed to remember when I was freaking out about little differences. I wouldn't trade my renewed relationship with Sarah for a million Wednesday chili dog buffets. And who cared if she cussed more than she used to? Words were just words. Actions were what mattered, and Sarah had proved what an amazing friend she was.

And I was going apple picking! I actually squee-ed aloud as I ran around the theater, heading toward the west parking lot.

Who cared that Rachel had stung me yet again? I was going to relive a precious moment from my childhood with two of my favorite people in the world. Rachel probably wouldn't know a precious moment if it came up and bit her on her perfect little butt. She probably . . . wouldn't . . .

Mitch waved at me from across the lot. He leaned against the door of the family van, ready for wholesome, fruit-picking fun in a white, long-sleeved shirt beneath a pair of faded overalls. He looked like an overgrown Huckleberry Finn, which shouldn't have been cute, but it was. Really cute. It made me wish I'd thought to dress up too. My jeans and blue-and-white-checked button-up were definitely farm friendly, but Mitch had taken this to an entirely different—and awesome—level.

If Isaac had been sporting overalls too, it would have been a moment of such preciousness I would have been forced to grab my cell and take a picture. Of course, if Isaac had just *been there*—regardless of his state of dress—that would have been good too. But he wasn't. It was only Mitch.

I slowed, crossing the last few feet to Mitch's van at a trudge, my feet clearly wanting to avoid the inevitable. "He's not coming, is he?"

"He called a few minutes ago. Practice is running late."

"Great." I wanted to rant about the fact that Isaac should have called *me*, not Mitch, but I knew why he'd done it. He didn't want to deal with me "nagging" him about basketball consuming his life. Basketball came first and he was sick of me pressuring him to change that. "This stinks."

"We don't have to go, if you don't want." Mitch shrugged. "I know you wanted this to be a three-of-us kind of thing, so—"

"No way." I smiled and grabbed the bandana out of the front

pocket of his overalls. "We're going. And we're going to pick apples and keep them all to ourselves and not give Isaac any." My fingers trembled a little as I tied the bandana around my hair, but I pushed my anger and disappointment away.

I wasn't going to let basketball ruin another day. Mitch and I were going to go and have fun, and we'd be back when we got back. Isaac had talked about watching a movie at his house tonight, but if I didn't get back in time, he could watch it by himself. It was probably some stupid boy movie he'd ordered from Netflix anyway.

Basketball and boy movies. They could both go suck it.

"Hell, let's get some cider too," Mitch said, playing along. "And we'll warm it up and go sit right in front of his house and drink it."

"And when he smells it and comes begging for a sip, we won't give him one."

"Not even *one*. And then he'll cry," Mitch said, absolutely serious, so serious I wanted to laugh, but I didn't. It was more fun not to.

"That's right, but we still won't give him one." I narrowed my eyes, doing my best Mom impression. "And he'll learn not to stand us up ever again."

Mitch nodded sagely. "It will be a bought lesson."

"That's right." I fought a smile as I walked around to get into the passenger's seat. "Sometimes you have to show people a little tough love."

"Speaking of, I love you in that bandana." Mitch hopped into the car, the light in his eyes making me glad we hadn't canceled.

"Thanks. I love your overalls."

"All the ladies do, Katie." He winked at me and fired up the van. "All the ladies do."

We laughed as Mitch pulled out of the parking lot and down the street lined with fire orange trees. Crisp fall air rushed in the windows and a demo tape Mitch had scored from one of his music connections blared from the speakers. It was going to be a perfect afternoon, whether Isaac was there or not.

Chapter Eight

*M*itch sneezed again, and the little girl with pigtails seated next to him in the hay-filled trailer scooted a few more inches away. At this rate she was going to fall off the back of the cart before we reached the apple orchard.

I pressed my fist against my mouth and fought the urge to laugh.

"This is picturesque." Mitch motioned toward the cornfield flowing down the hill away from the tractor trail and the pumpkin patch beyond. "I'm glad we—decided to—take the hayride—to the—"

Mitch lost the battle with another sneeze, making the little girl shoot first him, then her mother—seated on the opposite side of the trailer—an outraged look. *Somebody needs to do something,* the look said. This diseased sneezing was unacceptable!

Clearly a little Rachel Pruitt in training.

"Sorry," Mitch said, turning to whisper in my ear. "I'm allergic to hay."

"I sort of figured," I whispered back.

"I would have taken my allergy medicine this morning, but I forgot about the whole hayride thing. Do you think I'm bothering anyone?"

"No, not at all." I bit my lip to keep from smiling.

Mitch squeezed my knee right at the ticklish place, making me jump and giggle before slapping his hand away. "I take back every nice thing I ever said about your acting. You are a bad actress. Very, very bad."

"I'm not a bad actress, I'm a bad *liar*. There's a difference."

Mitch reached for my knee again, but I dodged him with a karate chop and a handful of hay to the face. He sneezed again and we both started laughing.

"This is embarrassing." He sniffed.

I pulled his bandana out of my hair and pressed it into his hands. "Here, I think you need this more than I do."

"Thanks, Mom."

"No problem." I was still grinning when I turned back to watch the apple orchard come into view and caught the mom of the little girl giving me and Mitch "the look"—the same "aren't young people in love the cutest thing" look old people had always given me and Isaac. She turned and kissed her husband on the cheek. He wrapped his arm around her, pulling her close.

A chill slipped into my chest, tamping down my giddiness to a nice, respectable level. This was a friendly trip. A *friend* trip. Mitch and I had always been physical with each other—a side effect of becoming friends when we were little enough to think wrestling in our swimsuits on the Slip 'n Slide was completely acceptable—but maybe we should tone it down a little. We wouldn't want to give anyone the wrong idea.

Not that it really mattered on a hayride in the middle of nowhere, surrounded by a bunch of families and little kids, but still . . . It would probably be a good habit to get into.

Mitch sneezed again, and the little girl made a face like she'd been sprayed with monkey pee. "It should stop once I get away from the hay," Mitch said apologetically, loud enough for the girl and her family to hear.

"It's fine," I said. "You can't help it. And we'll walk back when we're done picking. It's not that far to the van."

I could see Mitch's relief on his face. In that moment, I knew he'd done the hayride thing for me, because I'd been so excited to see the faded green tractor pulling the hay-filled trailer the same way it had when we were little. It kind of made me want to hug him, in spite of my non-touchy thoughts.

"Here we are." The old man driving the tractor—the same ancient, crooked-faced farmer who had helped me and Mitch lift our apple baskets into our red wagons when we were little—turned around at the end of the gravel trail. "Baskets are at the beginning of each row and ladders at the end. Children, be sure to watch your parents. Don't let them get lost."

The mom and dad across from us laughed. The little girl rolled her eyes. Still in pigtails and already with the eye rolling. Good thing her parents were gross in love because she was going to be a heck on wheels. I didn't think I eye-rolled until I was at least old enough to wear lip gloss.

Farmer Funny killed the engine. "Last tractor leaves in forty-five minutes."

"I forgot about the ladders," Mitch said as he jumped off the end of the trailer and turned to offer me a hand down. "I was so scared of those when we were little. My dad had to climb up behind me."

"Really? You were scared of ladders?" I'd forgotten about the ladders too, even though I'd nearly been crushed by one an hour earlier. Still, climbing a little apple-picking ladder should be a piece of cake after braving the light grid.

I followed Mitch through the trampled grass, heading toward the last row of the orchard. The sun was going down and everything was bathed in a rosy pink light, blushing like the ripe apples peeking from the tree branches. It was beautiful, but the fading light meant fading warmth. We were going to have to pick fast if we didn't want to freeze on the walk back to the car. It was starting to get cold at night.

"I'm *still* scared of ladders," Mitch said. "Heights, really. Terrified of them."

"Me too! " I studied him out of the corner of my eye. Was this something I hadn't known about Mitch or something new, something that was different this time around? I'd been lulled into relaxing my guard by the utter sameness of the farm and had almost—for a blissful thirty minutes—forgotten I was living in do-over land.

"I know." He grabbed a basket and headed down the row.

"Remember swim lessons? When you wouldn't jump off the high dive and the lifeguard had to push you off the end into the water?"

Thank God, I *did* remember that. It was the first time I'd ever really thought I hated someone. I'd plotted the pimply-faced teenage lifeguard's death for the rest of the summer. "And you hid under the bleachers so you wouldn't have to jump. You big chicken," I said as we walked by a pair of little boys struggling with a basket of apples as big as they were. They couldn't be more than four or five years old.

"You're just jealous that you lacked the forethought to hide with me," Mitch said, stopping in the middle of the row as I doubled back to check on the boys.

"I was *seven*. Who has *forethought* when they're seven? And you don't count, Mensa boy." I threw the words over my shoulder before bending down to take one side of the giant basket. "Do you guys need help?" I asked the two boys, smiling at the almost identical freckled faces that looked up into mine. Aw, man, these two were precious.

And trouble. Before I knew what was happening, both of them had narrowed their eyes and lifted their fists.

"Stranger danger!" the one on my right screamed, aiming a karate kick at my knee that I just barely avoided.

I backed up, holding up my hands. "No, I—"

"Stranger danger! Mom!" The slightly bigger boy joined his brother and they both rushed me like mini-ninjas.

"Run!" I grabbed Mitch—who was, of course, laughing his ass off—by the arm and busted a move down the row.

Thankfully, however, our flight was short lived.

"Ashton! Amos! Stop chasing those people!" a female voice yelled from the other end of the row. We turned to see a tired-looking woman with a little girl propped on her hip pulling a second red wagon toward the boys. She dropped the handle to wave in my and Mitch's direction. "Sorry about that! They take karate."

"No problem!" I smiled and waved back, relieved to have been spared some kind of preschool smack down. Sheesh. The perils of trying to be nice!

Mitch chuckled again as we headed back down the row. "Stranger danger. How awesome was that? I'm totally going to teach Ricky to do that. It's hysterical."

"So you're getting used to the little-brother idea?"

Mitch shrugged and his smile faded. "Maybe."

Hmm . . . sounded like that was still a topic best left alone if we wanted to enjoy the rest of our afternoon. I reached up to grab an apple from a low-hanging limb. It snapped off easily in my hand, still a little warm from the sun. Yum.

I bit in, tasting sweet and sour, simplicity and sin, all in the first crunch.

"That apple is probably coated in pesticides."

"Mmm . . . pesticides." I took another big bite and grinned at him around the pulpy white flesh.

Mitch snatched the fruit from my hand so fast I made a yipping sound and juice ran down my chin. I swiped at it and swallowed while he finished off the rest of the apple in three huge bites.

"What about the pesticides, thief?"

"You made them look so yummy, I couldn't help myself." He tossed the core into the grass and stopped to stare at the last tree in the row. It was much bigger than the others, with three gnarled main branches that twisted at least twenty feet in the air and dozens of longer, thinner limbs reaching down to kiss the ground on every side. A ladder was already positioned beneath a break in the foliage, near a clutch of particularly delicious-looking fruit.

"Is it wrong that even looking at that ladder kind of makes me want to puke?" Mitch asked, tossing our basket on the ground with a sigh.

Crap! He really *was* scared of heights. This could put a major dent in my tree house plan. Dad was nailing the platform on the lowest limb, but still . . . it was at least twelve feet up. How ridiculous would it be to have a tree house between our yards and both of us be too scared to sit in it?

Ugh. No way. I wasn't going to let phobia win. I'd beaten my fear once today and survived a mini-ninja attack. I could do this. Mitch could too.

"I climbed out on the light grid to replace a spot at the fashion-show practice this afternoon," I said, grabbing the discarded basket from the ground. "All by myself."

"You're kidding. That's, like, forty feet up."

"Fifty." I stuck my nose in the air, playing up my pride in my accomplishment.

Mitch laughed. "Wow. Aren't you the badass?"

"I am the badass. *The.* Badass. I am so badass I'm going to climb that ladder even though I am much less coordinated than you are and much more likely to break something doing it."

"That's not true." Mitch followed me over to the base of the ladder, but he didn't look happy about it.

"It is true. You used to be almost as jocky as Isaac," I reminded him. "And I get B's in gym. Nobody gets B's in gym. Coach Miller gives A's for showing up and dressing out."

Mitch grunted as he looked up, his dark eyes flitting from the ladder to the apples and back again. "Yeah. You aren't the most athletic Katie I know."

I snorted. "How many Katies do you know?"

"At least ten, and they're all better at sports than you are." He grinned a crooked grin and nudged me with his shoulder. "You were pretty bad at swimming too. Did you ever learn to do anything but doggy paddle?"

"Nope."

"That's sad. Poor baby." He started to pet my head like I was a puppy-pound reject, but I growled and snapped at his hand. He pulled away with a laugh. "Hey, that's okay. I like sad clowns."

"Thanks, but you know what's really sad? *I'm* not the one who's too chicken to climb a little ladder." I propped the basket on my hip and started to climb, ignoring the gazelle-like leaping of my heart in my chest as my brain complained that it wasn't safe to climb a ladder without both of your hands free.

People had been picking apples for hundreds of years, maybe thousands, and you never heard of anyone falling off a ladder and dying at their friendly local pick-it-yourself farm. This was perfectly safe. Besides, I was only five feet in the air, six . . . seven . . . eight.

Oh . . . man. Nine . . . ten . . . eleven. Gulp.

I plunked the basket down on the top of the ladder, gripped the top rung with both hands, and took a deep breath. It didn't help. It was getting harder and harder to breathe as I imagined myself toppling backward, breaking my neck when my body connected with the hard ground. In my mind's eye, I saw the unnatural bend of my limbs and my blood splattered on the dust—tiny spots of crimson dwarfed by the red apples scattered around my broken body.

I was about to cry uncle and scurry back down the ladder when Mitch started up behind me.

"Fine, I'm not going to let you out-manly me," he said, an edge in his voice, though he was obviously joking around. "But if we die, I'm going to say I told you so a hundred zillion times."

"That's fine. Jews and Catholics don't go to the same heaven, right? So I won't be able to hear you anyway," I said, feeling a marked loosening in my chest when Mitch's hands grabbed the ladder just below mine. His body surrounded me on every side. He wouldn't let me fall. And even if we did, he was in prime impact-softening position.

"So you believe in heaven? In the white-wings-and-fluffy-clouds kind of way?" he asked, his tone light, but with an undercurrent of seriousness I couldn't ignore.

"No, not really." I shrugged. "I don't know what heaven will be like."

"But you don't think I'll be in yours?" He stepped up another rung and his mouth was in my hair, his breath warm against my neck.

If I turned my head, his lips would touch my cheek. My pulse picked up again, and I was suddenly very aware of how close Mitch was. The heat from his body seeped through my clothes, warming my skin, making my bones ache in a disturbingly pleasant way.

When I spoke again, I didn't sound like myself. "Of course not. If there's a heaven, I think all good people will be there." I swallowed, struggling to get a hold on the quiver in my voice. "I was just joking around." I shifted to the right, but that only brought Mitch's lips into my peripheral vision.

Bad idea. *Bad.* I tried to shift back, but Mitch moved closer, until we were nearly nose to nose.

"So you don't think it matters which religion you are?"

Wow. Heavy question. I'd been raised Catholic, but did I believe I was right and everyone else was wrong? There were parts of my faith that seemed to demand I think that, but . . . those parts had never felt right to me.

"I'm sorry," Mitch said, moving back a few inches. "Am I getting too—"

"No. I don't think it matters." I met his gaze and held it, even thought I knew I shouldn't, even though every second I stared into his eyes made me more and more aware of the not-just-friends energy licking at every bare inch of my skin. "Do you think it matters?"

"What matters?" he asked, lips parting slightly. "Did you know you have a blue swirl in your left eye?"

"No, I didn't." I tried to laugh, but it came out as a sigh. I needed to move. I had to get away from Mitch. Now.

"You do. When the light hits it just right, you can see it." His mouth moved a little closer to mine. My head spun and my lips tingled, every traitorous nerve ending urging me closer, closer. "It's pretty."

"Thanks." My breath was coming faster. I wondered if he could tell.

Tension spiked the air, making each breath a shot of rum I shouldn't drink. Mitch's smell—honey shampoo and incense from the air freshener in the van, mixed with the salt and cinnamon scent of his skin—teased at my nose. He smelled so good, so amazingly good. I wanted to brush my face against his neck and suck in his scent, feel his pulse beat beneath my lips. I wanted to—

For the first time since my rewind, the locket grew hot beneath my shirt. Terror blossomed in my chest—sharp and fast, like a shot of adrenaline straight to the heart. This couldn't happen! I didn't want to go anywhere! I didn't want another do over. I wanted things to stay the way they were—with Isaac still in love with me and Mitch my good friend.

I clutched wildly at the burning locket, grabbed a fistful of my shirt instead, and would have tipped over backward and made my bloody, head-splattered vision of a few minutes before a reality if Mitch hadn't steadied me with a hand on my shoulder.

"Hey," he said, fear in his voice as the ladder swayed for a moment before growing steady once more. "What's wrong? Are you—"

"I don't know. I . . . I . . ." The locket cooled, its temperature dropping rapidly. Too bad I couldn't say the same for my racing pulse. It took several seconds for me to regain control and convince my heart to stop trying to crawl up my throat.

Finally, I sucked in a shaking breath, wondering if my inappropriate thoughts about Mitch had triggered the jewelry's power. There was no way to know, but I could make darn sure I didn't trigger it again. No more thoughts about kissing anyone but Isaac.

"I thought I saw a bee. It's gone now." I thrust my arm into the air between us, fumbling for the closest tree limb. "We should start picking. We've only got like twenty minutes, and that's if we catch the hayride. But you wanted to walk, right? So you wouldn't start sneezing again?"

Mitch's lips pressed together and he swallowed hard, but then his hand reached up to grab a mostly ripe piece of fruit. "Yeah. That would probably be better."

"Cool. We're still good. This shouldn't take long." I snatched at anything red and thrust it into the basket, attention trained on the tree limbs, ignoring the feel of Mitch's eyes still on my face.

"Good. Following my manly ladder-climbing display, I wouldn't want to ruin your image of me by having another allergy attack," he said, sounding mostly normal. "Allergies aren't manly."

"Nope. Not really." I smiled, a fake smile that I hid by twisting around to pluck an apple on my left.

"Wow, thanks, Minnesota." Mitch grabbed the nearly full basket and backed down the ladder with a dramatic huff. "That's a nice thing to say."

I followed him with a tight laugh, doing my best to relax. The tension was fading, the locket was cool and calm, everything was going to be fine. "I didn't say it, *you* did! I was just agreeing with you."

"Whatever. My rock-god guitar playing and cool hair and unusually awesome tallness make up for my delicate health and fear of heights. Completely." He reached the bottom and moved around the side to watch me finish climbing down. "You should really think that. That I'm awesome and adorably flawed."

"Since when do you care what anyone thinks?" I rolled my eyes as I stepped off the ladder.

"I *don't* care what anyone thinks." Mitch's lips quirked at one side, but his eyes were soft, telling. "I care what you think."

My mouth opened and closed with no words coming out. What could I say to that? To the sweetness and scariness and heaviness of *that*? I didn't even want to think about his words. They were dangerous.

I just shook my head and grabbed the apple basket from his hands. "I think you're almost perfect, dork. You're my best friend."

The way my voice lingered on the word "friend" made it echo through the orange-and-pink-streaked orchard, down the trail past the pumpkin patch and cornfields, all they way into the van. It was still whispering in the air when we pulled into my driveway forty-five minutes later.

"Mr. Almost Perfect will see you later," Mitch said, shifting the van from drive straight into reverse, clearly intending to drop me and go.

I bit my lip, wondering if I should leave the tree house for tomorrow. It was almost dark and—after the weirdness between us—it seemed better *not* to let Mitch know I'd spent my every free minute this week working on a secret project for him. He might get the wrong idea.

And maybe he should. You didn't spend any time making something for Isaac.

I blinked, trying to erase the realization from my mind.

"Um, right. It's late. I'll call you, then?" I sounded as unraveled as I felt. I was so confused, so—

"Katie!" Dad stuck his head out the front door, smiling and waving when he saw Mitch. "You two come on in, Katie's gran is here."

Gran! She was here. A day early! It was the answer to a prayer.

"Bye, see you tomorrow!" I was out of the car so fast I almost tripped and fell flat on my face. Thankfully, I didn't. I didn't have time for skinned palms. I had to talk to Gran. Now. Yesterday. Five days ago!

"What about your apples?"

"I'll get them tomorrow!" I called over my shoulder, giving Mitch a little wave. "Yay! Gran!" I squealed to my dad as I ran past him into the house, following the smell of lavender and rotted peaches into the living room.

There Gran sat, right next to my mom, wearing the same pink and black turtleneck dress she'd been wearing when she arrived the first time. I'd never been so happy to see her crazy 1970s wardrobe or her silver bun and muddy green eyes. I opened my mouth, ready to tell her how happy I was that she was here, how I'd been dying to talk to her, but she beat me to the punch.

"My Katie!" She laughed and tapped my mom on the knee. "Lord, girl, your hair is as red as it was when you were a baby!" Her friendly green eyes were flat, empty of everything but the usual good humor, and I knew right then . . .

She didn't know that I had the locket.

Chapter Nine

Just keep swimming, just keep swimming, just keep swimming. As I flicked switches up and down, working the board in the light booth, the fish from *Finding Nemo*'s mantra played on an endless loop in my brain, powered by fear and anxiety and the need *not* to think about last night.

I couldn't think about Gran's complete confusion when I'd asked her about the locket. I couldn't think about Dad's insistence that he'd never seen his mom wearing the piece of jewelry. I couldn't think about the hours I'd spent digging through the family photo albums after everyone else had gone to bed, searching for some proof that Gran had worn the necklace and coming up empty.

And I especially couldn't think about the pictures inside the locket.

My fingers worried the clasp, a part of me sickly tempted to open it again, to check one more time and make certain I hadn't been imagining things at three in the morning. Finally, I gave in to compulsion, but even in the dimness of the darkened theater, I could see that Grandpa wasn't Grandpa anymore.

It was a picture of a different man. A. Completely. Different. Man.

I stared at the blond hair and mustache and fought the urge to scratch the stranger's face away with my fingernail, anything to destroy the evidence that reality was crumbling all around me.

I snapped the locket closed with unnecessary force. Destroying the picture wouldn't solve anything. I had to calm down and keep it together. "Okay. It's okay," I mumbled under my breath as I punched in the next light cue and the stage warmed, blue light fading into bright yellow. Everything was okay.

Ugh. No, everything wasn't okay. I couldn't begin to wrap my head around what this latest wrinkle in time meant in the greater scheme of things. How could that be my grandpa? How could Dad still look like Dad if he'd had a different father? How could I look like me? What the hell was going on? And why didn't Gran remember the locket?

"And where are the pictures? I know there were pictures of her wearing it."

"Are you talking to me?" Sarah asked over the headset, making me realize I'd actually said the words in my head aloud. "What pictures?"

"Nothing. Sorry." I tried to laugh, but ended up sounding like a strangled muskrat. "Just having a minor mental breakdown."

Minor. *Right.* There was nothing *minor* about the way I'd been feeling since last night.

"You want me to come up there?" she asked.

The light booth was at the rear of the theater looking down onto the stage and the sound booth was in the wings stage left, so Sarah and I couldn't see each other. Which was probably a good thing. I knew I looked like death. I'd barely slept last night. I'd spent hours tossing in my bed, stressing about the space-time continuum and other time-travel dangers I had pushed to the back of my thoughts until my "Gran will explain everything" hopes crashed and burned.

"The sound is cool for another five minutes, Katie. I can—"

"No, it's okay. I was just kidding. Mostly. It's just some family stuff." I turned my attention back to the stage, hitting the next light cue as Ally completed her last pivot turn and disappeared behind the stage right curtain. I could do this. I could get through the fashion show rehearsal and then go home and hide in my room and sleep the rest of the day.

Heck, maybe I'd sleep for the next *week*, just stay in bed with the covers over my head and hide until this do over was finished.

"If you want to talk, I've got time after this run-through," Sarah said, her voice comforting me the same way it had yesterday. "I don't have to be at the Rep until two today."

"Yeah. That would be great. Maybe we could get coffee or something?" I couldn't talk to her about what was really bothering me, but still . . . girl time sounded good.

"Perfect." Sarah sighed. "Now if only this torture would end already."

"We're almost to the finale. It will be over soon."

"If Rachel will quit giving walking lessons." Sarah growled into her mike and cut the music as Rachel once again raced out onto the stage to give Natalie Bean grief about leading with her pelvis. Or *not* leading with her pelvis . . . or something.

I was so under-caffeinated I hadn't figured out if Rachel wanted her to stick her hips out further or pull them back in, but I had never been more happy to be hidden in the darkness at the back of the theater.

"Who does she think she is, anyway?" Sarah asked. "Tyra?"

"Well, she is pretty *fierce.*"

Sarah giggled softly, before continuing in a whisper. "No, she's just a bitch. You should hear the stuff she's been saying back here when she thinks only her underlings are listening. I wish I had a tape recorder. Her sweet-pea image would be ruined forever."

"Really? Like what?"

"Like telling everyone that Natalie had an abortion last year and still has some horrible case of crotch cooties."

"No way!" Natalie was a beautiful blonde and one of the best cheerleaders on the BHH squad.

She'd also dated Rader—Rachel's ex—for a very brief moment last year, before Rachel had started flirting with him again, leading him on until he broke up with Natalie. Afterward, Rachel had lost interest in her ex in a few days. She hadn't really wanted Rader back, she'd just wanted to make sure her ex was never happy with anyone else, though she herself had been dating a young country music up-and-comer her dad had signed to his promotion company for over a year.

"I just can't believe that," I said. "Natalie's so nice."

"That doesn't mean she couldn't have crotch cooties. Sometimes bad cooties happen to good people."

I snorted. "You are bad."

"But I'm funny."

"True, but—"

"Um, hello? Earth to Katie?" Rachel covered her eyes with one hand and waved the other impatiently in the air. "Could you dim that light? I'm having a hard time giving instruction with that glaring in my face."

"Sure! Sorry!" I yelled, hurrying to dim the spot by fifty percent.

"Oh my God, give me a break," Sarah mumbled into my ear. "*Giving instruction.* I can't handle much more of this. She really thinks she's—"

A loud snapping from the ceiling cut her off. Sarah cussed, I jumped, and the two adult sponsors sitting in the audience stopped gossiping about who was getting kicked out of the PTA long enough to look around—searching for the source of the sound. My eyes flicked up in time to see something big and gray plummeting toward the stage, a hunk of metal my brain didn't even have time to process was one of the grid lights until *after* it had connected with Rachel Pruitt's head and was lying broken on the floor.

Right next to the Rachel's disturbingly still body.

Girls screamed and I was dimly aware of Sarah announcing that she was calling 911 as I scrambled through the narrow door of the light booth and ran for the stage. My mouth filled with the sour taste of fear and my hands shook as I ripped off my headset and threw it to the ground, freeing my mouth in case I needed to give CPR. I'd taken the babysitter's workshop down at the memorial hospital when I was fourteen and I was pretty sure I remembered how to do it.

I *had* to remember. Rachel's life might depend on it . . . if she wasn't dead already. I climbed up onto the stage, but froze a few inches away from the body.

God, there was a lot of blood. The light had hit her temple, leaving a deep gash that bled freely onto the black planks of the stage, shining like a rain puddle on asphalt in the theater lights. Her eyes were closed and her face so pale and still. She looked dead. She could *be* dead.

"Oh, no. Oh, no." Natalie stood staring down at Rachel, her hands fluttering in front of her face, looking like she was about to pass out.

"Sit down, Natalie," I ordered as I moved around her. She obeyed, her knees buckling and her butt hitting the stage with a thunk. She might have a bruised tailbone, but at least she wouldn't get a concussion if she fainted and fell off the stage.

I knelt beside Rachel, reaching out to feel the cool skin just beneath her jawbone. For a horrible second, I couldn't feel a thing. Nothing. Then faintly, just the barest pulse throbbed beneath my fingertips. She was alive, but maybe not for much longer.

Her wound was so bad I could see cracked bone peeking from the bloodied hair and skin. Even if the paramedics made it here in time, she could have brain damage for the rest of her life. Or worse. Though I couldn't imagine much worse than perfect Rachel damaged beyond repair, the razor sharpness that was the queen of BHH blunted and dulled forever.

No matter how cruel she could be, she didn't deserve this. She hadn't done anything wrong, just been in the wrong place at the wrong time when—

When the light you hung yesterday fell on her.

My eyes flew to where the light lay on the floor. Even shattered and broken, I could tell it was the spot. The same spot I'd hung the day before, the one I thought I'd made sure had the safety cable firmly attached.

But I must have screwed up. I'd been so distracted by my fear of heights and worrying about Isaac and Mitch that I hadn't done the job right. And this time, I'd made a mistake that might cost a girl her life. I couldn't believe I'd been so stupid, so care—

The locket suddenly went from zero to flesh melting, heating up so quickly it took my nerve endings a few seconds to catch up. When they did, the pain was blinding. I couldn't scream, I couldn't move, I couldn't think, all I could do was feel and pray to stop feeling as the locket ate away at me. It was so horrible, even worse than the first time, so bad I didn't remember squeezing my eyes closed or falling to my knees until the agony vanished as quickly as it had arrived.

Only then did I realize my hands were braced against the floor. The *carpeted* floor, not the slick boards of the stage. My fingers dug into thick blue fibers as my head jerked up, eyes taking in my new surroundings. I was back in the light booth. Outside, I heard the pulse of the fashion-show music and then Sarah's voice sounded in my ear.

"Oh my God, give me a break," Sarah mumbled, repeating the words she'd said only seconds before the light had fallen. Fear caught at my throat and squeezed. I hadn't gone back a week or even a day, I'd gone back a few *minutes*, to the moment right before the light set a collision course for Rachel's head.

"Giving instruction," Sarah said as I bolted to my feet—ignoring the flash of pain in my right knee—and scrambled for the light-booth door. My fingers fumbled with the slick handle for a few precious seconds, drawing a strangled sound from my lips. I had to hurry.

"I can't handle much more of this."

Finally the handle gave and I flung myself out into the aisle.

"She really—"

"Get off the stage!!" I screamed as I raced toward Rachel, arms pumping, legs churning, every second it took to close the distance between us making me feel like my heart was about to explode.

Natalie and Rachel turned; Rachel's face twisted in disapproval. "Aren't you supposed to—"

The screech of metal cut her words in half. In my peripheral vision, I saw the light begin to fall. I jumped, hurling myself the last few feet, tackling Rachel to the ground. We slammed into Natalie on the way, taking her to the stage boards with us, landing in a pile of tangled limbs and sharp, bony elbows. Seconds later, the light smashed into the floor where Rachel had been stand-ing, shattering in a dozen pieces, sending shards of glass flying through the air.

Instinctively, I hunched over, tensing for the impact of the debris. A moment passed, then another, until I finally felt safe enough to lift my head and look around.

None of the glass had connected with skin. Natalie and Rachel's flawless skin sported not so much as a speck of blood from the tiniest cut. A breathless look around the theater revealed Sarah standing wide-eyed in the wings—surrounded by the other fashion-show girls—and the two sponsors gasping in the third row of seats. None of them were hurt. We were all okay.

It had worked. The locket had worked its magic and saved the day again . . . but just *barely*.

The closeness of the moment made me shake. What if the locket hadn't taken me back? What if I hadn't moved quickly enough? What if the light had fallen in a different place the second time around? What if, what if, what if—round and round in my head until my teeth began to chatter.

Rachel and Natalie hurried to their feet, backing away from the destroyed light, but I couldn't seem to move. I was too afraid, as terrified of the locket as I was grateful.

"Come on, come with me." Sarah was suddenly next to me, helping me to my feet, looping my arm around her narrow shoulders. "I called 911. They're going to be here soon."

"But no one's hurt this time," I said numbly, stumbling a bit as she led me backstage.

"It doesn't look like anyone's hurt, but better to be safe." She snapped her fingers in Shawn's direction. "Go call Mr. Geery. Tell him we had an emergency at the theater and we need him here. Now."

"I have to tell him I messed up." I sucked in a breath that came out as a sob. "I didn't hang the light right. I almost killed people and—"

"Shh. Just chill for minute. We don't know what happened and you could be going into shock with all this shaking." She settled me into a chair near the girls' dressing room—which was now back on the same side of the theater as it was before, right next to the boys' dressing room.

The realization made me shake even harder.

"Relax, Katie." Sarah rubbed my back, then turned to yell over her shoulder. "Somebody get Katie a drink!"

"I'll get her a Coke." Natalie had followed us backstage and stood a few feet away. "You're, like . . . a hero, Katie. That was amazing." She smiled before running into the girls' dressing room.

"Yeah, how did you know that light was going to fall?" Sarah asked.

"I . . . heard it. I heard a screeching sound."

"I did too," she said, narrowing her eyes, hazel eyes that looked greener than usual.

Was that because of the green sweater she was wearing or another change in this second do-over world? What else was going to be different now? Was my grandfather my grandfather again? Were Isaac and I still together? Was the tree house in my backyard, waiting for Mitch to notice its presence?

"But I didn't hear it until a few seconds before," Sarah continued, shaking her head. "You must have amazing hearing."

"Or she has an amazing, and *sick*, need for attention." Rachel's voice was soft, but I heard every word. Every. Single. Word.

Chapter Ten

SATURDAY, OCTOBER 3, 11:02 A.M.

I looked up to see Rachel leaning against the wall just behind Sarah, glaring down at me. "You didn't get to be in the talent show, so you decided to find some other way to get attention, didn't you?"

"What?" She couldn't really think that. "No way. No, I'd *never* do that." I shook my head back and forth, willing Rachel to believe me.

"Oh come on, Katie." Her eyes narrowed. "You're Little Miss Do-gooder. You're always helping people. Maybe this time you decided to arrange for—"

"No. It was an accident. I was sure I put the safety on. I *swear*, I—"

"You could have killed someone," Rachel said, angrier than I'd ever seen her. She was usually the master of calm, cool, and collected. "You could have killed *me*!"

Natalie appeared behind Rachel with the Coke but froze when she heard Rachel's shout. Blue eyes darted between the two of us, and I could see that she wasn't going to take another step toward me. Pretty, popular senior cheerleader or not—even Natalie had a healthy fear of Rachel.

"Now, hold on," Sarah said. "Let's just wait. We don't know what happened."

I knew what had happened—I'd screwed up. It was only a matter of time before everyone else found out the truth. The locket hadn't saved my ass this time. This time, I was going to have to pay the price for my mistake. But that was okay. I'd take whatever punishment I had to take. Rachel was alive. I wasn't a murderer. I hadn't killed someone with my scatterbrained stupidity.

"We don't know if Katie forgot the safety cable or not," Sarah continued, "but if she did, I know she didn't do it on purpose. We just need to—"

"She didn't forget the cord." Shawn appeared stage right, making all our heads spin in his direction. He blushed and squirmed at being the focus of so much girl-tention, but finally managed to speak up. "I was just looking at the light. The safety cord is still locked and there are pieces of the grid on the stage. The grid broke. That's what made the light fall. It wasn't Katie's fault."

What? But . . . how could that be possible?

"Wow." Sarah let out a shaky breath and squeezed my hands. "If the grid was weak enough for a light to break it . . . you could have fallen through yesterday when you were up there. You're lucky you're not dead."

"Thanks," I said, trying to smile as Natalie hurried to my side, squatting down beside Sarah, evidently deciding it was safe to be nice to me now that I wasn't guilty of almost killing Rachel Pruitt. "That's really going to help with my fear of heights."

I clasped the Coke Natalie pressed into my hand and took a tiny sip, but couldn't taste anything but cold. My taste buds had ceased to function in the wake of this latest reveal.

It *wasn't* my fault. I *hadn't* made a mistake—one that was meant to last or otherwise.

Then ... why had the locket worked? Why had I traveled back in time? I'd been sure the locket had worked the first time because fate, or a higher power, or *something* out there in the universe that was bigger than me had decided my slipup with Mitch wasn't "meant to last" and given me a second chance. A second chance I'd put at risk yesterday with my inappropriate thoughts about Mitch.

But what if the locket didn't work that way at all? What if the inscription didn't mean what I thought it meant? What if—

"I want to go home." I needed to talk to Gran. Maybe now that I'd used the locket again, she would remember owning the piece of jewelry and be able to help me understand.

"I'd rather you stay until Mr. Geery takes a look at the light," Rachel said, her tone inferring she wasn't buying my innocence, at least not completely. "Just to make sure it's not your fault."

"Come on, Rach," Natalie said in a sweet voice. "Give her a break. Katie saved our lives. We should be thanking her, not giving her a hard time."

"Yeah," Ally said, piping up from the clutch of fashion-show girls hovering near the dressing room door. "We should totally give her a makeover."

"Because nothing says 'thank you' like implying you're ugly the way you are," Sarah whispered under her breath, just loud enough for me to hear.

I tried to smile at her joke, but my lips were having none of it. Nothing was funny, not yet, maybe not for a long, long time. I had to figure out what was going on with the locket. Now.

"Yes!" Yin, another senior girl with striking white stripes in her shiny black hair, clapped. "That would be awesome. We could take her to my mom's salon after practice on Wednesday."

"And I've got a bunch of True Religion jeans I can't wear since I started doing the Shred and lost those last ten pounds," Melissa said with a smile in my direction. "You could have them, Katie. They're, like, two hundred dollars a pair."

"Better yet, let's take her to Ziggies before the salon on Wednesday," Rachel said, her attitude doing a three-sixty now that it was clear her underlings were threatening mutiny. "You can pick out a couple of brand-new outfits. On me." She smiled, but all I saw was bright, white teeth. There was nothing friendly in that grin.

"No, I couldn't." I stood even though my knees still felt shaky. "I mean, I really appreciate the offers, but—"

"You should do it," Sarah said, surprising me. "I mean, it's your birthday next Saturday, anyway, and—"

"Perfect, then it's decided. We'll have makeover girls' night after rehearsal on Wednesday." Rachel wrinkled her nose and cast a nasty look at the ceiling. "I'll get my dad to call some people to make sure this death trap is repaired before then."

"Come on, Katie, I'll walk you out to your car," Natalie said, looping her arm through mine.

I cast Sarah a confused look, but she just shrugged and grabbed my backpack from the wall. "Drive safe. We'll do that coffee another day?"

"Yeah, for sure." I waved at the other girls, and they waved back, offering well-wishes and further promises that Wednesday would be a day of "pure awesome."

"Just wait until Wednesday. Yin's mom is a genius, she's going to make you look amazing," Natalie said, smiling as we pushed out the back door and crossed the lot to my car. "A few highlights will really bring out the depth in your hair."

My hair had depth? I had no idea. "Sounds great." Gray clouds hung low and threatening, making the red leaves on the pin oaks surrounding the parking lot look even redder, like the trees were bleeding into the sky. I shivered, suddenly cold. It had been a bright sunny day without a chance of rain before my second do over. Now it looked like a storm would hit any minute. "It's really nice of y'all to do this for me."

"You totally deserve it! I mean, if Isaac can't see how gorgeous you are, we'll just have to remind him, right?"

"Um . . . right." My mouth went dry and I forced myself to take another sip of the Coke in my hand.

What did she mean? Had Isaac said something about me to the senior girls? Something about thinking I wasn't attractive anymore? Despite my own doubts about my appearance, I had a hard time believing Isaac would *ever* say something mean about the way I looked. He'd always told me I was pretty—beautiful, even. And there was no mistaking the look in his eyes when I came down the stairs for a date wearing my tight jeans.

Or there'd been no mistaking the look in his eyes *before* this latest do over. Maybe, in this new world, Isaac didn't think I was the one who did the sparkling in our relationship.

The thought made my hand start shaking again as I dug through my backpack for my keys. I had to find out what Natalie was talking about, even if it made me seem like a freak.

"So . . . did he say something?" I asked, trying to sound casual and failing miserably. I sounded as anxious and pathetic as I felt. "About wishing I'd wear makeup more often or something?"

She shook her head, genuinely confused. "Oh, no. He never said anything, I just . . ." Natalie bit her lip and I watched her decision to lie play out behind her bright blue eyes. "You know, it's nothing. I was confusing Isaac with someone else."

Someone else. Someone who had done *something* to make her doubt that he was happy with his present dating situation. Something like . . . what? I didn't really want to know, but my lips were forming questions before I could stop them.

"Really? Are you sure?" I asked.

"Yeah, totally sure. Boy mix-up." Natalie twirled her hair between her fingers, giving her hand something to do while she lied to me. Again. Isaac had done something to make her believe he wasn't happy. There was no doubt about it. Natalie wasn't mean. She wasn't the kind of girl who tried to break couples up for no reason. She must have seen something. Or at least heard something. "I had to get up way too early this morning, my brain is fried."

But she wasn't going to tell me the truth. She didn't want to be the bearer of bad news. She'd only said something because she thought I already knew what she was talking about. Maybe in this life, I *should* know. But I didn't, because I'd traveled through time. Twice.

"Me too," I said, the sick feeling in my stomach spreading out across my body until even my fingers and toes felt wretched. "I think I'll go home and snag a nap."

"Good idea. See you Monday!"

"Monday." I waved goodbye and jumped into my car, a nap the furthest thing from my mind.

I had to go see Isaac. I had to see for myself if he still loved me or if I'd ruined my life when the locket decided I should save Rachel's, by fixing a "mistake" that wasn't even mine to begin with.

Chapter Eleven

We don't have to watch the game, we can watch something else," Isaac said, but he made no move to reach for the remote control. Usually, I would jump at the chance to watch something other than football. Today, I just pulled him closer, snuggling my face into the soft fabric of his sweatshirt.

We were lying on the couch in his basement under the Bearcats fleece blanket I'd given him for Christmas last year, just like we'd done a hundred Saturdays before. He'd been happy to see me and sincerely concerned when I'd told him about the broken light grid. He'd hugged me so tight my spine had popped in a couple of places and made me promise never to climb up there and put myself in danger ever again. All very loving, good-boyfriend-type behavior.

Still, I couldn't get Natalie's words out of my mind.

"Isaac . . . you've never said anything about the way I look to anyone, have you?" I asked, keeping my eyes on the television and my tone light.

"Um . . . something like what?" He grabbed his Gatorade from the table and took a drink.

"I don't know, like, you've never said you don't like my hair or . . . whatever?"

Isaac laughed, a completely innocent sound. "Babe, guys don't talk about stuff like that."

"So you've never said anything?"

"No. I don't talk about you to other guys. You're none of their business."

"Even Mitch?" I lifted my head from his chest, staring into his face.

Isaac shrugged. "Maybe. When we were first dating, I'd ask Mitch things. Like, what I should say to you and stuff. But not for a long time."

"Okay." I stared into his eyes, seeing nothing that made me doubt him. The tightness in my chest eased the slightest bit. "I just wanted to make sure we were good. Me and you."

"Of course we are. We're great." He ran his hand through my hair, a serious look on his gorgeous face. His blue eyes focused in on mine, making me feel more solid than I had a second ago. "Is this because I didn't make it to the apple-picking thing yesterday? You know I couldn't help it. Practice ran late and—"

"I know. It's not that. Mitch and I had fun," I said, then hurried to add, "It would have been better with you there, but—"

"So why don't we all do something together Wednesday night?

After you get fabulous?" he asked, obviously trying to make nice. "They're setting up for career night in the gym so we don't have practice. We could go ride bikes again, or whatever."

"That would be great. I want us all to stay good friends."

Isaac turned back to the TV as the referee announced a flag on the field. "Sure, we'll always be friends. I always thought Mitch'd be the best man when we get married."

"Yeah. That would be perfect." But for some reason Isaac's casual mention of our future married life didn't make me feel warm and safe the way it usually did. It made me . . . anxious. After a few minutes, it was impossible to stay snuggled under the blanket. It was hot, smothering. "I'm going to head home, okay? I've got some homework I want to finish before tomorrow."

"Okay." He didn't take his eyes from the game as I untangled myself and crawled off the couch. "You want to go get dinner later or something? Maybe pizza?"

"Sure, call me."

"I will. Love you."

"Love you too." I hurried out the back door that led into Isaac's mother's garden and circled around the house to get to my car. I didn't want to go upstairs and out the front door. I wasn't up to another visit with Isaac's mom and dad. I just wanted to get home and talk to Gran.

But when I pulled into my driveway a few minutes later, I knew grilling my grandmother about the locket was going to have to wait a little longer.

Mitch had found his surprise.

Music drifted through the yard, something sweet and aching

that Mitch played so soulfully I knew it had to be one of his own songs. How he'd gotten both himself and his guitar up into the tree house, however, was something I couldn't imagine.

The music stopped, and Mitch turned, almost as if he could feel me looking his way. "Hey! There you are. You are the best friend in the world, Minnesota," he called, waving his arms from on top of the platform.

The platform that was *way* higher in the tree than it had been when I left for fashion-show rehearsal this morning. The limb where my dad had nailed my creation had vanished completely. Now the lowest limb was thirty feet in the air and the entire tree was bigger, scarier. Using the locket had added at least fifty years of growth to a tree in my backyard.

How was that even *possible*?

I'd altered one thing, one *tiny* moment, and the ripple of change had affected everything in my life, even things not in any way related to me or Rachel or that stupid light. It didn't make sense . . . but then, what did I really know about time travel? Or fate? Or magic?

Nothing. I knew *nothing*. And it was scaring me more and more.

My hand drifted to my chest, where a second, ridged scar was nestled next to the first. At this rate, I'd never be able to wear a V-neck shirt, let alone a bathing suit. If the locket pulled me back too many more times, I'd look like a burn victim.

How was I going to explain to Isaac what had caused the marks on my skin? We hadn't been together since my do over, but we were bound to get the chance sooner or later. What would he say when he saw the locket-shaped burn marks? What would he do when I told him I couldn't get the locket off, no matter how hard I tried?

"Hey, Katie, you okay?" Mitch yelled.

Forcing my hand away from the locket, I took a deep breath and tried to focus on the bright side. Rachel was alive, Isaac still loved me, and Mitch had a new tree house. It was selfish to worry about a few scars when the locket had done nothing but great things for the people in my life.

And in a crazy way, the scars were almost comforting. They were the sacrifice I made for a miracle. Nothing came without a price. I'd be even more anxious if the locket seemed to cost me nothing.

"Katie, are you—"

"Hey! I'm fine." I waved and started across our sloping backyard to the giant tree. I had a clear path since our fence had vanished along with the low tree limb. But that was fine, *more* than fine. Who needed a fence in a safe, suburban neighborhood like ours?

That's right. Thinking positively. Looking on the bright side.

"I thought you were afraid of heights?" I asked, tilting my head to look up at Mitch. "How did you get up there? With your guitar?"

"I strapped it on my back and climbed. Fear could not keep me from my tree house." He smiled down at me, his dark eyes sparkling, so happy I couldn't help but smile back. "Your dad said you made this all by yourself."

"I did. I'm handy with power tools, turns out."

Mitch shook his head. "Just when I thought you couldn't get any hotter."

"Right." I rolled my eyes, ignoring the heat rushing to my cheeks. This was Mitch joking around, nothing more. I could see in his face that we'd never kissed in this version of reality either. "I should be even 'hotter' come Wednesday." I filled Mitch in on the theater drama and my impending makeover.

"Don't let them ruin you," Mitch said, suddenly serious. "I like you the way you are."

"Thanks." I looked down at the leaves beneath my feet, flustered. Isaac had seemed excited that I was going to get renovated by the popular girls. Shouldn't *he* have been the one telling me I didn't need new hair or clothes?

"So are you coming up or not?"

"Um . . . not." I lifted my face, wincing at the thought of starting up the ladder nailed to the side of the tree. "After the light-grid thing I'm feeling my height fear in new and powerful ways."

"Understandable. Later, then?"

"Much later. Like, maybe this summer? Maybe . . . or not?"

He laughed. "Okay, but still . . . thanks. This made my day, my month. I can't believe you did this."

I shrugged, uncomfortable with Mitch's gratitude. I knew I didn't deserve it, not really. I hadn't been a very good friend to him before the do over. "It's no big deal."

"It is a big deal. Just say 'you're welcome,' okay?" Mitch's voice was tight, like a guitar string about to break.

"You're welcome." I paused, searching his face, finding that same sadness I'd seen in the coffee shop lurking beneath his smile. "Are you okay?"

"I'm fine," he said. "Just getting a few minutes to myself.

Lauren and Dad are working on their guest list for the wedding reception. I was in charge of watching Ricky, but he had a melt-down because I couldn't get the PlayStation to play his Elmo game. Then Dad freaked out because he thought I'd yelled at Ricky, but I didn't yell *at* Ricky, I yelled to be heard over *Ricky's* yelling and . . . yeah."

"Not the best babysitting gig ever, huh?"

Mitch shrugged. "It wasn't that bad. Just a charming reminder of how unskilled we are at being a family of more than two."

Guess his dad and Lauren were still getting married and Ricky still existed. I didn't know whether to be pleased or nervous. "So, is the adoption stuff still bothering you?"

He shook his head. "No, not as much. Dad really loves Ricky, as much as he does Lauren, and I'm leaving anyway, so . . . I guess it makes sense." He smiled and his tone lightened. "Besides, there's always family therapy, right?"

"That's what I always say," I said, trying to play along.

"Right, Minnesota. Like you and your perfect family need therapy. You're probably the only functional people on the street."

I laughed, but it was strained, thin. Mitch had no idea how much I'd appreciate a little therapy right now.

"Anyway, the wedding seems like it should be fun," he continued, not seeming to notice my angst. "I get to have an entire table at the reception for my friends. You and Isaac are invited, of course."

"That should be fun."

"Yeah," he said, eyes drifting across the yard. "And I was thinking of inviting Sarah too if you don't mind."

143

"Why would I mind? I love Sarah."

Mitch's eyes flicked back to mine. "So you two are still good?"

"Yeah, why shouldn't we be?" I asked.

He paused a second too long before shrugging. "Cool. Then I'll invite her and the rest of the band and we'll have a full table."

"Great." But it wasn't great. There was something Mitch wasn't telling me.

Just like Natalie. Could I afford to keep letting people lie to me?

"I've got to go. My gran's here and I'm supposed to be visiting and catching up and stuff." I backed away from the tree house, eyes on the ground.

Maybe people *were* lying to me, but right now I couldn't handle the truth if it meant Sarah—or Isaac—had betrayed me. And besides, I knew Isaac well enough to know he hadn't . . . *cheated* on me. He's like an open book. I would know. In any event, I had to keep thinking the locket had made mostly positive changes in my life or I was going to lose my mind before this do over was finished.

"See you," Mitch said. "And thanks again. For real."

I forced a little smile and hurried back to the house and in through the sliding back door, grateful for the warm air and the someone's-been-cooking-good-things smell that always lingered in our kitchen. At least my house had stayed the same, no matter what. The giant oak table still glowed faintly gold in the dining room, the wallpaper still sported way too many red flowers, and the grandfather clock near the stairs ticked comfortingly in the silence.

Grandfather. I was suddenly possessed by the need to look at the picture of Gran and Grandpa again. It was obvious no one was home—Gran must have decided to go to work with Dad this morning, and Mom had to go to a baby shower this afternoon—but I could at least look at the picture and see if *something* was back to normal.

I pulled the locket from beneath my shirt and flipped it open, rushing through the anxious moment like a kid ripping off a Band-Aid. It hurts less when you rip them off.

But seeing the picture didn't hurt any less than it would have if I'd taken an hour to open the locket. There was no way to lessen the impact of seeing Grandpa's picture flicker, shifting from my clean-shaven, brown-haired Grandpa to the blond man with the mustache and back again, right before my eyes. It was like one of those hologram stickers I'd had when I was little, the ones you tilt back and forth to change the image, but I wasn't touching the picture.

It was changing all on its own, as if reality couldn't make up its mind which version of events it should go with this time around. As if time itself were short circuiting, skipping like a scratched CD.

The impact of such a thing was almost too big to comprehend, but it wasn't too big to fear. I slammed the locket closed, pulse thudding erratically in my throat.

Trembling, I fumbled at the clasp of the locket, but I should have known better by now. It wasn't going to come off the normal way. I was going to have to try more extreme measures.

I grabbed a pair of scissors from the junk drawer in the kitchen and hurried to the downstairs bathroom. In the mirror, my eyes were wider than I'd ever seen them, like an anime sketch brought to life. It looked like they'd bulge straight out of my head as I slipped the locket's chain between the blades of the scissors and squeezed.

Again and again, I sawed away at the delicate links. Ten minutes later, I had nothing to show for it but sore fingers. The locket wasn't the slightest bit damaged, despite the fact that my scissors looked like they'd lost a battle with a garbage disposal.

I might never get the locket off. *Never.* Even though the necklace had saved someone today, the thought was terrifying. What if I had to wear it for the rest of my life? What if it kept pulling me back into the past with no warning? What if the world never returned to normal, but was always changing, flickering back and forth like a candle I couldn't trust not to blow out at any second? What if waiting for that flame to die really made me crazy?

The scissors fell into the sink with an ominous clatter. I buried my face in my hands, praying the world as I knew it wasn't about to come crashing down around me.

Chapter Twelve

*P*opularity, I was discovering, was a lot like the plague. It triggered fever, chills, unexplained sweating, was highly contagious, and might be the death of me within seventy-two hours.

I'd been a "heroine" for less than four full days and I already felt like hurling myself off the Shelby Street Bridge. I wasn't meant to sit in the spotlight for so long. It made me a mass of symptoms. *Plague* symptoms.

I'd alerted my mother to the fragile state of her daughter's health this morning, but not even my *slight* fever of 99.2 could convince her to let me stay home. The Catholic school where she taught first grade was on fall break and she and Gran—who was still suffering from amnesia regarding the locket—had plans to cook ten zillion cran-apple pies for the fall festival.

Mom didn't want me lurking in the kitchen stealing piecrust—

which is totally what I'd be doing if life were normal. Of course, life *wasn't* normal, but Mom didn't know that and there was no way I could tell her. So I'd been forced to drag my anxiety-ridden self to school after thanking her for spending one of her days off ensuring I did my part for the Junior League.

I was working the Junior League bake sale at the Belle Meade fall festival on Saturday instead of the cakewalk table, compliments of my newfound platinum status and Rachel Pruitt's continuing favor. Mom had stepped up to contribute twenty of her famous pies to the charity of the moment . . . whatever that was. I'd been told, but I'd forgotten. It was the kind of thing I'd usually be really interested in, but I couldn't seem to remember anything lately. I wasn't sleeping and when I did, I had horrible dreams, nightmares of looking into the mirror and finding my face covered in locket-shaped burns, my mouth sealed shut with scar tissue.

A part of me was certain life as I knew it was over forever.

My new friends, however, had bigger things to worry about.

"Seriously, Khaki is really letting herself go." Ally brushed on another coat of I Don't Do Dishes polish and blew on her nails. "Her roots are at least two inches long."

"I don't think she's been waxing either," Melissa said, flicking the leftover sprinkles from our cupcake project off the table onto the floor. Antara and Anika, my old tablemates seated the next row over, glared at the orange and white specks. They were both clean freaks. I avoided catching their eyes, knowing I'd feel obligated to pick up Melissa's mess if I did. "Her eyebrows are about to meet in the middle."

"Maybe you guys should give her the makeover this afternoon,"

I said, as nervous as I always was whenever I dared speak in my present company. Years of platinum-inspired terror didn't vanish in a few days. I still braced myself for eye rolling every time I opened my mouth. "The hair on my face is so blonde, I don't even look like I have eyebrows, so—"

Melissa laughed and flicked a sprinkle my way. "You are hysterical. I love you."

"Me too," Natalie agreed. She was actually eating a cupcake, the only one of the senior girls willing to risk sugar intake so close to the fashion show tomorrow night.

"Me three. I'm so glad you sit with us now!" Ally grinned at me, artificially whitened teeth so bright I had to squint a bit to look her full in the face. "But of course we're making you over today. You look fine now, but come six o'clock tonight, you are going to be drop-dead fabulous."

"Made of awesome with wicked hot on the side," Melissa concurred, then turned the conversation back to Khaki, the cheerleader in need of bleach and wax. "So we have to stage an intervention with Kak Attack. She's becoming an embarrassment to the squad."

I nodded along with the rest of girls and tried to think of some way to contribute to the conversation. Like it or not, I was now seated at the popular girls' table in family and consumer sciences—aka home economics. Our teacher, Mrs. Van Tassel, refused to acknowledge her class's more politically correct title. And why should she? We baked cakes, poached eggs, and sewed aprons, just like my mom did when she was in Van Tassel's class however many years ago.

Today, we'd made harvest cupcakes that were supposed to look like pumpkins. Being icing challenged and not really motivated to improve, my half dozen looked more like deflated basketballs than pumpkins. But who cared? The space-time continuum was probably on the verge of collapse. I had more important things to stress about than cupcakes.

I'd put some extra sprinkles on mine and called it quits.

Now I just had to survive another fifteen minutes of socializing before the bell rang without making a fool out of myself. Rachel was gone—she'd snagged a pass to go check on the state of the theater—so it shouldn't have been as difficult as usual. But still, no matter how nice it was to fit in with Isaac's crowd . . . I couldn't help but shoot a longing look at my old table.

Antara and her twin sister, Anika, spent most of the period talking to each other in their weird twin language and cleaning the table obsessively, but they'd never made me feel this on edge. I kept ducking my head, hoping no one would notice my blond brows had been allowed to go free range all over my forehead. I'd never waxed a single part of me. "Live hairy and let live hairy" was my motto. I was the type of girl who considered winter an excellent excuse not to shave my legs. Who was I to judge Khaki?

I found myself twisting the chain of the locket around my finger until it cut off the circulation, a bad habit I'd gotten into ever since the night of my failed locket amputation.

"Great necklace! I love it." Natalie leaned over and tapped the locket with her pencil, jolting me back into my body.

"Thanks. It was my grandmother's." My fingers brushed across the locket's cool, smooth surface.

I'd started wearing it outside my clothes, a part of me hoping that other people seeing it might take away its power. At least enough to allow me to take it off and put it somewhere safe.

Stress about the fragility of time aside, I couldn't deny the locket had made my life better—I had Isaac back, Mitch was my friend, Rachel was alive, and I was on my way to being a fully accepted and popularity-approved platinum. I didn't want to get rid of the locket . . . I just wanted to know that I *could* take it off. If I wanted to.

"It's gorgeous," Natalie said, snagging another cupcake.

At this rate she wouldn't have any cakes left to grade when Van Tassel finally made it to the back of the room. Not that it mattered. Everyone got an automatic A in this class. It was a big reason I'd taken it in the first place—aside from wanting to learn how to bake as well as my mom. I needed every A I could get this year if I hoped to get into whatever Division I college offered Isaac a scholarship.

"And it's going to be perfect with your dress for the finale," Melissa said, leaning in for a closer look.

"My dress for the finale?" I squeaked, praying I'd misheard her.

"Oh my God, you're right," Ally said. "It's a different color, but with the same swirly things and everything."

"But I'm running the lights," I protested. "I can't be in the finale."

Natalie paused mid-cupcake lick and turned to me. "Sarah said she'd do the lights for you, remember? Because the sound is already programmed and all she has to do is hit play?"

"She did?" My heart did the seizure thing that had become horribly familiar lately.

"Yeah, silly. Remember, right after practice on Saturday?"

"Oh. Right." I nodded, but I didn't remember that conversation at all. Was that because I'd been distracted and freaked out by Rachel's near death experience and not paying attention? Or was Natalie confused?

Or was reality tipping back and forth like kids on a teeter-totter, flickering like my grandfather's picture?

"It's an awesome dress," Melissa assured me, mistaking my terror for fashion-related anxiety.

"Just a sec. Rachel made me take a picture of it to show Yin's mom this afternoon," Ally said, digging in her purse. "She wants to make sure your highlights won't clash." She punched a few buttons on her iPhone and pushed it across the table. "Here. Gorgeous, right?"

The burnt orange silk dress was a 1960s cocktail number with a flared skirt decorated with brown filigree embroidery. It was intricate, expensive looking, and a little ridiculous but probably one of the most beautiful things I'd ever seen. It would certainly be the most beautiful thing I'd ever worn.

But Ally was right . . . the filigree pattern mimicked the swirls on the outside of the locket exactly. *Perfectly.* As if they had been made to go together.

Maybe, once I put the dress on tomorrow night, I wouldn't be able to take it off either. Maybe I'd spend the rest of my life wandering around in a cocktail dress, wearing a locket no one could remember giving me, raving to myself about what things "used to be like" before I'd traveled through time. I'd probably end up in a homeless shelter with a bad bedbug infestation, smelling like I was brought up in a barn.

"You okay, Katie?" Natalie asked, big blue eyes concerned, though she continued licking orange icing off her cupcake.

"Just need to run to the bathroom. Girl time. Be right back." I stood and hurried to the front of the room, grabbing the oversized pink key that served as the girls' bathroom pass for Van Tassel's room, silently berating myself for giving too much information.

Why did I have to say that? Who even called their period their "girl time" anymore? Dorks like me, that's who. It was only a matter of time before Ally and Natalie and Mel figured out I wasn't funny or cool but the same awkward doofus I'd been before. If I wasn't so messed up about the locket, the stress of waiting to be dork-scovered would probably have driven me off the deep end anyway.

Out in the hall, the air was a little cooler, quiet, more breathable. Only a couple of people wandered from their classrooms to the bathroom and back. For the first time all day, the anxiety that had been my best buddy since Saturday faded a bit.

There were only three more days to go until the do over was over and I would once again be living in a time I'd never lived before. *Surely* that would make a difference. Right now, two different versions of reality were existing side by side, layered on top of each other like phyllo dough, and that could be causing weird things to happen—or at least that's what I'd come to believe after several hours of late night Googling. Come Saturday night, all of that would change. Life would return to normal . . . or the slightly altered version of normal my time travel had helped create, anyway.

I just had to make it through until then. Just a few more days and—

"Ow!" I slammed into someone, driving my bathroom pass into my gut.

"Watch it!"

"Sorry." I blushed and backed away from the boy I'd just collided with. Apparently I couldn't *think* and walk a clear path to the bathroom at the same time. "I wasn't paying—"

"Katie?" the boy asked, shuffling a little closer, bringing a pungent, tangy aroma with him. He smelled . . . strange, and his long, frizzy red hair brought back a wave of longing for the old boys-must-have-shorn-locks dress code. "What's up?"

"Nothing much." I gazed up into the boy's face, still unable to place him despite the familiar voice. Only after he blinked, drawing my attention to the freckles across the bridge of his nose, did his identity slide into place. I should have known. There was only one other redhead at our school, and it wasn't like I hadn't stared into those gray eyes in confusion often enough. Theo had been my math tutor for over a year, ever since my pre-ACT test had showed a marked failure in my ability to comprehend mathematical concepts. "Theo! Hey! Sorry, I didn't recognize you. Guess I've been smoking too much crack again," I joked, nearly swallowing my own tongue when he squinted at me like I'd just farted on his shoe.

Guess we didn't make crack jokes in this life. Stupid, Katie. Stupid!

"Sorry?"

"I—I'm sorry," I stammered. "It's nothing, just a bad joke."

"Right," he said, running a hand through his matted hair. He must have been growing it for years. In the world I remembered,

Theo had a buzz cut and an almost military-like attention to personal hygiene. "I just wanted to make sure you got my note."

"Um . . . no, I didn't." At least I didn't remember getting any note. That didn't mean he hadn't sent one.

"Oh, well . . . I'm not going to be able to tutor you tomorrow."

"Okay." I wrinkled my nose as another wave of Theo odor wafted toward me. If I didn't know better, I'd think he smelled . . . weed-ish. But Theo didn't drink caffeine or eat sugar, and certainly didn't smoke up. I'd never even seen him consume food. I'd assumed he was so brilliant he'd learned to keep his body running on cranial electricity or something. "Well, we can reschedule if—"

"No, I can't reschedule." He shifted on his feet, obviously uncomfortable. "I'm not going to be able to tutor you at all. My mom wants me to spend more time on my own work."

"But . . . you already got into your dream school." Theo had applied to a bunch of nuclear-physics programs, and this was the week he found out he'd been accepted into MIT. I'd been certain about that a second ago, but the blank look in his eyes made me second-guess myself. Did I have my weeks mixed up? Or maybe college-acceptance letters went out at a different time in this new reality? Crap! I should know better than to assume anything at this point!

"What are you talking about?" he asked, a wary, hurt note in his voice that made me feel compelled to tell the truth. The last thing I wanted was Theo to think I was making fun of him.

"Um . . . MIT," I said. "I thought I heard that you got in."

Theo snorted, a shocked sound. "With my attendance record,

I'll be lucky to get into Brantley Hills community college, even if I spend the rest of the year studying to bring my grades up."

"No way," I said, the hopelessness in his tone making me want to grab him by the shoulders and shake him until he went back to being the brilliant, condescending nerd on high I'd always known. "You can get in somewhere great. You're the smartest person I know."

"You sound like my mom." He rolled his eyes. "She thinks I'm some sort of genius."

"You *are* a genius. You're a math prodigy and know more big words than I've ever read." Acid burned at the back of my throat. I swallowed the bitter taste, wishing I'd brought my backpack. I'd started keeping antacids in my makeup bag. You never knew when a bout of time-travel angst was going to hit. "You were the tri-state mathlete of the year."

"In *ninth* grade. I haven't done those competitions in years, Katie."

"Oh . . . oh." No, this couldn't be happening! Theo couldn't be someone completely different in this world. He just couldn't. "I—I forgot."

"Don't worry about it. It's no big deal." He turned to glance over his shoulder, looking for an escape route. "I don't even care if I go to college."

"Don't say that! You're too smart to—"

"Listen, I've got to go or I'm going to get it from Mr. Dillingham." He backed away, lifting one long, thin hand in the air. "See you around, okay?"

I stammered wordlessly for a second before forcing my mouth to form the expected response. "Okay." But it wasn't okay.

Theo hadn't gotten into MIT! Theo wasn't even going to go to college. His big, huge, beautiful brain was going to go to waste and he'd probably grow up to be one of those frustrated geniuses who blew things up instead of a talented physicist unraveling the secrets of nuclear power. And it was all my fault.

The knowledge made my head spin and my skin break out in a cold sweat. I burst through the heavy door to the bathroom and rushed into the last stall, kneeling on the tile, assuming the position just in case my stomach decided to put on a repeat performance of last Monday's barf fest.

"Please. Please." I leaned my forehead on the toilet lid, too dizzy to care about public-bathroom filth.

Theo's life was ruined. Was that because I'd gone back in time the first time or the second time? And was there any way to undo it? Or would undoing Theo's misery simply pass the misery buck on to someone else? Was this my punishment for messing with fate?

I shivered and clenched my jaw, fighting the wave of nausea that threatened to overtake me. I wasn't going to be sick. I wasn't going to—

"No way, of course I didn't." It was Sarah's voice. Sarah was in the bathroom! She would make me feel better. Or at least do me a super-favor and go get my backpack and antacids from Van Tassel's room. "I wouldn't tell."

I was about to call out to her when another girl spoke up. "Actually, you *would*. The normal you would, anyway. What about the whole 'tell the truth even if it hurts someone' thing?" Whoever her friend was, they sounded tight, probably tighter than me and Sarah. I was kind of glad they were staying by the sinks, away from the stalls. I suddenly didn't want Sarah to know I was here.

Sarah sighed. "I know. Believe me, it's bothering me, but this is for the best. Katie and Isaac are really happy together."

Oh, no. No. I squeezed my eyes shut, wishing I could do the same with my ears. I didn't want to hear Sarah's bathroom confession. I couldn't deal with having my suspicions confirmed right now. I needed Sarah to be my friend, not the girl who helped my boyfriend cheat on me.

"True," the other girl said. There was a spraying sound and the air bloomed with melon and flowers. My stomach gurgled in protest. Whoever invented fruity body sprays should be drowned in rotten-apple cores. "But even if you stay quiet, don't you think Rachel's going to say something sooner or later?"

Oh . . . crap. Rachel. *Rachel Pruitt*, Isaac's perfect platinum counterpart, the queen bee who should have been homecoming royalty last year. Who *would* have been homecoming queen if she'd been dating Isaac instead of an older guy, who might have decided she wanted a high school boyfriend after all.

I'd been such an idiot.

"I don't think so," Sarah said. "If she were going to tell Katie, she would have done it the other day at the fashion-show rehearsal. As hard as it is to believe, I think even Pruitt realizes Katie and Isaac have something special."

Riiight. And snakes felt sorry for the rodents they devoured whole.

"So everything's going to be fine," Sarah said. "Isaac's still crazy about Katie. He's planning to drop an obscene amount of cash on her birthday present, apparently. I mean, if Hunter is to be believed."

"Which he is. He's totally trustworthy. And *hot*."

"Ew!" Sarah laughed and I thought I heard a little fist connect with the other girl's body. "That's my brother! And he's a freshman!"

"I don't care." The girl giggled, a high-pitched sound that clashed with the squeak of the bathroom door as it opened and she and Sarah headed back into the hall. "He's still . . ."

I missed the end of her sentence, but it didn't really matter. I didn't care if she thought Hunter was hot. I had much bigger things to worry about.

I should have known Sarah wouldn't try to snag my boyfriend. I should have been smarter, but I was as stupid as Rachel had assumed when she'd set my brain down the path to suspecting Sarah in the first place. Sarah was just trying to avoid being the bearer of bad news.

I'd been so dumb.

But that didn't mean I had to *keep* being dumb. Nothing had happened between Rachel and Isaac yet, nothing that would constitute actual "cheating." If Isaac had cheated with Rachel, he wouldn't be acting so normal around me. I knew him well enough to be *almost* one hundred percent sure about that. He had a guilty conscience and wasn't a man skank, no matter how much he liked to flirt.

No, nothing had happened yet. But something was brewing between Isaac and Rachel, something Rachel was keeping quiet about for now. Probably because she wanted to keep seducing Isaac without any interference from girlfriend number one.

I took a deep breath. Girlfriend number *one*. I'd always assumed I'd be girlfriend number *only*. The first, the last, the one Isaac stayed with forever. It's what we'd promised each other. It was what I'd held on to when I suffered good Catholic girl guilt about having sex before marriage, when I stressed about our relationship not flowing as smoothly as I'd like . . . when I was tempted by other options . . .

And now, the boy I'd counted on might have let me down.

The bell rang, but I stayed on the floor, too afraid to get up and rejoin the living, too afraid of all the new and horrible things waiting out in the big, uncertain world.

Chapter Thirteen

They should tear that thing down," Isaac growled, in a foul mood for reasons of his own. His blond hair stood up from his forehead in jagged wisps that fit perfectly with his brown and black leather jacket, giving him a bad-boy look that was ... unusual. He seemed harder tonight, more grown up. Maybe it was the snarl on his face that eerily resembled his dad's when Mr. Tayte was in angry mode. "It makes the city look stupid." He shook his head in disgust and turned away from the Parthenon.

Most casual tourists have no clue, but Nashville, Tennessee, is home to a historically accurate, *exact* reproduction of the Parthenon from Athens, Greece—what it would have looked like before it fell into ruins, anyway. It's the centerpiece of Centennial Park and serves as our city's art museum. In the foyer stands a two-story replica of an ancient statue of Athena that's just plain scary.

When I was six, it made me cry. I'd thought it was the giant from "Jack and the Beanstalk" and was going to crush my bones to make its bread. The memory made me sigh. What I wouldn't give to be that little girl again, to be back in a time when turning to my dad and having him pick me up solved everything.

But you could be back in that time, couldn't you?

I shivered and clutched the thankfully cold locket in my fist, scanning the darkening lawn where we'd parked our bikes. "What time did Mitch say he'd meet us?"

"Eight." Isaac pulled his phone out of his pocket and flipped it open. "Five more minutes."

Mitch had to drop some paperwork off at Vanderbilt admissions and meet his dad—whose doctor's office was only a few minutes away—for dinner, but had promised to ride his bike over to meet us after.

I couldn't wait for him to get here. Isaac had been in a mood since he'd picked me up at the salon. He'd said he loved my hair, but he'd barely looked at me on the way into Nashville, making me nervous about my new look. My hair was gone, hacked to just below my chin and streaked with light blond and a golden honey color. It was gorgeous. The highlights made my eyes look bright green instead of muddy-frog hazel and should have thrilled me to pieces.

Instead, my makeover was just another source of angst. I didn't look *me* anymore and it scared me. Maybe it scared Isaac too, or at least turned him off. Or maybe he had other reasons for refusing to look at me—Rachel-type reasons.

Suspicion pinged around in my brain and pressed against the

backs of my eyes, slowly driving me crazy. So crazy, I'd almost said something to Isaac a thousand times, but hadn't. I was a coward who didn't really want to know if I'd messed with the fabric of time for a boy who had cheated on me.

But maybe he didn't *cheat the first time. Maybe that's just one of the things that have changed.*

How cruelly ironic would that be? If I'd scarred myself for life to keep from cheating on Isaac only to discover my time travel had somehow caused *him* to cheat on *me*? It would be awful, a horrible twist at the end of the story, a punch line no one would find funny.

Except maybe the locket. Maybe the locket made *bad* things happen. Maybe that's what it had been up to all along. Rachel had almost died, Theo's future was destroyed, and I was losing my mind, as evidenced by the fact that I was seriously considering a nose job in the name of getting the damn thing *off* of me.

The chain was the tiniest bit too short to keep me from slipping it over my head. If the tip of my nose were a little smaller, however, I just might be able to—

"Really?" Isaac gave the Parthenon the back of his hand as the night lights flicked on behind the white columns. "They make it glow *green* now? Since when?"

"Since when do you hate the Parthenon so much?" I asked with more frustration than I'd intended. But I couldn't help myself. Didn't we both have bigger things to freak out about?

"I don't hate the Parthenon."

"You sound like you hate the Parthenon." I pulled my knees into my chest, contemplating fetching the jacket out from underneath me and slipping it on. It was getting colder every minute. "You sound really angry."

"I *am* angry. It's dumb."

"It's just a building. And it's a museum. People go there and see art. It's a good thing." My words were clipped and tight, little darts thrown at Isaac's face, hoping to pop him open, make him spill whatever was really bothering him out into the cold air. "And it's pretty."

"I don't think it's pretty."

"You don't think anything's pretty this afternoon."

"What's that supposed to mean?" he asked.

"What's wrong with you? What's bothering you so much? You were scowly for over an hour before we even saw the Parthenon. I'm . . ."

I'm freaking out that our future—the entire reason I started this nightmare in the first place—isn't going to happen. That everything is crumbling because of this evil locket I can't take off and I don't know how to put the world back together again.

But I didn't say any of those things. I just reached over and took his hand, holding it tight, willing him to feel how much I still cared about him, how much I wanted him and me to work. "I'm worried about you."

"I'm fine," Isaac said, shifting his attention back to the object of his scorn with a sigh. But he didn't drop my hand. He held it, tight. A minute passed, then two, and when he spoke again, his voice had lost its heat. "I'm sorry. I just . . . I had a fight with my dad before I left the house."

"About basketball?" As if I had to ask. It was always about basketball.

"Yeah. Since practice was canceled for that career-night thing, he thought I should stay home and work on my free throw in the driveway." He shook his head, and a muscle jumped near his jaw. "When I said I would rather go see my girlfriend, he freaked out. He tried to take my car keys."

"Oh, man." I could imagine how that had gone down, Isaac's dad red faced and screaming and his mom trying to calm everyone down. "Then how did you—"

"I told him I'd quit basketball if he didn't stop giving me shit about spending time with you," he said, perfect blue eyes meeting mine for the first time all night. "I told him you were as important to me as sports and he'd just have to deal with it."

My heart squeezed in my chest, love for Isaac edging out a bit of the fear and doubt. Maybe some girls wouldn't have been flattered by hearing they were valued as much as a sport, but after years of feeling like I came second to a gym full of sweaty boys and bouncing balls, his words meant a lot. "I love you. You know that, right?"

"I love you too. And I mean it. I'm not going to be about basketball all the time anymore." He squeezed my hand one last time before letting it go. "But I should probably get home before too late. I'm sure Dad will be waiting up." Isaac stood and shook his legs before turning around to help me to my feet. "You want me to call Mitch and tell him we're bailing?"

"Let's wait a few more minutes. He'll be here and we don't have to take a long ride."

Isaac sighed and shoved his hands into his jeans pockets. "I just don't know how much bicycling energy I have left."

This from the boy who could play basketball for hours—until his entire body was dripping sweat and his face mottled red—and still want to stay another ten minutes on the court. But I couldn't argue with him about it being rude to set a date with Mitch and then leave, especially not after the night he'd had with his dad. It was better to let Isaac go sort things out at home feeling good about him and me.

Besides, our anniversary was in a few days. It would be the perfect time to rekindle our old heat and show him he didn't need anything Rachel had to offer.

"Then why don't you head home?" I grabbed my jacket from the grass and shrugged it on. "I'll wait for Mitch and get a ride with him."

"Really? You don't mind?" Isaac asked.

"No. It's fine. I know you've had a big week." I leaned into him, hugging him around the waist, trying not to think about how easy it was for him to leave me.

Isaac hugged me back, the feel of his strong body against mine so familiar, yet strange at the same time. He hadn't even tried to get under my shirt lately, let alone anything more. I'd been so worried about everything else, I hadn't had time to stress about it, but now—despite the stand he'd made against his dad—I did. Big time.

What if Saturday was too late? What if something had already happened, something Sarah felt compelled to keep from me in order to make sure Isaac and I stayed together? What if that something had changed the way Isaac felt about me? What if Isaac didn't want me in that way anymore?

Suddenly desperate to feel his lips on mine, I tilted my head and threaded my fingers through his short hair, pulling him close, kissing him with everything inside me—every ounce of fear and longing and sweetness and sadness, everything I'd ever promised him and everything I'd been too afraid to say.

And he kissed me back . . . the way he always did . . .

But it wasn't quite the same. He stayed at a safe distance, out of my reach, the heart of him hiding someplace I couldn't touch. As he pulled away, I wondered if I'd ever touched it, touched *him*. Or had I only imagined we fit together perfectly, like missing pieces of the same puzzle?

Isaac laughed under his breath. "Wow. That was . . . wow." He cupped my face in his hands, smiling that smile that had always made me feel beautiful.

It meant Isaac was pleased with me, happy with his choice. Usually that was all it took to make everything in me light up. At the moment, however, it only made me feel vaguely canine, like a cute puppy Isaac adored but didn't totally consider his equal.

But then I *wasn't* his equal. I wasn't as gorgeous, as talented, or as charming. I didn't know many people who were . . . except maybe Rachel. Maybe that was why the kiss hadn't felt the same. I was too busy thinking about Rachel. Wondering, worrying, stressing about whatever it was that had happened.

"I like this new haircut," he said.

"It's not the haircut. It's me," I whispered, needing him to really *see* me, to say something that would make me believe my doubts were foolish, the product of stupid insecurities.

So I wasn't perfect or extraordinary—did I really have less

intrinsic value than someone else because I lacked the qualities that made someone platinum? Didn't people like Isaac know, deep down, that they wouldn't *be* platinum if people like me didn't adore them, watch them, cheer for them?

"I know." Isaac brushed his thumb across my bottom lip. "You're my girl."

His girl. Defined by my connection to him. That never would have bothered me before the do overs. I'd loved being Isaac's girl. I *still* loved it . . . but now I wanted to be more. I wanted him to know I was *worth* more. And maybe he did. Maybe whatever had happened with Rachel wasn't the huge deal I was imagining. Maybe if I got up the guts to ask Sarah about it, I'd know for sure.

I shivered, just the thought of having that talk with Sarah making my body revolt. I didn't want to hear ugly things, I just wanted to move on and have the future I'd dreamt of with the boy I loved.

"I love you." Isaac leaned in, kissing the tip of my nose, his warm lips making me realize how cold I was. Bike riding didn't seem like such a great idea anymore. "You sure you don't want to come with me? We could go sneak in your window and spend some time in your room. Alone."

"I'd feel bad . . ." I said, though a part of me was tempted by Isaac's offer. If only he'd been the one to instigate the kiss and hadn't been so ready to leave me a few moments before. "One of us should stay to meet Mitch."

"Okay," he said, hesitating only a second before pulling his bike from the grass. "But it's you and me on Saturday. I'll pick you up before the party and we'll get early dinner anywhere you want. Okay?"

"The party? I thought we were just going to dinner?"

Isaac winced. "Shit. I'm sorry. Ally talked to me tonight about throwing a party at her house for your birthday. I didn't realize it was supposed to be a surprise."

These inconsistencies shouldn't shock me anymore, but they did. It was all I could do to hold on to the ghost of a smile. "Don't worry. I'll act surprised."

"Awesome." He grinned the grin that made his dimple pop, the one that made his whole face come together in a way that made grown women stop and stare. "I hear you drama dorks are good at that acting stuff."

"Ha ha." But it wasn't funny. Nothing about this day was funny.

"See you tomorrow, babe." Isaac kissed me on the cheek and then swung onto his bike and rolled down the trail, pausing only once to wave before he disappeared around a curve and a clutch of nearly bald bright orange trees.

The leaves were almost gone. When had that happened? Fall had just started and now all the orange leaves were gone? Had that happened every year? Did the orange leaves always fall first? And so soon? It was barely the second week in October.

Even though I'd lived it twice, autumn seemed too short, an abbreviated parody of itself. Or maybe it was my mental outlook clouding everything shades of scary.

At that exact moment, four giant horses plodded around the corner where Isaac had just disappeared. They were mammoth animals with white stripes down their faces and huge mouths that puffed crystalline air into the cold night, and they were pulling a carriage twice the size of any I'd ever seen.

Their appearance would have been crazy enough if the horses weren't wearing red and yellow floral headpieces or being followed by three men in togas playing fiddles. But they were. Wearing headpieces. And there were men. In togas. With fiddles.

I looked around the park, searching to see if anyone else was seeing this or if I'd finally lost my mind. If someone else saw, if someone else thought this was completely out of the realm of normal, everyday experience, then—

"Hey, sorry I'm late." Mitch's voice in my ear made me scream so loud a man jogging by ripped off his headphones and shot me a nasty look.

"You scared me," I said, spinning around, intending to smack Mitch on the chest but finding myself grabbing the collar of his navy peacoat and holding on for dear life instead. "Do you see that? The horses and . . ."

"And the men in togas playing 'Amazed' by Lone Star on fiddles to a carriage full of people dressed like they're headed to a Greek orgy?" His eyes flicked over my shoulder and then back to mine. "Yeah, I see that."

I heaved a sigh of relief that emerged sounding more like a hysterical gasp for air. "Good. Okay, good."

"You okay?" Mitch asked, propping his forearms on my shoulders. "Did Isaac ditch us again?"

"No, he was here, but he—"

"Come with us, young lovers!"

I turned just in time to catch the rose a pink-faced woman in a red and yellow veil threw from the carriage as it passed by.

"Come, and celebrate our union!" She raised a red plastic cup that I strongly suspected held something alcoholic and pointed toward the Parthenon. "Everyone is welcome, everyone is—" Her sentence ended in squeal-giggles as an equally red-faced man in a red toga pulled her back into her seat and kissed her.

"I think we just got invited to a wedding reception," Mitch said.

Duh. Ancient Greek–themed wedding, the Parthenon—it all made a cheesy kind of sense. Except the Clydesdales. And the country music. But who was I to say what was or wasn't part of a traditional, ancient Greek wedding?

"Well, then." Mitch nodded toward my bike. "Jump on, we'd better get going."

"You're kidding, right?"

"No way. It's bad luck to turn down an invitation to a wedding reception. Especially a Greek wedding reception at the Parthenon." He reached out and freed a newly short and blond strand of hair from what remained of my ultra-sticky lip gloss. "And my dad took me to the Indian place for dinner so I'm starving."

"You still don't do curry?"

"I don't do anything that looks like bright yellow dog food."

"It tastes really good," I said. "You shouldn't judge a food by its color."

"I don't, I judge it by the weird smell and the fact that it contains okra, the most disgusting southern food ever to slime its way onto a plate."

"Don't talk smack about okra. I'd kill for my mom's fried okra."

Mitch laughed. "Come on, I bet there'll be snacks. And drunk people dancing badly. Those are two of my favorite things."

"Food and drunk people?"

"Not just drunk people, Katie dear. Drunk people *dancing badly.*"

Then a minor miracle occurred in Centennial Park. I laughed. A real laugh. In spite of the doubt and the fear and the fact that a possibly evil piece of jewelry still hung around my neck, I laughed.

It was decided. "Okay. Let's go, I'll race you to the bike racks." And then I was gone, smiling as the cool wind whipped my hair around my face, comforted by knowing Mitch was right behind me, doing his best to catch up.

Chapter Fourteen

An hour later, Mitch and I were holding our glasses of champagne aloft for the tenth toast to the newlywed couple. Turned out the bride and groom were both from big Greek families, so there was a *lot* of toasting to be done. My head was buzzing a little, but it was a good buzz, a light, drifty feeling that helped hold the heaviness of the past week and a half at a distance.

"Uncle Alexander talks more than Bubbe Birnbaum," Mitch whispered out of the side of his mouth.

"At least he speaks English," I whispered back.

"True. But look at the old guy behind him. He's going to toast in Greek for sure." He nodded to the line of men and women waiting to take their place on the small stage next to the bride and groom's table.

Or the bride and groom's *pillows*, rather. The pair reclined on yellow and red pillows, laughing at the toasts even when they weren't funny, feeding each other grapes and sips from the red plastic cup I'd first spotted in the carriage. The caterers had supplied glass champagne flutes, but the bride and groom seemed to prefer whatever hooch they'd brought with them.

It was pretty cute. They were so in love they didn't need any of the fancy reception food or drink they'd obviously shelled out quite a bit of cash for—one entire side of the Parthenon's "porch" was encased in a clear tent, decorated with explosions of red and yellow flowers and elaborate tables covered in exotic fruit, and the three fiddlers had been joined by a live band. Add in all the food and drink and a two-hundred-plus guest list and we were easily talking fifty thousand dollars or more just on their reception. But all they wanted was a red plastic cup and some pillows to lie on while their family talked about how happy they were that Sacha and Peter had finally gotten married.

Just thinking about it was enough to make me tear up for the third or fourth time.

"I won't be able to drive if I drink any more champagne." Mitch turned and set his flute on one of the bar tables behind us. There were about dozen of them, surrounded by families in jeans and sneakers, college girls in jogging clothes, men in biker spandex— all the people the bride had summoned to the Parthenon on her ride through the park.

It was . . . magical. Everyone seemed so happy to be there, to be included in the wonderful, unexpected celebration of two people who really loved each other promising to be together forever, through better or worse, good times and bad—

"And you're going to cry for real if we listen to any more." Mitch plucked my drink from my hand and sat it next to his own.

"But I don't want to leave," I whispered. "I love them."

"Are you drunk?"

"No. I just love them. They're so . . . perfect."

Mitch smiled and looked back at the bride and groom. "They are. I'd like to be like that someday."

"Yeah?" I asked, not realizing Mitch had his arm around my shoulders until I instinctively leaned into his warmth and felt the soft scratch of his wool coat against my cheek.

Clearing my throat, I stepped away as casually as possible, retrieving my champagne glass and taking another swig. "I didn't know you wanted to get married."

"Of course I do," he said, sounding a little offended, though he turned to smile and clap with everyone else as Uncle What's-his-name finished his toast. "Just because I haven't dated anyone seriously doesn't mean I don't want to—"

"You haven't dated anyone at all." I hiccuped and blushed at the same time. The champagne was sneaking up on me. Time to stop. Hadn't I learned my lesson about alcohol and Mitch and me the first time around? I set my glass down.

"I don't need to date anyone. I know what I want," he said, stepping closer, hand coming down over mine, pinning my fingers to the tablecloth. "I think you've had enough, don't you?"

My skin sparked and my breath caught. It wasn't a kiss. It wasn't even a hug. But there it was, that awareness of Mitch, that aching in my chest. There was a part of me that didn't want to stay at a friendly distance, that wanted to know what it would feel like to kiss Mitch again.

"I wasn't going to have any more." I pulled my hand out from under his, cheeks hot, eyes glued to the buttons on his coat. I couldn't look him in the eye, not yet, not until I pulled myself together.

An hour ago, I'd been desperate for Isaac to do something to convince me I didn't need to worry about Rachel ruining our future. That's all this was, a reaction to how insecure I'd been feeling. I loved Mitch, but not in that way. Mitch was my goofy best friend who laughed at my fart jokes. Isaac was my future. He was everything I'd ever counted on. He was my steady, beautiful, talented, loving boyfriend and I was *not* going to ruin that a second time. We'd get past this tough time and go on to live the dreams we'd dreamed together, just like Sacha and Peter.

"I want to go home," I said, suddenly ready to leave the wedding. My own happily ever after might never happen if I didn't get out of here. And away from Mitch. There was definitely a weird energy hovering in the air between us.

Mitch's hand fell lightly on my shoulder. "Do you feel sick?"

"Yeah. A little," I lied, happy for the excuse to head for home.

"Champagne goes straight to my stomach if I haven't eaten," he said, grabbing my hand and pulling me toward the cheese-and-cracker spread at the end of one of the giant fruit tables. "Let's get something in you."

Ugh. No! "Mitch, I really don't—"

"I swear it will make you feel better."

"No," I hissed, waving an apology to the woman whose toes I'd stepped on in our dash to the cheese tray. "I don't want—"

"If you don't eat, the pukey bubbles will just get worse," he said, dropping his voice to a whisper as the next toaster began his speech—which was, as anticipated, in Greek. "And I don't want yack in my van."

Sigh. "Fine, but just a little bit. I already had a sandwich after school," I whispered, fidgeting as Mitch loaded a plate with enough cheese and crackers to constipate a baby elephant.

"Come on." He jerked his head toward the door to the Parthenon's lobby, heading off before I could protest a change of location.

I stomped after him, feeling both cranky and calmer at the same time. Being annoyed with Mitch for big-brothering me was a good way to keep from thinking of him as anything but my best, oldest, bossiest friend.

Smiling a little in spite of myself, I pushed through the door and into the lobby of the museum. The rest of the Parthenon was closed, but the lobby was almost always open. The better to scare the crap out of little kids with the giant statue.

Athena still stood in the center of the room—as big and brightly colored and creepy as I remembered—but the rest of the cavernous space was nearly deserted. Only a single guard paced slowly back and forth on the opposite side of the statue and a couple of touristy-looking families circled Athena, speaking softly out of respect for the wedding taking place outside.

Or maybe they were just afraid to talk too loud and risk offending the goddess of wisdom.

Wisdom . . . I could really use some of that, Athena. If you've got any extra hanging around.

"Over here." Mitch motioned me over to the bench near the wall. "Sit. Eat."

"You're like an old woman, you know that? Always trying to feed people." I sat down next to him and took a few crackers from the plate he held out.

"I get it from my bubbe," he said. "She'll put the food in your mouth herself if you don't eat fast enough."

I laughed around a mouthful of rye. I loved his grandma, but he was right. I'd seen her physically stuff food in Mitch's dad's face like he was a two-year-old. Mitch snagged a cracker and stuck the entire thing in his mouth. We chewed in silence for a moment, watching Athena watch us.

"I was so scared of that statue when I was little," I said, grabbing another cracker and a slice of something white with little green flakes in it. I was hungrier than I'd realized.

"Me too," Mitch said. "I cried the first time my dad brought me."

"Me too!" I laughed, spraying a bit of cracker crumb, then laughing again.

"We have so much in common. Fear of heights, fear of giant statues. It must be love," Mitch said, tossing the *L* word out like it meant nothing. It made me wonder if I'd been overestimating his interest. Maybe the awkwardness between us was all in my head. "Now, if only you had horrible allergies and weirdly bony knees and elbows, then we'd be a match made in heaven."

"Only if you had hellishly red hair," I said, joking along with him.

"I could dye it. I think I'd look awesome with hellishly red hair."

"So you're agreeing that my hair is hellish?" I leaned over, nudging his shoulder with mine.

Mitch surveyed me critically from the corner of his eye. "Well, it used to be. Before you did this whole blond thing."

Blond thing? My hand shot self-consciously to my newly chopped locks. "Everyone else likes the highlights."

"Hmm."

"What's 'hmm' supposed to mean?"

"I prefer you hellish. Your natural color is cool."

"Well, thanks. I guess." I frowned and shoved another bite of cracker in my mouth.

It was nice that Mitch appreciated my "natural beauty," but the condition of my hair was permanent—at least for the next year or so until the blond parts grew out. It was like he'd told me I'd be an unsightly blemish on the face of humanity for the next twelve months. But whatever. Who cared if Mitch thought I was ugly? He wasn't my boyfriend.

Still, I had to work hard to wipe the scowl from my face.

"You're welcome. The beauty advice is free," Mitch said, clueless that he'd just hurt my feelings. "The love-life advice, however, will cost you."

"Good thing I don't need love-life advice," I said, more defensively than I would have liked.

"Hmm. Right. So everything is sparkles and unicorns with you and Isaac?"

My pulse picked up and swallowing the last bit of cracker left in my mouth felt like I was downing an ostrich egg whole. Mitch knew something. But what did he know? And did I really want to hear it?

"I . . . I don't know," I said evasively, wishing I'd brought my drink with me. My throat was so dry. "It's mostly sparkles."

Mitch nodded, as if I'd confirmed his suspicions. "You need to be meaner to him."

"Meaner to him?" I asked, with a laugh. "Yeah, I'm sure that would make him really happy."

"He might not be happy, but it would probably help your relationship," he said, completely serious, not even the ghost of a smile on his lips. "You need to do the tough-love thing you were joking about the other day. Let him know that he can't get away with ditching you all the time."

I breathed a little easier. This wasn't about cheating. Thank God. I'd had enough angst about that for one day. "He doesn't ditch me all the—"

"Let's see—the play, the cast party, apple picking, um, tonight," he said, setting down the plate of cheese and crackers and ticking the occasions off on his fingers. "Those are just a few examples off the top of my head. It's ridiculous."

"Basketball season just started, he's busier—"

"What about this summer? How many times did he say he was going to pick you up and not show?" Mitch's voice was soft, but I could hear the anger hidden beneath the reasonable tone. "I know of at least two. I saw you standing in your driveway for almost an hour both times."

"So you're spying on me now?" I asked, angry with Mitch, even though he was simply stating the facts.

These weren't "new" memories, these were things that had really happened in my version of reality. Isaac had stood me up four times this summer, left me waiting in my bathing suit cover-up at the end of the drive when he'd promised to come get me to go swimming. Sure, he'd actually come to get me dozens of times—but did that make up for the fact that he'd "spaced" and forgotten to get his girlfriend because he was too busy playing Xbox 360?

But then, why was Mitch so eager to convince me to be mean to my boyfriend? There was a good chance his motives were not as pure as he'd have me believe.

"Yeah, I'm spying on you, Katie." Mitch sighed and rolled his eyes. "Because it takes a lot of effort to look out my window and see your house."

"You don't have to be mean."

He grabbed my hands, squeezing them with a frustrated sound. "I'm not being mean. I'm trying to be nice."

"By telling me my hair looks awful and my boyfriend treats me like crap?"

"By telling you that you're too good to let your boyfriend treat you like crap. And I don't think Isaac *would* treat you like crap if you were meaner to him. Get tough, show him you won't put up with his shit, and he'll respect you for it." Mitch's fingers laced through mine, sending a shiver across my skin. "And I don't think your hair looks awful. It's really pretty."

"Thanks." I sniffed, pulling my hands away from Mitch's. "But I think you're wrong about Isaac. He had a fight with his dad tonight about spending more time with me. He's really trying."

"Good. I'm glad." He grabbed my hand again and pulled me to my feet.

"I'm glad you're glad," I said, strangely breathless as I tilted my head back to stare up into Mitch's face.

"I'm glad you're glad I'm glad," he said, pulling me closer, wrapping my arms around his waist, then releasing my hands. His arms came around me a second later.

All the little hairs on my arms stood up and I was suddenly keenly aware that less than three inches separated me from Mitch. What was happening here? Friendly hug or more-than-friendly hug? How could I tell?

"Isaac loves you," Mitch said. "As much as Isaac is ever going to love anyone."

Ugh! Mitch was so confusing. One second it seemed like he wanted to be more than friends, and the next he was giving me advice on how to keep Isaac in line and assuring me my boyfriend loved me.

"What is that supposed to mean?" I asked, breathing a little easier when Mitch began swaying side to side. We were *dancing*; that's all this was. It wasn't a "moment." It was a perfectly natural response to the music drifting into the lobby. The toasts must finally be over.

"Exactly what I said." He spun me in a little circle, closer to the door. The music became clearer as we moved. The band was playing a popular country song from a few years back, something about all the roads traveled before you find the one who's your perfect match. It had never been one of my favorite songs. I didn't like to think about traveling "other roads." Isaac was my first road, my *only* road, my straight, clearly marked path.

Mitch grabbed my wrists and looped them around his neck

before putting his own hands back on my waist. Very proper, very gentlemanly, but still . . . there was something there . . . something in the way his fingertips pressed into the small of my back that made it hard to breathe.

Surely I wasn't imagining it. Was I?

"He loves you the way Isaac loves people," Mitch continued.

"Which is different than the normal way of loving people?"

"What is normal?"

"I . . . don't know," I confessed.

We both fell silent as we swayed even closer to the lobby door, until we could hear every word the lead singer sang. The air shivered with long, sweet notes pulled from the fiddle, and through the glass we could see the wedding party spin on the dance floor.

Everyone looked so happy, so sure that the partner in their arms was the *right* partner. I'd always been sure too. So sure. And I was sure *now*, wasn't I? *Isaac* was the one for me. The feelings I had for Mitch were because he'd been my best friend for years, because I'd loved him from the first day I'd seen him crying on the swings and wanted to hold him in my arms and tell him everything was going to be okay. I loved Mitch, but I didn't *love* Mitch.

Mitch wasn't the one who'd given me my first kiss when I was fourteen, Mitch wasn't the one I'd lost my virginity to on my sixteenth birthday, Mitch wasn't the person who I'd daydreamed about the future with for three years.

That person was Isaac. And "normal" or not, I treasured his love.

"I love Isaac," I said, my voice strong and sure.

"I know you do, but I'm pretty sure Isaac's way of loving is different than your way of loving. You see more, you want more," he said. "You go all the way for people—your family, your friends, even people you don't even know. Isaac wants to be a star, you want to be an impoverished social worker."

"Not all social workers are impoverished. And I could major in business and still work for a nonprofit," I said, hurrying on before Mitch could speak again. "And the only reason I don't want to be a star is because I'm not star material. Everyone likes attention. There's nothing wrong with that."

"Everyone likes different kinds of attention." He pulled me a little closer, seemingly oblivious to how stiff I'd become. "You wouldn't want to be famous, you know you wouldn't."

I shrugged, uncomfortable with how close he was to the truth. Hadn't I just been thinking about the plague-like nature of popularity?

"I'm not slamming Isaac." Mitch stared out at the dancers, a distant look in his eyes. If I hadn't known better, I wouldn't have thought he was talking to me at all. "He's a great guy."

"I know that," I said, a creaking sound making me turn and look over my shoulder. There, Athena glared down at me and Mitch, like the goddess herself disapproved.

I suddenly had an image of the base beneath the statue breaking in half and the marble giant crashing down. I could see the shock on Mitch's face as he was knocked to the ground, hear the shattering glass as Athena broke through the doors and smashed into the wedding party. The music cut off, the singer's soothing voice replaced by the sounds of people screaming as they struggled to lift the statue off loved ones pinned beneath. A little girl with ice cream spilled on her dress cried and—

"Katie?"

Mitch's voice made me jump, but it was a second creak from the statue that kicked my pulse into high gear. "Did you hear that? That creaking sound?" I asked, hands fisting at his collar, prepared to pull him to safety if the statue began to fall.

"Um . . . no. I didn't hear anything. Except the music," Mitch said.

Another glance at the statue revealed not the slightest hint of movement. I was just losing my mind, letting my childhood fears and time-travel stress get the better of me. Athena wasn't going to fall. Even if she did, the locket would help me go back and save anyone who'd been hurt.

The jewelry stayed cool and quiet against my skin, offering no argument but no comfort, either. I bit my lip, fighting the urge to pull it out and look at it for the millionth time. Staring at that silver *G* and the cryptic inscription wasn't going to help me any more now than it had a week ago.

Mitch cleared his throat and spun me in another circle. "I also heard my melodious voice telling you that, aside from the standing-you-up thing, there's nothing wrong with Isaac."

"I never said there was," I said, attention fully on Mitch once more. Why wasn't he letting this go?

"But there doesn't have to be something wrong . . . for something not to be right." His eyes met mine, and I knew in that moment that he was going to kiss me.

Even before his lips moved closer to mine, before his hands

clenched, digging into the small of my back—I knew the mistake was about to happen again. My entire body ached to kiss him back, my skin begged my brain to let this moment be whatever it was going to be.

Instead, I pulled away, breaking the circle of his arms. "I think you've been reading too many self-help books." My voice trembled, betraying how close I'd been to screwing everything up all over again. Some girlfriend I was. As things stood, I had no room to judge Isaac for being tempted by someone else. But that was going to change. Right now. "And I think I need to go home."

"Katie, I—"

"I really treasure your friendship, Mitch," I said, forcing myself to look straight in his eyes, to make it clear that this was the last time this was ever going to happen. "You'll always be so important to me. You know that, right?"

He stared at me, into me, searching for whatever he thought he'd found a few minutes ago, but it was gone. The weak Katie was gone. Forever. Never to return. Finally, he stopped looking and dropped his gaze to the ground. "Yeah. Me too." When he glanced back up, his smile was almost back to normal. Almost. "And sorry if I stuck my nose in your business. You and Isaac are great together, and if his disappearing act doesn't bother you, then who am I to start trouble?"

"You haven't started trouble." And neither had I. Not this time, and not ever again.

Using the locket had brought me closer to crazy than I'd ever been and maybe even *ruined* Theo's life. I wasn't going to let that be for nothing. Isaac and I were going to make it, no matter what.

Even if Isaac had done something with Rachel, we would get past it. I could forgive him. Even if—in another life—he *hadn't* been able to forgive me.

"I should get home," I said, taking another firm step away from Mitch. "I want to call Isaac and see if he and his dad made up after their fight."

Mitch sighed and fell in beside me as I walked to the door. "What were they fighting about?"

The story filled the space while we fetched our bikes and waved goodbye to the bride and groom, giving us something to talk about while the last of the awkwardness between us faded away, banished into the unrepeatable past. By the time we reached Mitch's van, we were just friends again. For now. For always.

Chapter Fifteen

Only one more day. One more day until my birthday. Then the do over would be over, the wrinkles in time would smooth, and I'd be able to take the locket off and move on with my life. I had to believe that. I had to believe the picture of my grandfather would stop flickering, and the weird inconsistencies would stop, and the—

"Katie, could I borrow a ponytail holder?" Rachel asked, sliding in next to me at the dressing room mirrors. In the new world, juniors and seniors had gym class together seventh period.

Because God was cruel and fate unkind and wishes come true didn't play out the way you thought they would.

"Sure." I fumbled for a few holders from my makeup bag and handed them over. "Take three. It's not like I need them anymore."

"I love the new look. It's so you." She ran her fingers along the bottom of my bob before brushing her own long brown hair into a ponytail.

I fought the wave of nausea inspired by her touch and forced a smile. I'd done my best to put my suspicions about her and Isaac out of my mind, but it wasn't easy.

Isaac hadn't helped shore up my wavering faith by skipping school today. After the fashion show last night, he'd disappeared and hadn't called me until a few minutes before class this morning. He was allegedly hitting the mall with his mom, but I found the excuse hard to swallow. In all the years I'd known him, Isaac had steadfastly refused to enter a mall with his shopaholic mother. Even getting to skip class wouldn't usually be enough to get him to agree to such a thing.

Then there was the fact that Rachel hadn't checked into school until lunch hour. She'd said she'd been too "drained" from coordinating the fashion show to make her morning classes, but it seemed horribly convenient—Isaac and Rachel gone at the same time when neither of them had missed school all year.

My imagination had been running wild, torturing me with scenes of Isaac and Rachel and what might have been.

And that had been *before* Sarah pulled me aside just before class and said she wanted to talk to me in private after school. The look in her eyes had promised I wasn't going to enjoy our conversation. I could only guess that she planned to tell me whatever she knew about Rachel and Isaac. In less than an hour I'd know the truth.

I struggled to swallow a rush of acid that surged into my throat. Ugh. I was falling apart. I probably had an ulcer, but I hadn't bothered to ask my mom to make a doctor's appointment. I kept hoping it would go away, just like I hoped everything that hurt or scared me would go away. Just like I'd wanted the mess I'd made with Mitch to go away.

Seemed like I would have learned my lesson about wishful thinking by now, but I hadn't. I still didn't want to hear whatever it was that Sarah was going to tell me. It made me wish for a fire drill or a bomb threat . . . *something* that would allow me to slip out to the parking lot without having that conversation.

"And I really like the color," Rachel continued, adjusting her ponytail a little higher on her head. "It's a lot more interesting than plain red."

"Thanks. Yin's mom is so great."

"Totally," Rachel agreed.

I turned back to my own alien reflection, ignoring the perfectly made-up face staring back at me, trying to stay calm as I brushed on a coat of lip gloss. I didn't know why we put on lip gloss *before* gym class, but the popular girls did, so now I did too. Last night's fashion-show performance had cemented my platinum status. The dress I'd modeled had sold for four thousand dollars, the highest price fetched by any outfit in the show.

"Isaac must love it. Did he tell you he loved it?" Rachel's tone was filled with so much fake sweetness that I nearly turned and walked over to Sarah.

I could see her reflection in the mirror. She was already dressed out even though we had five more minutes until we had to be in the gym. I could go to her and ask for the truth right here, right now.

Instead, I plunked my lip gloss back in my bag and dug around for some hair spray to keep my new bangs out of my face.

One more day. The locket would come off in one more day and who knew what the "truth" would be then? Maybe things would stay the same, but maybe they'd be different. Maybe I wouldn't have to worry about Isaac and Rachel because there wouldn't *be* any Isaac and Rachel. Maybe—

"Oh my God!" Rachel screamed, and knocked my hair spray out of my hands. "What's wrong with you?"

"What's wrong with *you*?" I shook my stinging hand and glared openly at Rachel in a way I never would have dared before. But I couldn't help it. I was just so stressed out and scared.

The locket was making me crazy, stealing every ounce of joy and hope from my life, making a joke of the second chance it had given me, twisting every dream I'd had into some sad, pale imitation of what I'd thought I'd wanted, showing me what a failure I was.

"I was trying to keep you from spraying deodorant in your *face*, but if you're going to be a bitch . . ." Her eyes flicked to the ground and then back to me. "Then Dove it up."

I looked to my feet, wincing when I saw that she was right. It was a can of Dove spray deodorant on the ground, not hair spray. Failure. More failure. Even at fixing my stupid hair.

"I can't believe you even use that stuff," she said, turning away from the mirror with a disgusted sniff. "Aerosol is so bad for the environment."

I knew that. That's why I *didn't* use spray deodorant. I used roll on. Degree roll on, but no one would believe me if I told them the truth. Who believed in time travel? And even if they did, who would believe that traveling through time changed stupid little things like which kind of deodorant you used or the color of a coffee shop door?

No one. That's who. Especially not Rachel, a girl who had always reveled in my mortification, a girl who was only being nice to me because of a freak accident, a girl who would stop being nice to me as soon as my popularity faded or—

The locket warmed against my chest, shocking me from my thoughts. I stared—wide-eyed—at my reflection, praying for the metal to cool down again. I didn't want to go back and relive anything ever again. Let Rachel think I was a freak. I just wanted my life to go back to normal. I didn't want any more scars or mistakes that weren't "meant to last."

The locket gave second chances I wasn't sure anyone was supposed to have. I was beginning to think there was a reason we only got one opportunity to do things right. Knowing nothing was set in stone made the whole world topsy-turvy, terrifying. Wrong.

Slowly, the locket cooled, and I drew a slow, calming breath.

"Hey, don't worry about it," Ally whispered as Rachel threw her makeup bag into her backpack and left the room. "One time, I almost drank lighter fluid. I was so drunk I thought it was vodka. *So* embarrassing."

"Thanks." I worked on a shaky smile. Ally was much nicer than I'd given her credit for.

"No problem," she said, grabbing my deodorant from the floor and shoving it back into my bag. We both dropped our makeup on the bench and headed for the door. "And Rachel will be cool. Just tell her you like her new bracelet or something."

I followed Ally out into the gym and settled between her and Rachel on the bleachers. I didn't want to compliment the girl who was probably after my boyfriend, but I couldn't afford to have her mad at me either. I needed my life to stay calm, not get any more crazy, and having Rachel Pruitt mad at you was a good way to end up in Crazyville.

"Nice bracelet," I whispered, my voice so soft I wasn't sure she'd be able to hear.

Surprisingly, she did, and smiled right away. "It's from Tiffany's, a gift from my dad for excelling at charity work," she said, holding it up for me and Ally to admire.

"So gorgeous!" Ally squealed.

"Really pretty," I agreed, focusing on the delicate gold-and-diamond bracelet, deliberately avoiding Sarah's eyes as she walked by.

She loathed my new friends, so there was no chance she'd try to sit with us. A cowardly part of me hoped she might also rethink her plan to tell me the truth I didn't want to hear if she saw how tight I was with Rachel and Ally. Surely she didn't want to mess things up with me and Isaac *and* ruin my new friendships all in one big swoop.

"I wish my dad bought me jewelry. The last two things he got me were a four-wheeler and a pink shotgun for hunting season. He totally wishes I'd been a boy." Ally sighed and popped her gum. We weren't supposed to chew gum in Coach Miller's class, but she got away with it most of the time.

"I can't believe you even go hunting with him. So gross." Rachel watched Coach head out of the equipment room, wrinkling her nose when she spied the cart of big red balls. "No! Not dodgeball."

"I hate dodgeball," I agreed, neglecting to add that I usually hated it because Rachel had a surprisingly accurate—and powerful—right arm.

In my old life, I'd cried with relief on the last day of gym the year before. Sophomores and juniors had class together, but seniors had their own, separate class. No more leaving gym with my cheek throbbing bright red because Rachel had "accidentally" thrown the ball right at my face . . . or so I'd assumed.

But at least today I had a decent chance of being on Pummeling Pruitt's team.

"I'll choose you first, Ally, then you choose Katie," Rachel said, automatically assuming she'd be one of the team captains, which she no doubt would be. Coach Miller loved Rachel. "Katie, you can choose either Sammy or any of the jock girls." Rachel stood up, brushing an imaginary piece of lint off her black shorts. "Just don't pick Sarah Needles. M'kay?"

"Why?" I asked, even though I knew I shouldn't. Underlings didn't question the queen's authority, especially so soon after a deodorant misunderstanding.

"I want her on the other team." Rachel smiled. "She's so cute and tiny and I like a challenging target, don't you?"

"Um . . . yeah . . . but, she's my friend." I couldn't aid and abet Sarah's face smashing, especially when I guessed Rachel's reasons for wanting Sarah as a target had little to do with her "challenging" size. Whatever Sarah knew, Rachel knew that she knew—she'd made that clear that day in the theater—and she wanted Sarah's mouth to stay shut.

Rachel shrugged, an ultra-feminine lift of her shoulder that sent boys into rabid drool fits. "Okay, you can pick her for our team. No worries."

I should have known right then that something awful was going to happen. Rachel had agreed too easily, without so much as a wrinkled nose or a narrowing of her melty, baby-deer-esque brown eyes. Looking back, I could see trouble coming a mile away. But at the time, I was just pleased by the way Sarah's face lit up when I called her name.

"Thank you," Sarah mouthed as she scampered to our side of the gym, casting a pointed look at Rachel, grateful to have been spared.

I forced a smile. Sarah was a good friend. I didn't like the way it felt to have a secret between us, but I liked the idea of having Isaac's infidelity confirmed even less. If I didn't hear the cold, hard facts, it was so much easier to pretend everything was fine.

"You know the rules, girls." Coach Miller lovingly arranged the balls along a thin white line she'd had painted on the court specifically for her yearly dodgeball tournament. "Play tough, but play fair."

As if she cared about fair. I would swear Coach enjoyed seeing us hurl things at each other with intent to do damage.

"Be prepared to suffer!" Ally giggled and ran to the center-court line. Rachel, Sarah, me, and the two other girls on our team lined up beside her, facing down our opponents, who had reluctantly arranged themselves beneath the basketball goal.

They were condemned prisoners facing a firing squad, but . . . twitchier. Prisoners knew it would only take a bullet or two to get the job done. These girls had an entire forty minutes of brutality ahead of them without the promise of death to cling to.

"I'm starting the three-minute timer . . . now!" Coach blew her whistle and our team bolted toward the balls like starving children swarming a food-supply van. I'm not much of an athlete—neither is Sarah—but we both knew better than to hesitate.

Rachel's team didn't lose. Not ever.

We were both right there with the rest of our team as they bent down, snagging all of the balls but one. As we spun—heading back to our line to take aim at our opponents—Rachel was on one side of Sarah and I on the other. So I saw what happened, saw it *perfectly*, though Rachel moved so fast I was sure no one else had.

I watched Rachel's foot dart out at the last second, tangling in Sarah's ankles, bringing her down. I watched Sarah's eyes fly wide and her hands release her ball a second too late to block her fall. I watched my friend's chin smash against the hard wood of the court and blood fly from her mouth, splattering across the floor like we were at a boxing match instead of a girls' high school gym class.

Sarah screamed—a thick, liquid sound—and rolled over onto her back, pressing her hands to her mouth. Blood leaked through her fingers and trickled down the sides of her face, cutting a curved, crimson trail from her lips to the gym floor.

Couch Miller's whistle screeched and everyone froze—balls falling from hands and soft cries from lips—as Couch raced to the center of the court to kneel beside Sarah.

"Let me see, Needles. Let me see," she said softly, but Sarah only moaned. Coach turned, searching the eyes of the horrified onlookers. "Did anyone see what happened?"

"She fell, Coach. I think she might have tripped on one of the balls or something." Rachel was innocence personified. She didn't even look my way. She was that certain no one had seen what she'd done.

"Sarah, come on. Sarah, let me see," Coach said, finally coaxing Sarah into removing her hands long enough for Miller to sneak a peek into her mouth. "Shit. Pruitt, go get the nurse."

My eyes flew from Sarah's bloody mouth to Rachel's face just in time to see the shock etched on Rachel's features before she nodded and ran for the door. She hadn't meant to hurt Sarah so badly . . . but she wasn't too broken up about it either.

Not like I was. This was all my fault. *Again.* I'd made a big freaking mistake when I'd insisted Sarah join our team.

The locket warmed against my skin, as if sensing the direction of my thoughts.

I could go back in time and fix this, make sure Sarah ended up on the opposite team and Rachel didn't have the chance to hurt her. I could make it all go away. I could make life better for a girl who mattered to me in the same way I'd made life better for a girl I loathed. I'd saved Rachel; I *had* to save Sarah, no matter how frightening the side effects of time travel.

Hotter, hotter, until I could feel the scar tissue on my chest ache and twitch. This was it. I was going back.

I fought to keep my eyes open as the metal edged into the burning zone. I had to be ready to act fast, just in case the locket did what it had done last time and put me only seconds ahead of impending danger. Every muscle in my body tensed, preparing for the pain . . .

But the pain . . . didn't come.

A sharp knock on the steel gym doors made me jump and clutch at my neck, hands fisting around the locket through my shirt. It was cold now, so icy it made my fingers seem feverish.

"Mottola, go open the door. It's probably the EMTs," Coach said, before turning back to Sarah.

The locket hadn't worked. This couldn't be happening! I had to go back, I had to fix this! It *had* to take me back. I squeezed the metal harder, silently pleading for another chance, imagining how I would pull Rachel away before she could trip my friend. But nothing happened. No temperature change, no time travel, nothing except another shout from Couch Miller.

"Mottola! Move it!"

I took one last look at Sarah's face—tears streaming down her cheeks, blood painting her chin like something out of a horror movie—then ran to let the paramedics in. As I watched them load Sarah onto a stretcher and wheel her out into the crisp, perfect day, the locket grew cold enough to make me shiver.

Chapter Sixteen

FRIDAY, OCTOBER 9, 3:23 P.M.

The school parking lot was emptying fast. Only a smattering of cars, trucks, and luxury SUVs littered the vast expanse. The emptiness made me feel smaller and smaller as each vehicle pulled away, leaving me and my little Hyundai stranded in one lonely corner.

The student parking at BHH was at least three times the size of any student lot I'd ever seen. Everyone had a car. *Everyone*, even the "poor" kids who lived in the oldest subdivision on the north side of town. Brantley Hills poor wasn't like real-person poor. We were all so over-privileged and under-appreciative. We were self-absorbed jerks.

And I was the worst one of all.

How could I have spent so much time and energy stressing about Rachel and Isaac? And worrying about avoiding Sarah?

There were bigger things at stake here—life-and-death things. People were getting seriously hurt, lives were being ruined. I'd been able to hold the horror and guilt at a distance when I believed I could go back and fix the past if I really needed to, but now . . . the locket hadn't worked. Even when I'd *begged* it to take me back in time.

My teeth began to chatter, despite the warmth of the autumn sun on my face. I had to get to the hospital. I had to see Sarah and make sure she was okay. Maybe her injuries weren't that bad, maybe that's why the locket hadn't—

My phone buzzed in my coat pocket. I pulled it out but let it go to voice mail. It was Mitch. Again. He'd called half a dozen times today, four times in the past hour. He must have heard about the "accident" in gym class. I knew I should answer, but I didn't want to talk to him right now. I didn't want to talk to anyone except Sarah.

I'd already be halfway to the hospital if I hadn't locked my keys in my car like a total idiot. I hadn't even realized they were gone until I'd made it out to the parking lot and seen them sitting in the driver's seat, where I must have dropped them while I was talking on the phone with Isaac this morning.

Isaac. He was on his way with my spare key. He'd be here any second. A part of me dreaded looking into his face. It was loving him and being so afraid to lose him that had put this terrifying series of events in motion in the first place.

No. You put this in motion. *You and your mistake.*

I squeezed my eyes shut as a tsunami of self-loathing swept over me. I fought against it, struggling to breathe past the shame that did its best to level me where I stood.

I'd made mistakes, yes, but this wasn't my fault any more than it was Isaac's. I hadn't known what the locket could do or how my do over would affect other people. If I had, I never would have put the jewelry around my neck. I was selfish and wanted the happily ever after I'd dreamed of, but not if other people had to pay the price for my happiness. I wasn't that type of girl.

I was a good person, and I was going to do my best to make things right, starting with being there for my best girlfriend. If only Isaac would hurry . . .

"Hey, Katie! You need a ride?"

My eyes flew open to see Theo hanging out the passenger's window of a beat-up VW Bug idling a few feet away. His long hair was even more tangled than it had been a few days ago and his eyes so bloodshot they matched the rusted paint of the car.

"No thanks," I said, the sight of the new Theo triggering a fresh wave of regret. How far back in time would I have to go to fix Theo's life? A year, maybe more? Was I capable of that, even if the locket would let me? The past two weeks had been crazy enough. I couldn't imagine reliving a *year*, even to get Theo his MIT acceptance letter.

Maybe I wasn't as good a person as I'd thought . . .

The locket warmed for a split second before cooling again—just enough of a temp change to make my hand clutch at my throat and my left eyelid twitch. I was really starting to lose it.

"You sure? We're headed your way," Theo said.

"No." I fought to keep my voice level, normal. "Isaac's bringing my spare key."

"Isaac! He's so cool. He told me to swing by your party tomorrow," he said, laughing like he'd made some huge joke. The driver, a long-haired blond boy I didn't recognize, laughed too. "I'm totally going to come. Cool Band Name is hysterical. I saw them at the Bean a few weeks ago."

Mitch's band. They were playing at my party? I'd had no idea. Maybe that's why Mitch had been trying to call me. I'd been dumb to assume it was about Wednesday night or that he even cared that I'd been avoiding him since our strained ride home from the Parthenon.

"Yeah, they are funny."

"Indubitably," he said, the hint of the old Theo's vocabulary making my eye twitch even worse. "Later, Katie."

"See you tomorrow." I watched the Bug disappear and wondered who had decided to invite Cool Band Name to play.

It had to have been Isaac. None of the other platinums even knew about Mitch's band. Bar mitzvahs and obscure coffee shops were far from the coolest music venues in Nashville. It had been sweet of Isaac to think of his friend and give him a chance to show the school what he could do. Mitch's band was getting really good. I knew everyone would be impressed.

The realization made me a bit more patient when Isaac's truck roared into the lot a few minutes later and a laughing Isaac made a joke of nearly running into the back of my car before slamming his brakes on at the last minute. This wasn't the time for dumb boy stunts, but then again, Sarah wasn't one of Isaac's good friends. He probably hadn't been that upset to learn she'd been hurt.

"Hey!" He practically bounced out of his truck, happier than

I'd seen him in weeks. "Sorry it took so long. I couldn't remember where I put your key for a few minutes."

"That's okay," I said, taking the key and turning back to my car, ignoring the voices in my head screaming that shopping with his mother could never make Isaac this giddy. I didn't have time for suspicion and jealousy right now.

"Then my mom was freaking out that I couldn't be on campus after missing class all day." He walked up behind me, lingering by my elbow as I unlocked the car and grabbed my keys. "She made me call Coach and make sure it was cool for me to come to practice."

"You're going to basketball practice?" I spun around, glaring up at him.

Isaac's mega-watt smile faded the slightest bit. "Yeah. I can't miss it. We've got our first game next week."

"So you can skip school to go shopping, but not skip practice. Nice priorities, Isaac," I said, angry that he could be so oblivious. "Good thing I didn't plan on asking you to come with me to the hospital."

"Why are you going to the hospital?" he asked, worry creeping into his eyes. "Are you okay? Is it that puking thing again?"

"It's not me. I'm fine. It's Sarah." The confusion on his face took a minute to register in my cracked-out brain, but when it did, I felt awful.

Isaac wasn't being an asshole. Isaac had no idea my friend was hurt. I'd evidently placed way too much faith in the BHH gossip machine. *I* was the asshole, the freak who was losing her mind.

"Sarah Needles got hurt while we were playing dodgeball last period." I pressed my spare key back into Isaac's hand. "They had to call an ambulance to—"

"Oh, man. That sucks. Is she okay?"

"I don't know. There was a lot of blood and it seemed like she was in a lot of pain. That's why I really need to get to the—"

"Shit." Isaac shook his head. "How do you get hurt like that playing dodgeball?"

"Dodgeball is dangerous when you play with Rachel Pruitt," I said, mentioning the one name I'd promised myself I'd avoid. I just couldn't seem to help myself.

"What?"

"Rachel tripped Sarah." A sick part of me had to say the words, had to see the expression on Isaac's face. "She made her fall."

"No way. Rachel wouldn't do something like that."

"Yes, she would," I said, staring straight into his eyes, searching for the slightest sign of guilt. "I saw her. I was standing right next to her when it happened."

"Well, maybe it was an accident. Rachel's really nice. She wouldn't—"

"Rachel's really nice? You honestly think that?" I asked, my voice rising as I asked the question I'd been dying to ask for years. Was he really that oblivious? Couldn't he see how Rachel cut me down every time she had a chance, couldn't he hear the snubs in her saccharine voice? On some level, didn't he know we all pretended to love Rachel because we were afraid of her?

"Yeah, I do." His obvious indignation cut through me, bringing tears to my eyes. "She's a bitch sometimes and doesn't stress out about hurting people's feelings, but she would never hurt someone on purpose."

I shook my head, willing myself not to cry. His words were all the confirmation I needed. Whether it was just in the thinking stages or he'd actually done something with Rachel, I didn't know, but there was no longer a shred of doubt in my mind that the boy I loved had betrayed me.

Now I just had to decide what to do about it. Did I get in my car and leave him in a squeal of tires the way he'd left me? Or did I try to fight for him, for us?

"Listen." Isaac sighed and backed another step away. "You're upset. Why don't we talk about this later when you—"

"Do you really want to talk to me later?" I asked, my voice soft and bruised around the edges.

I couldn't believe I was going here, giving Isaac the "out" I'd never dared to give him before. I'd always feared that he'd figure out he was too good for me and leave, and I'd never wanted to make that easy for him. But now . . . I had to know if everything I'd been through had been for nothing. When I spoke again, I sounded like I was about to cry. "Do you even want to be with me anymore?"

Isaac's eyes narrowed. "Of course I do. What kind of question is that? My dad is barely speaking to me because of you."

Ouch. "So it's *my* fault that you and your dad—"

"No, it's not," he said, hurrying to reassure me, obviously freaked by the tear that had just slid down my cheek. "I'm sorry, but this is just stupid. Everything is good. We're . . . good." He stopped, searching for some further description he couldn't seem find. Finally, he threw up his hands in frustration. "You know I love you."

"I love you too." *But I'm not sure that "love" means the same thing to both of us anymore.*

Mitch's words that night at the wedding had squirmed their way into my brain and made me doubt. Was Mitch right? Did Isaac and I love differently? And did Isaac's way of loving include it being okay for him to mess around with other girls behind my back?

For a second I almost asked him point-blank, but then he reached out and pulled me in to his chest. His warm arms went around me, squeezing me so tight I could barely breathe. There was need in the way he held me, need for *me*, not anyone else. Need that felt real no matter what he'd done.

"Come on, babe," he whispered into my hair. "I spent all day shopping for your presents with my mom. I let her drag me into *two* malls." I could tell by the tone in his voice that he was telling the truth. I'd been driving myself crazy all day for nothing. "Let's not fight the day before your birthday."

I looked up at him, searching his face again, this time looking for reasons to stay. I found them in the clear blue of his eyes, the eyes I'd always hoped our children would have instead of my muddy green. Isaac and I had so much history and so many things to look forward to. I'd traveled through time and nearly lost my mind for him. I wasn't going to let that all be ruined.

"And our anniversary," I said, making my choice. It was time to let it go and move on, to get through the rest of this do over and reclaim my life.

"I got you a present for that too," he said. "I know you've had my presents for months."

I smiled, a small smile, but a real one. "Were you sneaking around in my closet?"

"Guilty," he said. "But you're going to forgive me, right?"

"I should have hidden them better."

"So we're good?" he asked, scanning my face.

"We're good." And we were. Or we would be. I believed Isaac loved me and wanted to be with me. Whatever he'd done with Rachel was in our past and it could stay there, buried with all the other secrets and lies of the past two weeks. "But I've got to go. I really want to go see if there's anything I can do for Sarah."

"I've got to get to practice, too," he said, backing away. "But I'll call you later."

"Okay. I love you."

"I love you too." He smiled as he opened the door to the truck.

The warmth of his smile kept me relatively calm on the drive across town to St. Mary's hospital. I'd gotten a text from Sarah's mom that they were taking her there, but by the time I finally found a place to park and made it to the emergency room waiting area, there was no sign of Sarah or her parents. It was barely four o'clock. No one ever got in to be seen in less than two hours . . . unless . . .

Unless their injury was really bad.

For a second I stood frozen in the waiting room, searching the seats full of people in various stages of pain and misery and sickness for a familiar face, thinking I'd see Sarah if I just kept looking. Surely I'd just missed her. But a few minutes later, I had to admit defeat. I was going to have to call Sarah's mom. Checking in with the overworked nurses at the front desk wouldn't do any good since I wasn't a family member.

"Hello? Katie?" Sarah's mom answered on the second ring, her voice as calm and collected as usual.

"Hi, Mrs. Needles," I said, my spirits lifting. Maybe Sarah had already been treated and sent home. "I'm at the hospital. I came to the emergency room, but—"

"We're upstairs on the fourth floor, room . . ." She paused and I heard footsteps. "Room 412. We're waiting for the plastic surgeon, but you're welcome to come wait with us. I know Sarah would be glad to see you."

"Sure," I said, my hope freezing into a hard lump in the center of my chest . . . right beneath the cold metal of the locket. "I'll be right there."

All the way out the door and around to the main entrance to the hospital, up the three floors in the elevator, and down the hall to room 412, I did my best to convince myself that Sarah's injury wasn't that bad. She wanted a career as an actress. Her parents knew that, and they knew even the tiniest scar could impact her ability to earn a living in her chosen field. They were probably seeing a plastic surgeon just to be absolutely sure Sarah received the best treatment possible.

The second I turned the corner and saw Sarah's pale, tear-stained face and hugely swollen upper lip, however, I saw my positive thinking for what it was—a hot, sloppy mess of lies.

"Come in, Katie." Sarah's mom motioned me inside but didn't

get up from her chair near Sarah's bed. "Sarah can't talk, but she's writing notes."

Sarah waved me in with a sad sniff. I crossed the room slowly, forcing my feet to move closer, though I really wanted to turn and run until I found someplace safe to hide from the misery in her eyes. The misery I hadn't been able to go back and take away.

"She's going to have stitches on her upper lip and need a bridge to replace one tooth the doctor said we wouldn't be able to save." Mrs. Needles still sounded completely calm, but I could see the tension in her face. She was trying to be strong for her daughter, but it was freaking her out to see chatty Sarah so quiet and broken. "Everything should heal in a week or two."

Sarah groaned and started to scribble something on the sheet of paper in front of her, but her mother stopped her with a gentle hand.

"But it won't heal in time for her to fulfill her obligations in *Romeo and Juliet*," she said softly. "Sarah's going to have to back out of the Rep production."

"Sarah, I'm so sorry." I started crying again when Sarah's eyes filled with tears. I took her hand, squeezing her thin fingers.

I knew how much earning her Equity card had meant to her. It wasn't an easy thing to get. You had to be cast in an Equity production and beat out hundreds of other union actors for a job. *Romeo and Juliet* was unique because it called for very young-looking actors, but another play like that might not come along for years. She could still audition for Julliard and go on to be a professional actress, but one important, life-changing break had been taken away from her.

A break she'd been allowed to keep the first time we'd lived these two weeks. It was my do over that had ruined this for her.

"Katie, while you're here, I'm going to step into the hall and try to call her dad one more time," Mrs. Needles said, rising from her chair.

"Sure, no problem." I squeezed Sarah's hand as her mom left the room, trying to think of something encouraging to say that didn't stink of look-on-the-bright-side stupidness. I came up with . . . nothing. There was nothing I could offer except another lame "I'm sorry" that she couldn't truly understand how much I meant.

She'd never believe this was *my fault* or the work of a horrible, cursed piece of jewelry.

All my doubts and suspicions, every dark thought I'd ever had about the locket surged into the tiny hospital room, burying me alive. It wasn't good. It didn't help people or make things better. It had taken me back in time to drive me crazy with worry and fear; it had nearly killed Rachel just for the kick of seeing me scramble to save her; it had ruined Theo's life and messed up Sarah's face and played with reality for its own amusement.

It was pure evil and was going to do its best to ruin my life before my do over was complete.

I stood there in silence with the weight of my fear wrapped around my neck, squeezing until I could barely breathe, sweating, shaking, my heart pounding in my ears until I finally broke under the terror pressing in all around me. "I'm sorry," I said, pulling my hand away from Sarah's. "I just can't stay. I'm . . . I'm so sorry, but I can't. I just can't."

Sarah made a noise of protest, but I'd already spun and raced from the room. I ran past Mrs. Needles, around the corner, and down the hall to the elevators. As I punched the down button, the locket flared hot against my skin.

"No, no way." I ignored the freaked-out stares of the two older men waiting for the elevator and clawed at the buttons of my coat. I wasn't going back in time. I didn't want to "play" anymore. The locket couldn't make me.

I pulled it from beneath my new gray sweater and flicked it open, determined to break it in half with my bare hands . . . until I saw the latest changes to the pictures within and froze. On one side, there was nothing but a hazy black and white blur. On the other was a black and white period-looking portrait of . . . me, wearing the same outfit I'd worn the night I made the mistake of picking up a seemingly innocent piece of jewelry.

My breath caught on a sob. I dropped the locket and stumbled toward the entrance to the stairs, ignoring the concerned grunt from one of the old men. I felt like I'd fallen flat on my back in the water and been swept out to sea. I couldn't breathe, couldn't figure out which way was up and which was down. I was lost and drowning.

This couldn't be real. It *couldn't* be!

The second the stairwell door closed behind me, I grabbed the chain of the locket and tugged, struggling to get it off, pulling until the metal dug into my cheeks and I wanted to scream with frustration. It wasn't coming off. I *knew* it wasn't coming off. It was mine. My cross to bear, my curse.

It really was mine now, in a way it hadn't been before.

Hands shaking, I thumbed it open again, my knees buckling as I saw the picture was still the same. I slid to the ground beside an empty sack of chips and a few crushed cigarette butts, staring at my own face, wondering if I would be trapped inside there forever.

Chapter Seventeen

SATURDAY, OCTOBER 10, 5:45 P.M.

The sun was just going down, but my birthday party had been cranked up for an hour, ever since Mitch's band took the stage for their first set. They were playing a lot of songs I remembered from my "old" life, but with a new punk-rock sound that really worked for them. They were amazing, fun, and their music as infectious as a popularity plague.

Everywhere I looked, people were dancing beneath the Chinese lanterns strung in a crisscross pattern over our heads, even people I wouldn't have suspected knew how. Meanwhile, I was doing my best to pretend life was normal and praying it really would be come six o'clock.

The hope that I'd be able to unlatch the locket at the end of the do over was the last thread connecting me to my sanity. The jewelry certainly wasn't coming off any other way. I'd spent a few hours with my mom's collection of steak knives last night. The chain and the locket itself were as invulnerable as always.

"Rader is funny." Isaac whispered the words into my ear, gesturing toward the porch of Ally's pool house, where Rader was mixing it up with something vaguely resembling air-traffic-control signals accompanied by some pelvic thrusting.

"He's scary. I thought he was having a seizure," I said, doing my best to pretend I was having as much fun as I should be having.

Isaac laughed and pulled me closer, nuzzling his face into the back of my hair. "You smell so good. I love your birthday present."

"Me too. You did good work." I tilted my head back, giving Isaac better access to the curve of my neck where I'd sprayed my new perfume. He'd never given me something so grown up before. I loved it. I loved *him*.

He felt so *perfect* today, and it made me so, so *sad*.

What if taking the locket off took away my second chance? What if Isaac hated me again? My fingers crept toward my neck, but I forced them away.

It didn't matter. It had to go, no matter what the consequences. Just a little longer. Then the locket and I were going to undergo a permanent parting of ways. I didn't want anything more to do with it. And hopefully, come the start of "new" time, the locket would no longer want anything to do with me either.

Please, please let that be true. Please.

"Hmm . . . I can't wait until later tonight, when it's just you and me," Isaac said, running his hand over my hip and squeezing.

My cheeks burned. I was keenly aware of the fact that half the senior class was watching Isaac feel me up, but I didn't pull away.

Instead, I shifted closer, just in case this was the last time Isaac touched me like this. I was glad I'd had a couple beers before we'd snagged a place on the Persian rugs spread out on the grass at one end of Ally's massive backyard, as far from the stage as we could get. Isaac had chosen our spot due to its proximity to the keg, but I hadn't minded being away from the action.

From the second Mitch had arrived, he'd reeked of weirdness— from the look on his face to the stilted way he'd introduced the band—and the last thing I needed was any more weirdness, from Mitch or anyone else.

After dropping by the florist to send Sarah a bouquet and a note apologizing for bailing on her at the hospital, I'd spent half the day reliving my volunteer work at Belle Meade—but working the bake sale instead of the balloon table, and dressed in an 1800s ball gown instead of a servant's dress. In this version of reality, volunteers at Belle Meade dressed like members of the aristocracy. My corset had been so tight I'd nearly passed out on the veranda. Twice.

On the bright side, we'd all been set free at three o'clock instead of five, so there had been plenty of time to get ready for the party and have an early dinner with Isaac at Mama Theresa's. It had been wonderful, a perfect last dinner . . . if it was our last. The uncertainty made my skin itch and everything within me ache to be done with time travel and its consequences. Forever.

"You want another beer?" Isaac asked, hand still idly squeezing my hip in time to the music, a punk-infused cover of "You're the One That I Want" that had even the parents in attendance dancing.

"Not yet. I want to wait until closer to supper."

"It's almost six," Isaac said, pointing to the clock above the pool deck. "They should start grilling soon, and I can get us some more buffalo wings."

Almost six. Where had the last hour gone? It was time! We'd officially cross over into the never-been-lived-before zone in five minutes!

I jumped to my feet so fast little gray flecks danced in front of my eyes. "You're right. Another beer sounds good. But I have to hit the bathroom first. You'll refill my cup?"

Isaac stood and reached for me, pulling me in for a quick kiss. "No problem, birthday girl. Hurry back."

My lips buzzed and my head spun as I sent out a prayer that I would be back and that Isaac would still be as in love with me as he was right now. Of all the things the locket had changed, I wanted to keep this one thing . . . so badly. Isaac had made it clear today that I was the one he loved and wanted to be with. At the moment our future was as bright as it had ever been, with nothing standing in our way.

Or nearly nothing.

Rachel was standing near the oversized doors leading into Ally's house, holding a glass of white wine, talking with Ally's mom like she was already the ruling queen of a small fiefdom. She pretended not to see me, but I felt her attention brush against my skin before skittering across the lawn like a rock skipped along water, landing on the now solo Isaac.

Not on my watch, Pruitt.

It was time to let Rachel know she wouldn't be getting between me and Isaac. Not now, not ever. If I got this locket off and Isaac was still in love with me, he was going to stay in love with me. End of story. I veered to my right, raising my hand to catch Rachel's attention.

"Hey! Rachel!" I smiled at Rachel and at Ally's mom, ignoring the lack of response on Rachel's part. It was clear she'd rather I hadn't come over to say hello, but I didn't really care what she wanted. Not anymore. Something inside me had shifted when I'd seen the picture of myself in the locket last night, something that insisted I make it clear who I was, what I believed in, and that I showed the people in my life what I stood for. "Thanks so much for having my party here, Mrs.—"

"Call me Tooty." Ally's mom laughed and squeezed my arm, her bright, melon-colored nails digging into my skin a bit too hard. "All Ally's friends do. And it's no problem! We love to party with ya'll. It keeps us young."

The Botox probably wasn't hurting anything either. Ally's mom's face barely moved when she spoke. It was . . . creepy, and I was suddenly so grateful for my mom's laugh lines and taste in age-appropriate clothing.

"Cool. Well, thanks anyway, Tooty," I said, wincing at how stupid I sounded. But it didn't matter; Ally's mom was too wasted to notice. She almost tripped over Rachel's shoe as she excused herself and headed over to the patio table to get more wine.

"Having a good time?" I asked Rachel, smiling even when she curled her lip slightly at my loser line of questioning.

"Sure." She shrugged, lifting her glass of wine an inch or two into the air. "Ally's parents throw the best parties. How about you? How's the birthday princess?"

"Feeling very princess-y. Isaac and I had a great day."

"Good for you." The mocking note in her voice was enough to convince me to end the chitchat.

"It is good for me. And for Isaac," I said, looking straight into the eyes that had once made me so anxious without flinching. "We're happy together and I'm going to do whatever it takes to make sure we stay happy. I know everything, and I don't care. Just know that from here on out, Isaac won't be with anyone but me."

Rachel rolled her eyes. "Okay. Whatever you say."

"I do say." I kept my voice soft and firm, not rising to her bait. "And I mean it. And while we're being real, I saw what you did yesterday. I don't ever want to see you touch one of my friends again."

She shook her head and heaved a put-upon sigh. "Screw you, Katie. *I* was trying to be your friend, your *real* friend, but—"

"Hey, Katie! There you are!" Ally—who was already pink cheeked and as trashed as her parents—suddenly bounced over and enveloped me in a hug, cutting off whatever bit of evil would have spilled from Rachel's lips. But that was fine. I'd already made my point, and Rachel was clearly sick of talking to me. She heaved another disgusted sigh and stalked toward the beverage table.

"Hey. Thanks for the party," I said, hugging Ally back.

"No problem. You rock. And this band rocks! Let's go dance."

"I can't," I said, anxious to slip away myself. I had to ditch Ally before she dragged me to the dance floor. "I really have to hit the restroom if—"

"Okay. Go potty, and then we party." Ally laughed at her joke, then grabbed the sleeve of the boy lingering behind her—an older-looking guy I didn't recognize from school. "Come on, I'll introduce you to Katie's boyfriend. He's so totally good at basketball. You two are going to be best friends."

"I play football," the guy said.

"Right, whatever. Same thing," Ally said, proving once and for all that she had no idea what she was shouting on the sidelines when the cheerleaders started the "first and ten" chant.

"Be right back!" I waved at her, then hurried into the house.

Inside, the party was even louder. There were at least fifty people hanging out in the giant living room, laughing and dancing, shouting over the music being piped in through speakers so the band could be heard throughout the entire house. Mitch's voice—singing about chills and losing control—was everywhere as I hurried up the stairs and down a long hallway, hoping to find a relatively quiet place to test my locket theory.

He sounded so good. And the band was tight. I'd heard more than one person wondering if Cool Band Name was going to get a record deal. It was definitely a possibility, but what would that mean for Mitch? Was this a good thing—setting him on the road to living a dream? Or a bad thing—stealing a brilliant mind from the world of medicine and plunging him into the diseased world of rock and roll, drug addiction, and womanizing?

Girls—popular, beautiful girls—had been looking at Mitch differently tonight. If he wanted to hook up, there would be plenty of takers. But then, there always had been. Despite his relative scrawniness, Mitch was a good-looking guy, and sweet, and smart, and talented on top of it. He was going to make some lucky girl very, very happy . . . once he found the one who was right for him.

"As happy as Isaac and I are going to make each other," I whispered to myself, praying the words were true but knowing my doubts wouldn't be banished until I threw this locket into a shoe box and buried it in my backyard.

At the end of the hall, I found a blue room decorated in old antiques and in such a perfect state of order I figured it had to be a guest room. Hopefully, it was too early in the evening for any couples to be hunting for privacy and I would be able to snag a few minutes alone.

I slipped inside and closed the door behind me, inhaling the smell of roses and lavender and old wood. It smelled like the past, like aging love letters sprayed with perfume and wrapped up with a ribbon. I decided to take that as a good sign. My hands trembled only the slightest bit as I pulled the locket from my shirt and opened it. Time's layers had been peeled away and now—

"No . . . no, no, no," I chanted, alcohol-muddied thoughts clearing with the speed of fear.

The pictures were the same. Worse, even. My picture was still there, but my face had been scratched off, like some monster had clawed away my eyes, nose, and mouth, and the opposite picture had gone completely black. Being in "new" time hadn't changed anything. The world was still upside down, time and reality twisted around each other, a knot I might never untangle. The locket was a nightmare that burned and scalded, scarred and ruined.

Fighting back tears and struggling to find hope floating somewhere in the tidal wave of anxiety, I reached for the clasp of the locket. I still might be able to get it off. My fingernail caught and I tugged, but as usual the metal wouldn't budge. I was still trapped, still the locket's prisoner.

Maybe I always would be, until the day it used me up and moved on to the next victim. Until the day it found its way into a pile of jewelry and my own daughter or granddaughter found it, passing along the cursed family heirloom.

No! No way. I couldn't let that happen!

The locket was an abomination. It had given me something I was never meant to have. Now I was paying the price with scars and guilt and fear and little pieces of my sanity chipped away by changes in the world as I knew it.

"I should never have had a second chance." The words choked me, grabbing at my throat and squeezing, but they were true. Isaac should still hate me, Mitch and I should still be estranged, and Sarah and Theo should still have their lives.

Would the locket take me back to that night I'd put it on and let me choose not to touch it? Even if it would, would that make everything better? Would time return to normal and everyone I'd hurt be safe? Or would it be like Rachel and Sarah, one evil exchanged for another, reality still distorted and strange?

The locket stayed cool and quiet, mocking my failure, its lack of heat an assurance that it was an evil thing that would never help me undo any of the damage I'd done. If I wanted out, I was going to have to fight my way out with something a lot more serious than wishful thinking and steak knives.

Hope danced across my skin. Why hadn't I thought of that before? Something more serious . . . like wire cutters. Or some kind of heavy-duty tool. Gardening shears, even!

I spun and hurried out the door, down the hall, headed toward Ally's garage. They obviously had a gardener—the giant yard and flower beds were too much for Ally's mom to handle alone and I could tell she didn't get her hands dirty—but maybe they had a few tools lying around. If I could find a pair of shears, maybe I'd be able to get the locket off.

It was unusually strong and definitely supernatural, but it was still made of something created on earth. It was metal, and *something* would be able to cut through its links. Even if I had to hunt down a blowtorch or a blade made of diamonds, I'd get it off of me. Then everything would be okay. Pictures would stop changing, lives would return to normal, memories would become constant and true. If I could just get the locket off, then—

"There she is," someone said, the excitement in the harsh whisper making my head turn.

Under normal circumstances, I never would have assumed the person was talking about me, even if I *had* just walked into the living room. I didn't inspire scandalized whispers. But for some reason . . . I knew I was the "she" in question.

Maybe a part of me felt the attention of the room even before I looked around and encountered a dozen pairs of curious eyes. Or maybe a part of my brain had been listening to the song blasting over the speakers, processing the meaning of the lyrics, even while the rest of me was too busy freaking out about the locket to remember how my feet got down the stairs.

"In love with my best friend, in love with a girl I shouldn't have been, in love with my best friend. Again." Mitch's voice rang out, smooth and haunting over a pounding drumbeat. The song was one part rock ballad, one part punk anthem, but I still recognized the tune. It was the same one he'd been playing in the tree house. The one his best friend had built him, the one *I'd* built him.

I swallowed and turned away from the living room full of curious stares, nonchalantly changing my course, angling toward the back door, pulse mimicking the pounding of the drums.

Surely Mitch couldn't be singing about me . . . and even if he *was*, how would all these people know? Until last week, I'd been invisible to most of the platinums. They wouldn't know that Mitch and I were best friends.

"Oh, little girl, come sit for a while, hair like a Muppet, but it makes me smile. We'll talk about him, like we always do, but I don't care as long as I'm with you, oh, Kaley. Oh, Kaley. Ka-ka-ka-kaley, will you always be my best friend's girl?"

Kaley, not *Katie*, but it didn't matter. I could tell myself all the comforting lies I wanted, but I'd seen the signs. During the past two weeks—and even for months before in "real" time—Mitch had done everything but write his feelings down and shove them in my face. And now he'd done that too. Or at least written them down and sung them. In front of the entire school.

I knew this song was about me. Everyone knew. *Isaac* knew.

I froze just outside the back door, scanning the ground near the keg where I'd last seen Isaac but finding only men in white and black uniforms rolling up the Persian rugs, dragging them under the tent covering the band, dancing area, and food. The sky had grown considerably darker in the few minutes I'd been inside. It was going to rain any second, the sky burst open and cry like it had about this time two weeks ago, when I'd fallen to my knees in the mud, screaming in pain as the locket worked its magic for the first time.

Maybe the locket would work for me again and turn back the past few minutes, back to before Mitch started singing so I could pull him off the stage and—

I squeezed my eyes shut and shook my head. No! I didn't want the locket to take me anywhere. Not now, not ever. No matter how horrible this was, the locket's magic was worse. I had to make this better. Me, on my own.

"Kaley, you don't know what you do to me, when you touch me, I can't breathe," Mitch sang, his voice making the simple lyrics sound like so much more. They were a confession, a prayer.

A prayer I couldn't answer, and a confession that was going to ruin everything *again* if I didn't find a way to fix this. I jogged down the deck stairs toward the tent, too panicked to know what I'd do when I got there. I only knew I had to find Isaac. Or stop Mitch. Or find Isaac *and* stop Mitch.

"Kaley! Ka-ka-ka-kaley."

God, Mitch, *why*? Why here? Why now? Like *this*?

"Oh, Kaley, will you always be my best friend's girl?"

The crowd at the edge of the tent parted to let me through, guys staring, girls whispering, and Rachel Pruitt smiling like the cat who'd pooped in the dog's food and watched him eat it. For a split second, I regretted saving her life, wishing I'd left her where she'd fallen, head cracked open and blood spilling out to cover the stage.

"Come on, Isaac, where are you?" I whispered under my

breath, eyes scanning back and forth, looking for the signature orange shirt.

Finally, I spied Isaac at the edge of the dance floor, where a few dozen clueless people still thrashed to the rhythm, oblivious to the major drama ripping the party to shreds all around them. He was staring at the stage, at Mitch, so still he looked frozen. I followed his eyes, finding Mitch and his guitar bathed in blue and red light only twenty or so feet away.

"Kaley, will you ever tell me it's time? Will you ever tell me you're mine?" Mitch sang, his eyes meeting mine above the dancers. In that second, the tension in the tent shot to unbearable levels, the air so thick with what-the-hell-is-going-to-happen that it was impossible to move, to breathe, to think.

Mitch stared at me, *into* me as the drum cut off and the last note of the song hung in the air. His voice drifted out alone, even more naked without the accompaniment underneath. "Kaley, tell him you're through. Kaley, I love you."

He loved me. *Mitch* loved me and he'd written a song about it and sung it in front of the entire world as we knew it. For a second, the weight of that wrapped around my shoulders and shoved me into the ground, rendering my legs useless. All I could do was stare at the stage, at Mitch, my skin prickling as applause stung through the air.

"Did you know about this?"

Isaac. I turned, numb and ultra-sensitized at the same time, and shook my head. I couldn't seem to get my lips to move, couldn't think of what to say. One of the boys I loved was staring down at me from the stage, expectation hanging all over him like strangling vines. The other was glaring at me from a few inches away, an all-too-familiar anger growing in his bright blue eyes.

It hadn't happened yet, but I could see revulsion beginning to twist Isaac's features, to transform him into the boy who didn't love me anymore, the boy who had left me on the side of the road and ended three years together in a squeal of tires. No matter what, I couldn't let that happen, couldn't let everything we'd planned be ruined by a song.

So I did the only thing I could think of, the only thing that would make it clear who "Kaley" loved. I hurled myself at Isaac, arms around his neck, pulling his lips down to mine, pressing myself against him.

For one horrible second, he stayed stiff and cold, but then I felt his arm around my waist, pulling me closer, his hand fisting in my hair, deepening our kiss, his mouth moving on mine in a way it had only ever done in the privacy of my room. All around us, people hooted and cheered, but somehow I still heard the sound of footsteps running off the stage.

I still knew the instant that Mitch was gone.

Chapter Eighteen

SATURDAY, OCTOBER 10, 11:42 P.M.

Come on, no one's going to come in." Isaac's fingers fumbled with the button on my jeans, but he was too drunk to get it through the hole.

We were back in the blue bedroom where I'd hidden only a few hours ago, when I'd assumed life couldn't get any worse. Before I'd lost my best friend and my boyfriend drank enough beer to float an oil tanker and decided he didn't want to wait for a ride to my house to be together for the first time in two weeks, a month in "my" time.

"Wait, Isaac," I said, covering Isaac's hand with my own. "Everyone saw us come up here and I—"

"So what? They're all too drunk to care." He pushed my hand away. He was probably right—Ally's parents actually seemed to be encouraging everyone to get smashed—but this still felt wrong.

I didn't want to be here. I wanted to be at the Home Depot, buying something serious enough to cut through the hateful chain still looped around my neck. Besides, Isaac was so drunk he hadn't even noticed the two huge scars on my chest when he'd taken off my shirt. Did I really want to be with him when his mind was in a state like that?

"*I'm* not too drunk to care." I moved my hand back to his, squeezing his fingers until he rolled onto his back with a sigh. "It doesn't feel right."

"Like it 'didn't feel right' to leave without seeing Mitch Wednesday night?" he asked, a nasty edge to his tone that made the hairs on my arms stand on end.

"No, it *didn't* feel right," I said. "I didn't want to be rude."

"Oh. Right." He laughed and pushed himself up to sit at the edge of the bed. "You wouldn't want to be *rude* to Mitch. Since he's your best friend and all."

"He is my best friend . . . or was my best friend."

"Is that why you invited him on all our dates lately? Because you're such good friends?"

"We are *all* good friends." I sat up and reached for my shirt, suddenly wanting to be fully clothed. "We've been friends forever. You know that. I just wanted us to be close again, the way we used to be."

"Back when you had two little boys with crushes on you instead of one?"

"What?" I pulled my shirt over my head and tugged it down, crossing my arms over my cramping stomach. "No way, that's not it at all. I just wanted—"

"Mitch has always had a thing for you. You knew that. I *know* you knew that."

"That's not true," I said, even though Isaac was right. I *had* known, deep down, but I hadn't meant to hurt anyone. "I've always thought of Mitch as a friend." I reached for Isaac, running my hands in soothing circles on his back.

"A friend who, all of a sudden, you want to spend every waking second with?" He stood up, moving away from me, pacing around the small room. "A friend you built a fucking tree house for?"

"He was really upset about—"

"A friend who's so important to you that you let me go home alone Wednesday so you could spend more time with *him* instead of me?"

"*You* ditched *me* and Mitch. You're the one who wanted to go home!"

"With you! Not alone." Isaac whipped around, glaring down at where I sat on the edge of the bed. "So what, Katie? One boyfriend wasn't enough for you? You had to have two?"

The only light came from the Chinese lanterns glowing outside in the rain, creeping through the window blinds, but I could see the anger and doubt on Isaac's face. He was lashing out because he was scared. No matter how cool he'd played it in the hours following Mitch's song, he didn't completely believe that *he* was the one. He still wondered if a part of me hadn't wanted to run up onstage and kiss someone else.

"You are the person I love. You're the one I kissed tonight," I said, voice low and even. "I made it clear to Mitch that you're the one that I want."

"Well, you didn't make it clear to me."

"Why? Because I don't want to do it in some strange house while everyone we know is downstairs?" I asked, starting to get angry.

"No, because you don't want to do it at all."

My breath rushed out between my lips. "Yes, I do. I love you, I—"

"You've hardly wanted to touch me the past few weeks. And then, every time I turn around, you're hugging Mitch, leaning on Mitch, any excuse to hang all over him."

"That's not true," I said, but there was a part of me, a tiny little voice that wondered if Isaac might be right.

My mind flashed on the way it had felt to dance with Mitch, the minutes in the apple tree when we'd stood so close, the way his forehead against mine had made me ache to kiss him that night at the cast party.

And the way he'd made me feel that night—his lips on my stomach, his hand up my shirt, the longing in his voice as he said my name. He'd made me burn in a way as beautiful as the locket's burn was awful. In a way Isaac had never made me burn, never made me ache and yearn and *need* to be close to him more than anything else in the world.

Isaac was my first love, and being with him had been sweet and good. It had been a big decision for both of us—good Catholic girls and good Baptist boys were strongly encouraged to choose abstinence—but I'd rationalized a little rule breaking because Isaac and I had every intention of getting married. But now . . . a part of me wondered if Isaac and I were meant to be.

A part of me wondered if love—and sex—couldn't be something deeper, something more, with someone else . . . someone like Mitch.

"It is true," Isaac said, his voice breaking. He was going to cry. I'd never seen Isaac cry. Never. Not even when he'd broken his arm in three places doing stunt jumps on his bike in sixth grade.

I stood up, reaching for him, but he held up a hand and backed away. "You're only with me because you've always been with me."

"But I love you," I said, tears in my eyes.

"Well . . . I'm not sure I love you," he said.

The words cut straight into me, puncturing the place deep inside where I'd stored away my own jealousy and suspicion. "Is that why you messed around with Rachel? Because you don't love me?"

"What?" His brow wrinkled, his confusion so sincere I couldn't doubt that his next words were true. "I never touched Rachel."

My mouth opened and closed, my shock so complete I couldn't think what to say. I'd been wrong. How could I have been so wrong? "But I thought . . . and Sarah said—"

"Sarah said she wouldn't tell is what Sarah said. But I guess she changed her mind." Isaac shook his head, apparently disgusted with my best friend. "Whatever she told you, it's not true. Rachel and I were never together and with Sarah it was just that one time. One kiss at a stupid party, nothing else."

"Sarah . . ." I shook my head, my mind refusing to process this new information. "You and *Sarah*?"

"Just one time. One kiss. We were both really drunk."

Oh my God. My boyfriend had kissed my best girlfriend and

they'd both lied to me about it for weeks. I felt sick and sad and broken inside, like there was no one in the world I could trust and I'd been a fool to trust anyone in the first place. Something soft and sweet at my core soured, turning rotten and bitter.

Still, even as anger and hurt made my cheeks heat and my palms sweat, the irony of the complete turning of the tables wasn't lost on me. I couldn't help but wonder if the locket hadn't had some hand in making things work out like this, in making sure I learned firsthand what it felt like to be betrayed.

"I'm glad you know," Isaac said, a hint of shame in his voice. "Not like it matters now, but still . . ."

"Not like it matters now?" I repeated dumbly.

"It's over, Katie. You know it is." His words made a desperate, horrible mix of excitement and fear rip through my chest, tearing up my heart. We were breaking up. I *knew* we were and it terrified me. Losing Isaac was the worst feeling in the world, but it was also . . . almost . . . a relief.

No more trying to fit in with his friends, no more worrying that I wasn't as important to him as basketball, no more fear that he was going to decide he was too cool for me and dump me for someone prettier, better. No more searching for ways to connect with Isaac other than talking about Isaac.

And no blue eyes smiling just for me, no more Isaac hugs, no more Xbox marathons on rainy days, no more movie nights, no more kisses that feel so safe. No more first love.

Panic rushed in, banishing any shred of relief. "Isaac, wait. Let's just talk about this some more."

"I don't want to talk." He turned to the door and opened it

wide. The light from the hall made me squint and cover my eyes. "You can put my stuff on my porch. I want my homecoming shirt from last year back for sure."

"Please, Isaac . . ." But he was gone, stomping down the hall in time with some angsty song from the Lithium XM radio channel. Ally's dad had hooked up the XM to the speakers after the band bailed, and the party had continued like nothing much had happened. Like three people hadn't had their hearts broken and their entire world turned upside down.

The temptation to beg for the locket's help came again, tiptoeing into the quiet room, teasing me with the idea that all this pain could go away if the locket would turn back the clock. But I knew better. The locket didn't make the pain go away. Here I was, two weeks from the day I'd traveled through time to change and everything that mattered was still the same.

Isaac and I were over. Mitch and I were wrecked. And my birthday was going to end in a walk through the rain because there was no way I was going to ask Isaac or any of the people at the party for a ride.

The tears came, hot and fast. I was sobbing by the time I made it down the stairs and out the front door, but I didn't care. I didn't care who saw me, I didn't care what Rachel and her friends would say about me when I was gone or the fact that I'd probably be one of the "out crowd" again by Monday, once everyone learned that Isaac had dumped me. I didn't care about anything except getting home, back to the one thing in my life that was still standing.

My dad didn't have gardening shears that I knew of, but we

had the table saw, the one I'd used to build Mitch's tree house. Getting my face that close to a blade that could slice through a two-by-four in a few seconds was probably one of my stupider ideas, but I didn't care about that either.

The locket was coming off. Tonight.

Chapter Nineteen

SUNDAY, OCTOBER 11, 12:32 A.M.

$\mathcal{I}$was soaked through by the time I reached the end of my drive-way, so wet and cold I could barely feel my hands, but I didn't go inside to get warm. I couldn't wait. I had to get the locket off, I had to know this ended tonight.

Shivering, rain dripping off the end of my nose, I ran around to the side of the garage and shoved the sticky side door until it flew inward, banging against the wall. Inside, tools and boxes and bicycles and antiques my dad meant to refinish but rarely got around to touching fought for space in the dust. Dad and Mom and I parked our cars outside in the driveway. We always had, but in this new reality it was even more necessary. The clutter was insane.

I flicked on the light, a single bulb that cast our family trash in sickly orange and yellow, and hurried over to my dad's work-bench, hunting for the table saw.

But the saw wasn't there.

"No. No!" I yelled, not caring if my mom and dad could hear me over the thunder shaking the world outside. How could the saw be gone? How? I'd used it a week ago to build Mitch's tree house.

Rachel. The falling light. I hadn't used the saw since the *second* time I'd used the locket. Now my family didn't have a saw anymore.

On some level I believed the vanishing act was just another little shift in reality, but on a more powerful, gut-based level I suspected the locket had made the saw disappear on purpose. It had known I'd resort to extreme measures and hadn't wanted to make it easy for me to escape, to free myself from whatever hold it had on me.

"I don't want you anymore. I don't want to change anything, ever again." I sobbed as I stumbled around the room, searching for something, anything, to use to cut the chain around my neck and finding . . . nothing. Nothing.

"Get off of me. Get off!" I tugged at the locket, pulling it up and over my chin. I was talking to an inanimate object and probably half out of my mind, but I didn't care. I suddenly felt like I would die if I didn't get it off, if I didn't—

The locket slipped another centimeter, until it was pressed against the tip of my nose, balanced between the world of here and there.

"Oh," I whispered, afraid to move for fear I'd make the locket fall back down around my neck. I'd never gotten it this far over my head before.

But then, I'd never been this cold and wet. Maybe the cold and the rain . . .

Moving slowly, making sure not to release my tension on the locket, I walked to the door and out into the backyard, until I was once again alone with the storm. Freezing cold droplets stung at me through my soaked shirt, but I refused to flinch. Instead, I pulled harder on the chain, tilting my face back to catch the full force of the rain, letting the water swim into my eyes and out again, blurring the twisting tree branches above my head until I felt like I was going blind.

Still, I pulled and pulled, until the skin on my nose tore and the chain claimed hairs at the back of my neck, until it felt like my face might be cut in half if I didn't let go and allow the locket to fall back into place, back onto the warm chest it had already scarred twice.

No. No more. Not me!

I cried out and fell to my knees in the muddy grass, crying and shaking, but not giving up. I couldn't give up. It was going to come off, even if I had to ruin my face to do it. I didn't care about my face. I didn't care about anything except being free to be myself again, to make stupid mistakes and deal with them without all this shame and terror.

The locket gave under my pressure, sliding up and over my eyes. My trembling, frozen fingers worked it over my forehead, untangled it from my hair, and, in another breathless second, I was holding it in my palm. Breathing hard, I stared down at the benign-looking hunk of silver.

It was off. It was over.

Another sob shook my entire body. I pressed the back of my

hand against my lips, muffling the moan as it escaped, muting the damaged sound just enough for it to be bearable. It was okay. It was all going to be okay. It was off. It really was.

Now I just had to find somewhere to put the locket where no one could ever find it, where even *I* couldn't find it. Just in case.

I struggled to my feet. My last beer had been several hours ago and I had never felt more sober in my life. I was fine to drive. I'd just sneak into the house, grab my keys, and go for a drive out to the nearest bridge over the Cumberland. Let the locket get swept away in the current and swallowed by a catfish for all I cared. It belonged at the bottom of the river, where no one would be tempted to use it again.

I spun so fast that my boots slid in the mud, bringing me back to my knees. Suddenly I was face-to-face with the rusty drain near the entrance to the garage, the one with the miniature bars I'd pretended kept a troll under the ground when I was a little girl. Water rushed into the drain and disappeared, never to be seen again. I had no idea where it emptied out—into a stream somewhere or into the Brantley Hills sewer system—but even if I did, there would be no way for me to find the locket once I threw it inside. It would be swept away, out of my life forever.

For a moment, I hesitated, wondering if the river might be better, if maybe there was an even safer place I hadn't thought of yet, if maybe I should—

The locket burned a little hotter in my hand, making my decision for me. I flung the hateful thing into the drain and watched it slip between the narrow bars without a tinge of regret. The only thing I regretted was picking it up in the first place.

I crept a little closer on my hands and knees, peering into the drain. The glow from the garage light revealed nothing but pipe with some kind of slimy black stuff growing on the edges. It plunged deep into the ground and the storm was supplying plenty of cold, rushing water to carry the locket along through the drainage system to destinations unknown.

It was gone. Forever.

"Thank God," I whispered, burying my face in my hands, so relieved I felt like crying and laughing at the same time. I pulled in a deep breath and let it out slowly, a vague notion that I needed to get out of the rain and into a hot shower floating across my mind before I heard the music and tension threaded through my muscles once more.

It was the song. The Kaley song. This time there were no words, just harsh guitar chords fighting a vengeful path through the rain, but I recognized it immediately.

The cold settled deeper into my bones as I turned toward the tree house. There was no moon, no stars, only the slight glow of the Birnbaums' porch light to illuminate the treetops, but I could still see the vague outline of someone on the platform I'd made.

Mitch.

My heart punched at me from the inside and for a second all those memories swam inside me again. Me and Mitch—talking, laughing, riding bikes, dancing . . . kissing. He'd been a part of my life for so long, a constant I'd taken for granted, a friend who maybe . . . *maybe* . . . should have been something more. Who *could* have been something more if I'd made a different call a few hours ago.

But what about now? What were we now? What did I want us to be? Did it matter what I wanted? And was it my fault that he was playing his guitar in the rain? Did he hate me as much as Isaac hated me? Maybe even more?

Whatever the answers, I would deal with them. Just me. I could do this, I could face the mistakes I'd made. I didn't need supernatural intervention or magic, I just needed to be strong, and honest, and brave. It still wasn't easy to hear those angry notes or take that first step across the lawn, but I could do it. I *would* do it.

With one last look at the drain where the locket had disappeared, I started toward Mitch, and all those scary tree house steps that separated him from me.

Chapter Twenty

*I*t was raining so hard that I could barely see my hands as I wrapped my fingers around the fourth step and started to climb. Even the shelter of the leaves still clinging to the branches didn't offer much relief from the downpour. I was climbing blind, the lack of visual cues making the swaying of the massive trunk and the groans lurching from deep inside the tree even more disturbing.

It was a horrible storm, worse than it had been the first time around. Freezing wind whipped through the little valley between my and Mitch's houses, cutting through the tightly woven fabric of my fleece V-neck, plastering it to my skin with another layer of cold and wet.

But still I climbed, shouting Mitch's name as I went. I had no choice but to go to him. He hadn't heard me the first or second or *third* time I'd called from the ground.

Or maybe he was just ignoring me.

"Mitch! Mitch! I'm coming up!" I screamed again, the act of forcing my stiff lips to form words helping keep my mind off the fact that I was six . . . seven . . . ten . . . *twelve* feet in the air. I shivered, fingers clawing into the damp wood.

This was even worse than the light grid. I could feel the empty space behind me growling, a hungry void that wanted my slick hands to slip, wanted to watch me fall and gobble up my fear as I dropped. I licked my lips, tasting salt and something sticky, thinking for a second I must have bitten myself.

Cramped fingers dared a brush up and down my face, swiping away water and something hotter that rolled down into my mouth. The blood was coming from my nose, from the place where the locket's chain had scraped away my skin.

Bringing both hands to cling onto the ladder once more, I turned and brushed my face against my shoulder, leaving a spot of black on the gray fabric I could just make out in the dim light from the Birnbaums' porch.

I peeked at Mitch's house through the leaves. My parents were long asleep and trusted me so implicitly they'd never get up to check and make sure I was home in bed. Especially just after midnight on my birthday. But maybe Dr. Birnbaum or his new fiancée . . . maybe . . .

The porch remained empty and the house silent and dark. I wondered if Dr. Birnbaum thought Mitch was asleep or assumed his son was still out at the gig where he was supposed to have been booked until midnight.

Ally's dad had said something about suing Mitch and the band for half the fee he'd paid them, but Ally had assured me he was just drunk and didn't really care. She'd sworn he would forget the whole thing by tomorrow. She'd hugged me and told me not to worry and promised she'd come over Monday morning to help me do my zombie Little Mermaid makeup for the first day of Un-dead Disney homecoming week.

Then she'd turned and thrown up in the kitchen sink, right in front of me and Isaac and her football player friend, who was so drunk he didn't even seemed to realize she was puking. He'd just kept rubbing her back and playing with her hair, grinning at me and Isaac with this scary, empty look in his eyes.

No one at the party had been telling their friends that they'd had enough, no one had been looking out for each other the way Mitch had always looked after me.

The guitar strumming stopped for a second. "Mitch!" I screamed again, certain he would hear me.

But he didn't hear. Or at least he didn't care to respond. The guitar chords struck up again, this time playing a tune I didn't recognize at first. It was only when I'd coaxed my shaking arms and roiling stomach up another three steps that I heard Mitch's voice, soft and slurred beneath the rain and the wind, singing, "Deserves a quiet night . . . sure all these people understand."

R.E.M. "Nightswimming." He'd played it on the way back from our last cliff-diving trip the summer of my freshman year, just before school had started and he, Isaac, and I had begun to grow apart. The song had made us all sad, as if we could sense we were at the end of something innocent and wonderful and life was about to get a hell of a lot more complicated.

"Mitch? Mitch, it's me," I said, voice trembling as I reached the top step and stared across the platform.

The music stopped and Mitch's hand reached for a bottle near his hip. He took a swig, hissing before he dropped it back down onto the boards. I couldn't see the exact shape of the bottle, but the sickly sweet, burning smell of whiskey hung in the air, tattling on the kid who'd stolen it from his dad's liquor cabinet above the refrigerator.

Mitch was *drinking* up here. Really *drinking*, not just unwinding with a beer or two, but slamming back shots of hard alcohol. I'd never seen Mitch drunk before and had no idea how chugging whiskey would affect him. What if he passed out? How in the world would I get him down?

This wasn't good. Not good at all.

I licked my lips and shook the rain out of my eyes, struggling to get up the courage to climb out onto the platform. "Mitch, I—"

"Go away." Mitch inched farther away, swinging his feet to dangle over the side like he was sitting on the edge of the swimming dock down at the lake, not hanging thirty feet in the air. Just looking at him made my head spin and my guts threaten to turn themselves inside out.

Guess whiskey had helped cure *his* fear of heights.

"I'm not going away. You shouldn't be drinking up here," I said, shouting to be heard over a sudden gust of wind. The tree rocked back and forth, moaning, while my pulse raced and my hands gripped the ladder step so tightly my knuckles snapped and cracked.

For the first time since that night in Isaac's truck, I felt the obscene weight of holding the future in my own hands. There would be no more do overs. The locket was gone, every second counted, and I had to get Mitch out of this tree before one of us was seriously hurt.

"Come on," I called, trying to channel my mom's bossy voice. "Come down. We can talk."

"I don't want to talk. I don't have anything to say to you." He took another swig from his whiskey, tilting it back to suck down the last few drops before pitching the empty bottle out into the air. "Go away."

His words hurt, but I deserved them. Still, I couldn't leave him up here. He was my friend and he was obviously smashed or going to be smashed very soon. I had to get him down on the ground and into his house. "Okay, we don't have to talk. Just come down."

"I don't want to come down."

"Please, Mitch, I don't want you to fall."

He turned to look over his shoulder. His face was in shadow, but for a second, I swore I could see the loathing in his eyes. "Like you care?"

"I do care. You know I care, I—"

"Fuck you, Katie."

My mouth fell open and my hands spasmed around the wood in my hands. Mitch had never said anything mean to me. Ever. Not in our entire lives. I'd only ever heard him cuss a handful of times, and I'd *never* heard him tell someone to "eff" themselves. The shock of knowing he hated me enough to say those words stunned me into silence.

"You know, I thought you were so different, that you saw past all the superficial shit," Mitch said, his words vaguely slurred but still coming through loud and clear. "I thought you cared about people, *really* cared about them, whether they fit into the stupid Brantley Hills mold or not."

"I *do* care."

"No, you don't. All you care about is being Isaac's perfect little girlfriend," he said, the disgust in his tone making me flinch. "You're as stupid and shallow as Isaac and all his friends."

"I thought Isaac was a 'great guy,'" I said, finally getting the courage to crawl out onto the platform, anger dulling the edge of my fear.

"I said a lot of dumb things Wednesday night." He laughed. "No matter what you said, I was so sure . . . when we were dancing . . . I thought I could see it . . ." He turned back around. "Just leave me alone."

"No. You're the one who sang that song in front of Isaac and everyone," I said. "You don't get to tell me to go away. You have to talk to me."

"Good work on the confrontation skills, Katie, but you've got the wrong guy." He swayed to one side, making my heart lurch until he righted himself again. I had to get him down on the ground. Now. "Go argue with your boyfriend."

"I'd rather argue with you." I reached out, grabbing a fistful of his soggy sweater. "Come on. Come down and argue with me."

He turned, his face caught in sharp silhouette. "I don't care enough to argue with you. Not anymore."

Tears filled my eyes, mixing with the rain. "Mitch, please."

"You aren't the person I thought you were. Just . . . go away." He shook his head. "You're not worth it."

His words made me shake all over and my throat close up so tight I swore it made a whistling sound when I sucked in a breath of cold, wet air. He didn't think I was "worth it." He didn't respect me, care about me, or even value our friendship enough to put up the energy to argue.

The reality of it hit me hard enough to make my bones ache. I'd lost Mitch. I'd *really* lost him and it hurt so bad. So, so, *so* bad. It was like a light had gone out inside of me, like someone had died and I knew they were never, ever coming back—no matter how much I cried, no matter how long I begged. Regret filled up every place inside of me, until I could taste it on my tongue, smell the pain seeping through my skin and drifting in the air.

This was so much worse than breaking up with Isaac. Losing Isaac had broken a piece of my heart, but losing Mitch shook something loose in my soul. Something jagged that knocked around inside me, bruising and screaming and bleeding, until finally my stupid brain got the message my innermost self had been trying to tell me all along.

"But I love you," I said, bursting into tears as I realized how entirely true the words were. "I love you."

And I did. I loved Mitch. I'd loved him . . . always. When we were little, it had been the love of a dear friend, but now it was more. So much more. It was insane that I hadn't seen it, felt it, *known* it to be true before now.

But then I'd always suspected I wasn't the smartest person in the world.

"Please, Mitch, I—"

"Go away, Katie," he said, still not turning to look at me. I grabbed hold of his sweater with both hands, fists clinging tight, willing him to turn around and look at me.

"No, I'm not going away." I sucked in a deep breath, shouting to be heard over the howling of the wind. "I love you. I don't love Isaac, I love *you*."

"I don't care."

I cried harder, angry and hurt and sad and panicked and scared all at once. This *couldn't* be happening. It couldn't be too late. "Please, don't do this. I know I'm stupid. I know I've made mistakes, but I have been a good friend to you. I love—"

"Go away!" Mitch turned around too fast, yanking his sweater out of my hands, angling his body just a little too far to the right.

I knew he was going to fall before he did and dove for him, but it was too late. I screamed as he slid off the side of the platform, chin knocking hard against the edge before he dropped like a stone, long body rolling once in the air on the way down, sending his skull to meet the ground first.

It was over so fast, the thirty feet from platform to ground snapped away before I could move a muscle. The dull thud of Mitch's body connecting with mud and leaves came seconds after, a soft, innocuous sound that split something open inside of me, flooding every cell with pure, cold fear.

Suddenly the night went quiet, the rain and the wind and the storm muted by the rage and grief racing each other through my veins, trying to see which one would win, and whether I'd start to scream or cry.

Instead, I called his name.

"Mitch! Mitch!" I leaned over the edge, peering into the darkness, but I couldn't see anything in the shadows on the ground. There was nothing moving down there. Nothing. Not even leaves blowing across the yard.

"Mitch!" His name ended in a ragged sob as another gust of wind shook the platform.

I clung to the wood as my heart pounded in my ears—so fast and loud I couldn't hear myself think. I was so afraid, so horribly, terribly afraid. My fear was a giant crushing monster that laughed in my face, taunting me with my absolute stupidity. I'd thought I'd felt terror so many times in the past few weeks, but I hadn't known the meaning of the word. *This* was hopeless, mind-numbing fear—knowing Mitch might be hurt, broken, or . . .

"No. No, no, no," I chanted beneath my breath, the shattered note in my own voice making me bite my numb lip.

I couldn't lose it now. I had to get down there. I had to get to Mitch. I had to find help. It wasn't that far to fall. He *had* to be okay. Maybe he was unconscious, maybe bruised or worse, but okay. Mitch couldn't be *gone* because of this. Because of *me*. Because of the—

The locket. Oh, no, oh, God.

In my mind's eye I saw it slither between the rusty bars of the drain—a serpent stealing away from the scene of the crime.

The realization made me shake all over, my entire body trembling and twitching with pure, unadulterated fear. I knew in that instant that I was never going to make it down the ladder on my own. I was too afraid of those slick steps, of the vast, hungry darkness, and of the horrible permanence of whatever I'd find lying in the leaves beneath the platform I'd made.

"Dad! Dad! Help! Dad!" I screamed and screamed as tears spilled down my face, hot against my frozen cheeks. I screamed until my throat was raw and my body ached, I screamed until I was certain no one would ever hear but kept screaming anyway, too afraid to stop and confront the enormity of my sins.

Finally, someone answered my call, and a familiar voice called my name.

For a split second, I thought it was Mitch, but then the shout came again. It was Dad. He'd heard me. I inched forward, just far enough to peer over the platform. A flashlight cut a path through the rain, its beam wobbling as my overweight, out-of-shape father stumbled toward me in the slick mud and leaves. Even with his baked-goods belly and thin, balding hair plastered to his face, in that moment Dad was the hero he'd been to me when I was small, the strong, loving man who could heal every hurt with a kiss and a smile.

If only he could fix this. If only he could fix Mitch.

"Dad! Mitch is hurt! He fell!" I yelled, praying he could hear me over the wailing of the wind. "Call 911!"

I saw Dad turn and heard him shout for someone to call an ambulance. It was only then that I saw my mother struggling through the rain behind Dad, still wrapped in her pink housecoat. She only hesitated a fraction of a second before turning and hurrying back toward the house.

I realized then that my hands were bleeding. The tips of several fingers throbbed and tacky warmth made my skin stick to the wood even when I forced myself to relax my claw-like hold on the platform. I'd ripped some of my nails away from my fingertips.

I observed this detail with an odd detachment as I watched my dad take the last few steps that would lead him to Mitch. "He's in the leaves. Underneath me!" I shouted to my father, my words ending in a sharp intake of breath as his flashlight fell on Mitch.

My best friend lay in a tangle, his long limbs bent at unnatural angles, his neck twisted sharply to one side. It reminded me of the vision I'd had while we were picking apples, of my own damaged body after an imaginary fall off the stupid orchard ladder. But this wasn't a vision. It was real. Heart-stoppingly real.

A part of me knew Mitch was dead even before my father bent down and brought his fingers gently to Mitch's jawline, feeling for a pulse that wasn't there. Before those interminable seconds passed as Dad searched another place on Mitch's neck and then another. Before my father stood and his shoulders began to shake. Before he looked up at me, his eyes dark hollows I couldn't see inside.

But I didn't need to see. I'd already seen enough.

Chapter Twenty-One

SUNDAY, OCTOBER 11, 1:24 A.M.

I don't remember getting down the ladder. I remembered Dad's hands on my back, I remembered his soothing voice, I remembered the smell of wet leaves clinging to his clothes—but not the individual movements it took for him to help me from one place to another. I couldn't guess how long it took, only that it took longer than it should have.

By the time we reached the ground, the rain had stopped and an ambulance was pulling into the drive.

Red and white light pulsed through the air. Three high-powered flashlights that made my dad's seem pitiful in comparison were flicked on and trained in our direction. I squinted, momentarily blinded, but recovered in time to watch three large shadows and two smaller ones hurry down the gentle slope.

They were coming for Mitch, trained medical professionals.

They would see that he was okay, and that my dad's whispered words of comfort were pointless. Mitch wasn't dead. There was no need to be "so sorry."

I started in Mitch's direction, but Dad stopped me with a hand on my shoulder.

"No, Katie, you don't want to—"

"I'm going with him," I said, shrugging my dad off, knocking his hand away when he reached for me again. "I'm going with him to the hospital!"

I ran, suddenly needing to get to Mitch before the men rushing toward him. I needed to touch him, feel the life still inside of him, *know* that he was going to be okay before anyone else laid a hand on him. They didn't know him, they didn't love him, they didn't need him to be alive the way I did. That need would make a difference. It *had* to make a difference.

When I reached the place where Mitch lay so terribly still, I fell to my knees, jeans sinking into the mud, hands slipping in wet leaves as I braced myself and leaned over to peer into his face. I knew better than to risk moving him, but I needed to see his eyes, needed to see the pulse fluttering behind his closed lids. I'd be able to see it now. The flashlights were so bright, there was no way I could miss the slightest sign of—

The sound I made when my eyes met Mitch's wide, unblinking gaze was barely human. It was an alien wail of pain and grief and a regret so profound it nearly stopped my heart. It actually might have. It was only when the stretcher thudded softly onto the ground on Mitch's other side that the organ jerked in my chest, sending a jolt of agony flowing down into my arms.

"Move back. Get her back." It was a male voice but female hands that grabbed me and pulled me away.

"Come on, honey." It was my mom, her voice soft and thick, her hands as strong as they'd ever been, holding me tight even when I began to struggle.

"Let me go."

"Sweetheart, please, you have to—"

"No! Please, I need to be with him," I screamed, panic dumping into my blood as I watched the medics' fingers roam swiftly and efficiently over Mitch's still form and come away limp and lacking intention. I knew what those purposeless hands meant. They meant there was nothing they could do, no hope, no trick of medicine that could undo what had been done.

I heard the words "police" and "family" and my mother saying something about Dr. Birnbaum being on his way from the hospital in Nashville, but my mind couldn't seem to focus on anything but the sight of Mitch's body still lying twisted in the leaves, all the Mitch-ness drained out of it. All the wonderful, hilarious, talented, sweet, loving beauty of him gone forever.

I shook my head, hard enough to send my wet hair flying into my eyes.

This couldn't be real. This couldn't be how it ended. This was some sick joke, a tragic nightmare. I was going to wake up any second, my pillowcase wet from crying the way it had been half a dozen times since the locket came into my life, and thank God that this was only a—

"The locket." *The locket.* It hadn't been *that* long since I threw it into the drain. I could still find it, put it back on, and *force* it to give me the chance to save Mitch's life. I'd promise anything, suffer any depraved trick of fate, if only Mitch could be alive again.

I twisted in my mother's arms, my movement so swift it caught her by surprise. The second I was free, I dashed toward the garage, legs churning so fast I stumbled and fell in the slick leaves more than once. Maybe twice, maybe three times—I couldn't say for sure, only that I was up and on my way again in seconds, driven to reach that drain with everything in me.

When I did, I crouched down, swiping away the leaves that had clustered around one edge. I squinted into the darkness, praying for a flash of silver, but saw nothing more than I had the first time. The rain had stopped, but a steady stream of water still flowed from the adjoining yard, trickling into the drain on its way downhill. I could hear it falling and falling, dropping several feet before it rushed away in a different direction. The sound wasn't promising. The drain sounded clear of leaves and sticks and anything that would snag a piece of jewelry and hold it prisoner, but I had to try. Two large screws held the drain in place. They were rusty, but with the right tool I could twist them out.

I rushed into the garage, flicked on the light, and hurried over to Dad's toolbox, shocked by the relative warmth of the space. I hadn't realized how cold I was, so cold the heated air bit at my skin and made me hurry to get back outside, back to where the world was numb and frozen. I didn't want to feel anything, not until Mitch was back in the world and feeling with me.

My wrecked hands shook as they fumbled with the metal latch on the toolbox. The nails on my middle and ring fingers had been torn away from the quick, leaving trails of red that had settled into the wrinkles on my hand, highlighting every imperfection, making me look a hundred years old.

I felt a thousand. Fear rushed through my body like some super-virus, shredding me from the inside out. I had to get that drain open. I had to find the locket. I had to bring Mitch back.

I found the screwdriver I needed but tried to stand too quickly. The cold, tight muscles in my back seized, making me scream. I was bent over—hands braced on my knees, struggling for breath as I waited for the spasm to pass—when my family trudged through the door. Mom came first, followed by Dad, and then a bleary-eyed Gran, fresh from sleep. Her curlers were still in her hair and a quilted housecoat peeked from beneath her rain jacket.

"Katie, honey, what are you doing?" My mom's eyes were red from crying, and the light blue bags beneath them seemed deeper, harder than they ever had before.

"I lost the locket. I have to find it," I said, fighting to stand up and finally succeeding despite the clenching in my back.

"What?" She turned to Dad, who only shook his head. Sadly. So sadly.

"Gran's locket. I lost it down the drain. I have to find it."

"My locket?" Gran asked, with that same confusion I'd seen the other times I'd questioned her during the past two weeks. "I'm not missing any jewelry. I don't think I've ever even owned a—"

"Yes, you have," I said, willing Gran to remember. "The locket I've been wearing used to be yours. I know you don't believe me, but—"

"But Katie, honey, you never wear jewelry." Mom reached for me, as if she would pull me back into her arms. I stepped back, holding the screwdriver up between us, a silent warning not to touch me. I couldn't be touched or I'd shatter into a million pieces.

"I've been wearing the locket for two weeks straight."

My mom sighed and shook her head. "I'm sorry, Katie. I don't know what you're—"

"But I *talked* to you about it," I said, voice rising as my eyes flicked between the three of them. "You and Dad and Gran!"

Dad's crumpled face told me what all three of them were thinking. They thought I was crazy. That I'd lost my mind because of what happened to Mitch. Because Mitch was dead.

Oh, God. Mitch was dead. He was really *dead*.

I swallowed hard, fighting back a wave of hysteria. It didn't matter that my family didn't remember the locket. *I* remembered the locket. I knew it could help me. It had saved Rachel's life and now it would save Mitch's.

"Just let me go." I pushed past my dad and hurried back to the drain. I felt my family follow and stand in the doorway, staring down at me, but put all my focus into removing the screws standing in my way.

The cover came off relatively easily considering the age of the screws, and thankfully my arm was thin enough to fit down the pipe. I thrust my hand down, deeper and deeper, the despair in me growing with every inch that my questing fingers explored and found nothing. Nothing, nothing at all, not even a—

"I remember when Harold put in that drainage system," Gran said, a wistful note in her voice. "We were the only house in the area back then. Our closest neighbors were almost half a mile—"

"Grandpa put this here?" I pulled my arm from the pipe, the importance of her words sinking into my soggy, frozen skull. "Do you know where it empties out?"

Gran pursed her lips. "Well, I did . . . It's one of those French drainage systems, to carry off the extra water that kept flooding the low place in the backyard. I thought I remember him laying the pipes down the hill toward the street in that direction, but—"

I grabbed the flashlight from Dad's hand and was off before she could finish, running through our yard and into the neighbor's, setting a dog to barking as I went. The locket wasn't lodged in the drain—at least not anywhere that I could reach—but if I could locate the place where Grandpa's drainage system emptied . . .

Three yards, two more dogs, and one jumped chain-link fence later, I'd followed Gran's finger down the hill to Skylar Street. It was the road Isaac and I had taken out into the country the first time I'd lived through my seventeenth birthday, only a hundred feet or so down from Mitch's house, close enough that I could see the headlights as Mitch's father turned into the driveway.

Mitch's dad. He was about to view his only child's dead body. First his wife, and now the son who meant everything to him. I couldn't let this happen. I had to spare him that soul-destroying pain.

Frantic, I trained the flashlight on the ground. Thankfully, it only took a few seconds to find what I was looking for. For once, Gran's memory had been dead-on. An old pipe jutted slightly from the concrete curb, spilling water into the street, flowing more slowly now that the rain had stopped. I pinned its stream with my light and followed it along the side of the road for five, ten, fifteen feet, until the wide mouth of a modern drain swallowed the little river whole.

A bitter taste filled my mouth and my cold muscles cramped again. My plan had failed. The locket was either hung up somewhere in the maze of pipes beneath mine and my neighbors' yards or it had already vanished into the vast drainage system beneath Brantley Hills. There was no way I would be able to find it. It was over, there was no—

No. No! My jaw clenched tight. I wasn't going to give up on Mitch that easily. I wouldn't give up on him, period. Ever. I'd dig up every inch of pipe my grandfather had laid, search through every sewer from here to Nashville.

Starting with this one.

The end of the flashlight just barely fit between my teeth. I held it in my mouth and used both hands to brace against the pavement as I dropped to my belly and slid my legs into the rectangular drain. Refusing to think about rats and other terrifying things that lived beneath the streets, I wiggled backward, until the weight of my lower body pulled the top half of me down into the darkness.

I fell for scarcely half a second—no more than two feet before my shoes made contact with more concrete—but it was enough to send my racing heart skyrocketing into dangerous territory. The world swam black and red and the flashlight slipped from my tingling lips, rolling to a stop a few feet away. I struggled to stay upright through the dizzy spell even though everything in me wanted to drop to the ground and dig my fingers into the muck, clinging to something low and safe.

Falling. That was what I was *really* afraid of.

I was afraid that I'd lose control and fall and every watchful step I'd taken would be for nothing. It was why I'd avoided heights, and change, and conflict. It was why I stuttered through every audition, a part of me determined to sabotage myself. Better to ensure my own understudy status than to go for the part I wanted and be shot down. Better to stick to the plan than veer off course and fail, even if that failure was in the name of love.

I'd tried to be so, *so* careful, but I'd failed anyway. Spectacularly. Horribly.

Still, there was a chance I could make things right, a chance I could undo what had been done, go back and choose not to take the easy way out, not to break my best friend's heart, and not to build that stupid, *stupid* tree house.

I bent to retrieve my fallen flashlight and froze, afraid to believe what I was seeing. There, in the thin beam of light, a shy bit of silver shone among the mud and the leaves and the crushed beer cans. Between half a Dunkin' Donuts coffee cup and something soggy that might once have been a sock, the locket waited patiently for me to come to my senses. To pick it up and put it back on.

I snatched at it with shaking hands, praying my cold-numbed fingers would be able to work the clasp. After propping up the flashlight to illuminate more of the space, I brought the two halves around my neck, refusing to listen to the voice in my head screaming that the locket wouldn't make things better.

I didn't care if the locket made things better. I just wanted Mitch back. Alive.

"Come on. Come on," I whispered, crying out when I forgot about my ruined nails and tried to use one to capture the clasp. I swallowed the pain, ignoring the feeling of fresh blood trickling down my middle finger, using my pointer finger instead.

One try. Two. Three. Four. Five. My neck cramped and my hands shook and sweat beaded on my forehead despite the cold, but I didn't give up. I couldn't. I couldn't let—

My breath rushed out as the tiny metal loop finally slipped home and the clasp closed around it. The locket fell heavily against my chest, glad to be back. It would work now. It would give Mitch a second chance at life. It *had* to work. It simply had to.

"Please, please, please take me back," I whispered, squeezing my eyes shut and imagining myself back at the coffee shop, the day I'd first had the idea to build Mitch the platform that had been the death of him.

"Please. Please, help me make this right." My aching fingers wrapped around the locket, fisting tight, praying for the slightest change in temperature. But the locket remained cold, even colder than my frostbitten hands.

I was asking for too much, too much time, too many opportunities. I was being greedy. That's why the locket wouldn't take me back.

"Okay, okay." My words echoed in the closeness of the concrete drain, the desperation in my voice terrifying. "Then take me back an hour, to right before he fell. I'll catch him. I'll find a way to keep him safe." I waited, bringing both hands to wrap around the locket, funneling every ounce of energy I had left into the lump of metal, wishing harder than I'd ever wished before. "Please, I'll give you anything you want. You can ruin my life, wreck my future, anything, but please . . . please . . ."

My voice broke, tears so close I could taste them on the back of my tongue. I bit my lip and held my breath, refusing to give up hope. The locket would take me back. It would feel how much I needed this, how much I was willing to suffer for Mitch's second chance, and it would turn back time.

I had to be ready, I had to be prepared to grab on to him and hold him tight, to physically overpower him if I had to. I was shorter and smaller, but I could do it. Knowing Mitch was about to die would give me the strength I needed. People lifted cars off their children and performed super-human feats of physical strength when the people they loved were in danger. I'd take one look into Mitch's beautiful brown eyes, see the life still in him, and be able to move mountains.

Two seconds passed, then three, then five, and still the locket sat quietly, unmoved by my prayers and promises.

"Please. Please!" I brought my clenched hands to my lips and whispered into them, warm breath sneaking through tight fingers to heat the metal inside ever so slightly. But the heat faded when I pulled in my next breath and the last chance nestled between my palms grew so cold it felt like I was clutching a chunk of ice.

There was only one more thing to try . . .

I uncurled my hands, letting the locket fall back to my chest as I reached for the clasp. It took some time to find it beneath my wet, tangled hair and another moment to catch the tiny bit of metal beneath my fingernail, but when I did, the clasp gave under the slightest pressure. The locket's chain slithered from around my neck as the locket fell into my lap.

I reached down, thumbing open the clasp, not as surprised as I should have been when I saw a faded picture of me on one side and a grainy picture of Mitch on the other. The pictures were black and white, charmingly old fashioned, the kind of thing a girl couldn't help but pick up and put on.

The new girl, the next one in line, whoever she might be.

I knew then that it was over. It was really over. The locket didn't want me anymore. There weren't going to be any more do overs. From here on out, all my mistakes were meant to last. Including this one.

Mitch was dead. And he was never coming back.

The realization possessed me like some evil spirit, flooding into every cell and infecting it with the cancer of despair. The tears came, fast and furious, fierce sobs that rocked through my body, tightening every muscle as they grew harder and harder. I cried like I'd never cried before, salty heat rushing down my face like the rainwater that had rushed into the drain. They just kept coming and coming, more tears than I'd known my body could hold, pouring from me as if their sheer quantity could purge all my guilt and shame and heartache.

But they couldn't. Nothing could.

Dimly, I heard my parents' panicked voices screaming for me in the world above, but I couldn't bring myself to call back to them. I didn't want to rejoin the living, not when the person I'd loved more than anything was dead.

Chapter Twenty-Two

SUNDAY, OCTOBER 11, 4:54 P.M.

I open my eyes to sunshine, so much sunshine, like melted lemon-drop candy smeared all over the world. It takes my eyes a few minutes to adjust, but I know where I am immediately. The old community pool, the one where Mitch and Isaac and I learned to swim, the one the city had torn down to make a bigger, better pool by the time we were teenagers.

The smell of chlorine and sunscreen, hot dogs and melted orange Push-Up ice cream, is unmistakable. When I wiggle my toes, I can feel the hot, cracked concrete beneath my bare feet. A light summer breeze blows the end of my ponytail into my face, tickling my nose, making me smile.

"Are you going to jump today?"

I turn to see Mitch standing next to me. Little Mitch, the boy with tiny stick legs, teeth too big for his mouth, and short, shaggy hair that sticks up in a hundred different directions. But the eyes are the same—deep, soulful brown eyes that see right to the heart of me and know everything I'm thinking. He knows I'm scared of the high dive even though I haven't said anything out loud.

But for some reason . . . today I think I might be able to do it. I fist my small hands at my sides and stand up a little taller. I still only reach Mitch's chin. I must be little too. I look down, taking in my red one-piece swimsuit with the Strawberry Shortcake on my slightly rounded belly and smile again.

I turn back to Mitch and take his hand. "Yes, I'm ready. Let's get in line."

"Are you sure?" he asks, obviously surprised. "You don't want to go hide under the bleachers with me and Isaac?"

"Why would Isaac hide?" I ask. "Isaac's not afraid."

"Of course I'm not." Seven-year-old Isaac appears on my other side. His blond hair is bleached nearly white from the sun and his skin dark brown except for a single white stripe across his nose that refuses to tan. His blue eyes are full of trouble. As usual. "But I've got firecrackers. We can hide under the bleachers, wait until Tim's about to jump, and set them off."

Tim. The lifeguard who had pushed me off the high dive. The thought is tempting . . . "But what if it scares him?" I ask Isaac. "What if he falls?" For some reason the thought of someone falling terrifies me, makes me shiver despite the heat of the summer day.

Isaac wrinkles his nose. "He won't fall. Don't be a baby, Katie."

"Katie's right," Mitch says. "And my dad won't let me play with fireworks."

"You don't have to tell your dad," Isaac says, his words a challenge.

"He'd find out." Mitch's arms cross over his thin chest. "You know we'd get caught. There's a fence around the entire pool. It's not like we could set them off and run away. Tim would find out we did it and he'd tell our parents."

Isaac's eyes narrow and his lips push into a pout. He obviously hadn't thought that far ahead. "Fine, then let's just go do the high dive. Come on, babies."

I hesitate, suddenly not sure if the high dive is such a good idea.

"Don't worry," Mitch whispers. "I'll go first. When you see me jump, you'll feel better." Before I can answer, he turns and runs after Isaac, long feet flapping on the hot pavement.

"No. No, wait," I call after him, but it's too late.

Suddenly he's at the top of the high dive, waving at me. Panic streaks through my body, but I don't understand why, not until my eyes flick down to the pool. Oh, no. There's no water! Nothing but concrete painted blue and white to look like ocean waves.

"No! Don't jump!" I scream, but Mitch doesn't seem to hear. He bounces on the board one last time and—

I woke up with a gasp, eyes flying wide, sucking in deep breaths, staring blindly at the muted television across the room. Colored ribbons reporting the latest headlines and stock market numbers streamed across the bottom of the screen and a woman with dark brown hair motioned at a weather map with vigorous sweeps of her arms. In the flowered chair next to the television, my gran slept, snoring softly. Next to the chair, on the love seat, Dad frowned, unhappy with whatever awfulness the news ribbon had to share.

For a second, I wasn't sure why I was asleep in the living room, but then it came back to me in pieces—a policewoman slipping into the drain to pull me out because Dad and Mom wouldn't fit through the narrow drain opening, my parents half carrying me home and stripping off my wet clothes, my mom dressing me and putting me to sleep on the couch.

I vaguely recalled awakening once before, when Sarah had come by with a note apologizing for what had happened with her and Isaac. As if that mattered now. I couldn't care less what she and Isaac had done. Still, I couldn't help but wonder what would have happened if I'd been brave enough to confess and apologize instead of lying and wishing for something to make my lie the truth.

Mom had taken her note at the door and told Sarah I wasn't up to seeing visitors. Then she'd broken the horrible news. I'd awoken to the sound of Sarah crying and lost it, sobbing so hard I thought I'd be sick before Mom forced me to drink a tall glass of water and take a small white pill. Soon after, I'd fallen back into the oblivion, eager for the escape from conscious thought.

But the misery had found me, even in my dreams.

I closed my eyes, wishing desperately that the dream had been real, that Mitch and Isaac and I were little kids again and had the chance to make everything turn out differently. But wishing didn't accomplish any more than it had the night before, when I'd passed out with the locket still clenched in my hand.

The locket . . . it was still there, resting in a basket of my curled fingers.

I lifted my head from my pillow and stared down at it, hating it more than ever. How dare it still exist? How dare it lie so heavy and solid in my hand when Mitch was gone? When I'd never see him or touch him or laugh with him ever again?

I was suddenly possessed by the urge to destroy it. For real, this time. It had hurt so many people—Sarah, Isaac, Mitch, and everyone who had loved and lost him. Mitch's death would spread grief through this entire community, dimming the spirits of a hundred souls or more, teaching people who had never known what real loss felt like how painful death could be when it came too soon. The locket had done that, and there was nothing I could do to change the past.

All I could do was try to ensure the safety of the future.

"Katie? What's wrong? Where are you going?" Dad startled as I threw off my covers and reached for my boots. They were still cold and wet, but I barely noticed. So my shoes were wet. What did it matter? Mitch was dead. That horrible fact made all the little worries of day-to-day life seem ridiculous, trivial.

"I need to take a drive." I stood and did a quick scan. Long-sleeved homecoming T-shirt and black sweatpants. My body was covered. That was all I needed to know. I couldn't care less what I looked like. I couldn't imagine I ever would.

"Do you think that's smart, honey?" Dad rose to his feet and I could see him debating whether or not to call for Mom. "You took a Xanax this morning."

The little white pill. My mom must have been really freaked.

She'd never given me anything stronger than an ibuprofen, let alone one of her "only for long-distance plane flights" Xanax.

I grabbed my keys from the dish by the door. "I feel fine. I just need to be alone. I need to think."

"Why don't you go to your room? I can make sure no one—"

"Please, Dad," I said, pausing with my hand on the handle.

"Mitch's funeral is tomorrow morning. First thing." I could see how much the words hurt my father. He'd loved Mitch so much, even more than my mom had, I guessed, as a tear rolled down his scruffy face. "I wouldn't want you to miss that. I know it's not going to be easy, but—"

"Please, Dad." I swallowed hard, trying not to think about the reality of mourning Mitch in public with his casket sitting across the room. "I'm not running away from home. I just . . . Just let me go for a drive."

"I don't think—"

"Let her go, Andrew." Gran was awake and staring at me with sad green eyes. Eyes filled with understanding.

She knew what it was like to lose the person you loved, how it made you want to run and run and never look back. In the years since Grandpa's death, Gran had traveled constantly, not once coming back to the house she'd shared with her husband. I'd always thought she had better things to do than visit, but maybe it had taken her twelve years to gain the strength to sit in the rooms she'd shared with the man she'd loved so much and lost to cancer.

"Do what you need to do, Katie," Gran said, her words sending a shiver across my skin. It was almost as if she knew about the locket . . . .though I knew she didn't. Still, her words made me feel stronger. "We love you. We're here for you when you're ready."

"I love you too," I said, swallowing away the burning taste of tears teasing at the back of my throat. I couldn't cry anymore. Not until this was really over. I hurried out the door before my dad could utter another word of protest.

Outside, my car was in its usual spot, which surprised me for some reason. How could so many things be the same when the world was so changed? How could leaves fall through the air with that pretty whispering sound? How could the air smell so clean and bright? How could those kids across the street practically scream with laughter as they raced each other down the sidewalk?

I turned away from the two little girls on their bikes. They reminded me too much of what Isaac and Mitch and I had been.

Inside the car, I tossed the locket into my dirty, sticky cup holder, started up the engine, and darted out of the driveway, a part of me knowing where I was going even before I took the right onto Skylar Street and headed out into the country.

Water hadn't banished the locket. It was time to see what fire could do.

I pulled into the drive-in less than thirty minutes later and steered straight around to the back, finding a parking spot within spitting distance of the Pit. Lovelace's—the corn dog shack where Isaac had been bound the night of our anniversary—didn't just have the best shakes and dogs on a stick in the county. They also had an infamous fire pit, a sizable flame my dad had always said was a lawsuit waiting to happen.

During the day, families with little kids roasted the marshmallows that came with the kids' meals around that pit, warming up after a wholesome afternoon of fun at the nearby historical park. At night, the pit became a sketchier place. People from the surrounding towns clustered around the flames with pockets filled with cash, waiting for someone to come along with a pocket full of something more interesting.

Whether Mr. and Mrs. Lovelace—two old hippies who lived in a trailer not too far from the restaurant—realized their fire pit was *the* place to buy weed or not, I didn't know. But they certainly didn't seem to mind people hanging around their fire pit. They didn't even care if you bought food first.

I hadn't eaten all day, but the thought of a greasy corn dog wasn't the slightest bit tempting. It was as if my body had forgotten how to be hungry, how to do anything but focus on the ache deep in my bones, the physical pain caused by losing Mitch that felt like it would never go away.

The locket remained cool to the touch as I plucked it from the cup holder and started toward the fire that burned as high and bright as I remembered. The Lovelaces' adult son, a man who was "not quite right" but harmless except for his fascination with fire—which his parents had wisely funneled into fueling the Pit rather than torching barns—tended his flame well. I could feel the heat on my face when I was still a few feet away.

I prayed it would be hot enough to melt silver, to destroy the misery I held in my hand.

I stopped at the edge of the Pit, alone except for a mom and her little girl on the other side, both too absorbed in stabbing marshmallows with a wire hanger to pay much attention to me. Even when I tossed the still cool locket into the flames, the mother's eyes only flicked to mine for a second.

The little girl, an orange redhead like I'd been when I was small, with a trail of untended snot leaking down into her mouth, stared a little longer, but eventually she too looked back to the fire, seemingly curious to see what would happen next.

I stood there and stared, watching the flames lick at the locket until the little girl finished her marshmallows and her mother herded her back into their car, until two more families came and left, until finally, after thirty or forty minutes, the locket began to melt. The change was subtle at first—a barely perceptible smudging that I thought was my eyesight blurring—but soon it became clear that the locket was going soft, the connection of its particles breaking apart in the intense heat. In another ten minutes or so, the process was complete and the locket a puddle of liquid metal that might eventually harden if the Lovelaces' son allowed his fire to cool.

A part of me hoped he wouldn't. I didn't want that poisonous thing to ever be solid again.

Just in case, I grabbed one of the unbent wire hangers meant for marshmallows from the bucket nearby and stabbed at the coals around the melted silver. The liquid slipped away into the ash beneath, streaming apart, never to be whole again.

It was over. Really over. As much as it ever could be.

Suddenly more exhausted than I could remember, I turned away from the flames, just in time to see the flash of lightning strike above Lovelace's.

It hit so close I could feel the electricity on my skin, raising every little hair, making me gasp and lift my hands as if to block a blow, squeezing my eyes shut a second too late.

As the thunder clapped down, shaking the very ground beneath my feet, the red double of the lightning bolt burned behind my lids. Even when I opened my eyes, the image danced and teased in front of me, blurring my vision, making it difficult to understand what I was seeing until Isaac's truck had already pulled onto the main road and started back toward town.

Isaac's truck. His muddy truck ... pulling away in a squeal of tires ...

My mind couldn't process the information for a moment or two. It was only when I looked across the street and saw the familiar field of cows that a seed of suspicion was planted. I looked down—taking in the black shirt and skirt, lifting a strand of long red hair, noting the absence of a certain piece of jewelry—and that seed burst open, swiftly growing into a bean stalk I would have climbed into the sky to face that ogre I'd been so afraid of when I was a little girl.

I would face any ogre, any kid fear or grown-up misery, if only this were real, if only I was back to where I'd started and Mitch was still alive.

I ran, first in my high-heeled sandals and then kicking them off and running barefoot along the side of the road, feet slapping against the sun-warmed pavement. The sunset still painted the sky a hopeful, gentle shade of red, but I knew the storm would hit soon. If I ran all the way, I could be halfway home before that happened and calling Mitch another ten or fifteen minutes after that.

I might hear his voice within the hour. I might see him—alive and whole—before the night was through.

A vicious hope swelled inside of me, making me cry and laugh at the same time, giving me a wild strength, inspiring a speed I hadn't known I possessed. I had run over a mile and was nearly to the historical park by the time the storm hit. The sky opened up and poured, the way it had the first time around, but I didn't mind the cutting drops.

They were cool against my face, soothing to my stinging feet, full of wonder and faith. The whole world seemed brighter, sweeter, even the rain a kinder, better version of itself. Life and time were back to what they should be. I knew it. I could feel it with everything in me.

By the time I reached the end of Skylar Street, I was positive that Mitch was alive, even before I made it around the bend and saw the family van pulling into the Birnbaums' driveway or the long, lean shadow leap from the car and dash through the rain toward the garage.

Chapter Twenty-Three

He was alive! Mitch was alive!

I screamed his name—once, twice—but he couldn't hear. I was still too far away. But that was okay. I was nearly there. Soon, I'd be able to throw my arms around him and squeeze, to feel the heat and breath and *life* inside him, to know without a doubt that this nightmare was over!

The thought fueled my flagging muscles, soothed the numbness and pain in my scraped feet. I sprinted the final stretch, flying past the drain where I'd lost my mind the night before and the remaining houses before Mitch's. By the time I reached his driveway, I was breathing so hard little spots pricked at the edge of my vision, but I didn't slow down until I reached the garage, until I stepped inside and saw the boy I loved with my own eyes.

There he was. Mitch. *My Mitch.* Slightly damp and wrinkled, wearing an old pair of jeans and his faded red OMG, WTF, BBQ! hoodie. I'd never seen anything so beautiful.

I sucked in a deep breath and silently sent out a prayer of thanks. Even if he hated me, even if he told me to go away and never come back, everything was going to be all right. He was alive. The force of my gratitude was dizzying, making me sway on my feet. The emotion was so intense, so overwhelming, that it took a few seconds for me to realize that Mitch hadn't heard me come inside.

Or that he was singing.

"Hair like a Muppet, but it makes me smile." The lyrics echoed through the empty garage, haunting and sweet over the rhythm of the rain. Mitch was sitting on a stool with his back to me, strumming his guitar, singing that song I hadn't heard in this life. Not yet.

But I *knew* who it was about, and what it meant.

Hope curled in my chest, a thread of smoke in a pile of wet firewood. I tiptoed toward him, bare feet quiet on the concrete. I didn't want him to hear me coming. I wanted to listen, to soak in the sound of his voice. It was so lovely, so perfect. I'd never listened to something so intently, never felt music sneak into my soul and light me up from the inside. I would never take Mitch or his songs or his heart for granted again. Ever. The locket had made sure of that.

My fingers came to my chest, brushing against smooth skin. The scars were gone, erased, as if the past two weeks had never happened.

But they *had* happened. They had pulled me apart, nearly

destroyed me. They'd ripped my life to pieces and shown me I had the strength to put them back together again. I wasn't afraid to fall anymore. I was too grateful for this chance to worry about the danger lurking in the next step up the ladder. Nothing was going to keep me from telling Mitch how much he meant to me, how much I loved him, how much I hoped—

"Sarah, this song's for you. Sarah, the things you make me do." His voice was rich and smooth, but the words made me flinch. My stomach lurched. "Sa-sa-sarah, won't you be my girl?"

Sarah. He was singing about *Sarah*.

A choking sound filled the air, cutting off the music. I didn't realize it had come from me until Mitch spun around, nearly dropping his guitar. "Hey!" He ran a nervous hand through his hair and jumped to his feet. "You scared me. I thought you were out with . . . Are you okay?" His gaze tracked down my body and back up again, the concern in his eyes growing. "Why are you all wet? Where are your shoes?" He set his guitar in its stand and took a tentative step forward. "Katie?"

My tongue moved in my mouth, but I couldn't speak. All I could do was stand and stare as the pain of realizing he didn't love me seeped into my skin, chilling me in a way even the rain hadn't been able to manage. He loved *Sarah*. It was Sarah's name he'd whisper while they were kissing, Sarah's skin he'd run his guitar-calloused fingertips over when they were together. I'd had my chance and I'd lost it.

But . . . that was . . . okay.

My eyes squeezed shut. No, it wasn't *okay*. It was far, far from okay. It hurt like hell. But not the way losing Mitch had hurt, not even a shadow of that kind of pain. He was alive, and he was going to be happy and in love. I was just going to have to love him enough to put my feelings aside and be happy for him.

"Katie, I'm going to go call your—"

"No, wait," I said, stopping him before he could turn toward the door leading into the house. "I just wanted to say . . . I'm sorry. And to let you know that . . . Isaac and me . . . we're over."

"Oh, man. I'm sorry." He really did look sad to hear the news. The regret on his face twisted the knife in my chest another quarter turn. "Was it because of—"

I nodded. "Someone told him. *I* should have told him, but I didn't, but I should have," I babbled, failing to hold back the stream of stupid. "Anyway. It's okay. Breaking up was the right thing to do. It's for the best."

"No, it isn't. It never should have happened. I never should have . . ." His eyes fell to the oil-stained concrete beneath our feet, his hair flopping into his face. "You were really upset that night, and you'd been drinking. I knew that and I still . . . did what I did. I shouldn't have."

"I wasn't *that* drunk," I whispered. "I knew what I was doing."

"Yeah . . . well." He looked up, eyes so beautiful they broke things inside me and healed them at the same time. A wave of pure, unselfish love rushed through my chest, leaving me breathless.

He was alive. All that light and intelligence and silliness that was Mitch still sparked inside him. His father wouldn't have to grieve, all the people who loved him could go on loving him, and the world would be a better place because this boy was going to live a long, full life. In the end, it was all that mattered.

"Still, I'm sorry," he said.

"It's okay." And it would be. Eventually. "I just wanted you to know. You should probably talk to Isaac. Not today, but . . . soon."

"I will."

"So . . . can we be best friends again?" I sucked in a breath, so close to tears I sounded like I'd inhaled a helium balloon.

Mitch smiled, that soft smile that meant he still loved me the way he'd always loved me, as a friend, as chosen family. Maybe someday I'd come to love him like that again too. Maybe . . .

"We never stopped being best friends. Don't be crazy, Minnesota."

"Okay. Good." I tried for a smile and failed. "I'll work on the crazy." I pushed the tears pressing against the backs of my eyes away and kept them there, even when I realized I still owed my friend a final, painful thumbs-up. "And you should probably know that Sarah saw us . . . out by the pool that night."

"Sarah Needles?" he asked, brows drawing together.

"She told her little brother and he told Isaac. I don't know if that'll make a difference when she hears the song, but . . . I thought you should know."

"When she hears what song?"

"The song you were singing. The song you wrote for her." The words stabbed me on their way out.

"That song's not for Sarah." Mitch shook his head. "I mean, it *is* for her, but it's not for *me*. Not *from* me."

Every muscle in my body tensed. "It's not?"

"It's for Michael." Mitch stepped closer, a half smile quirking his full lips. "He wants to sing it to her at our next gig. We're playing Jukebox Java on Thursday and she said she'd come."

"But what about the Muppet hair?"

"Sarah kind of has hair like a Muppet, don't you think? In a cute sort of way?" he asked, so close I could smell the scent of cinnamon and apple tea and wet boy clinging to his hoodie. Nothing had ever smelled so good. Ever. "Do you think that will hurt her feelings? I thought she'd think it was funny, but—"

"I thought *I* had hair like a Muppet." I stared up at him, breathless, a part of me still afraid to hope. "Because it's red. And fuzzy."

"Well . . ." He reached out, smoothing a damp strand behind my ear, fingers lingering in my hair. "You have hair like a Muppet too." His tongue swept out to dampen his lips. "Does that make *you* mad?"

"No." I shook my head, gently, careful not to disturb his hand on my face. "I love it." The tears I'd been holding in spilled down my cheeks, silent and sweet, even as my lips trembled into a smile.

"You do?" His other hand came to my cheek, cupping my face. "Then why are you crying?"

"Because I love it. I really do." I made a sound that was half laugh, half sob and fisted my hands in his shirt, pulling him closer, knowing I'd never be able to get him close enough. "I love it *so* much."

Mitch's eyes were full of the same wonder that made my skin too small, that made me certain I'd have to grow a larger one to contain all the joy and amazement and hope and happiness being with him made me feel. "We aren't talking about Muppets now, are we? I really hope we're not talking about Muppets."

"We're not talking about Muppets."

"Then what are we talking about?" he asked, as breathless as I was.

"We're talking about you. About how much I love you." Mitch's face swam as tears filled my eyes again, but I ignored them. I wasn't upset, just too full. I'd never known love could feel like this, like a never-ending fall into blissful possibility and coming home to an old friend all at the same time. "I've probably loved you forever."

He smiled, happiness bursting out all over him until I could have sworn I felt the echo of it along my skin. "You have?"

"I was just too stupid to figure it out until . . . I . . ." How to tell him? What to say? How to explain a nightmare that began with a wish to undo something I knew now I'd never give up? "I . . . I started thinking about what it would be like if you really did stay away from me like I'd asked you to, if you weren't a part of my life anymore. It was . . . the most horrible thing I've ever imagined."

"Worse than breaking up with Isaac?" he asked, showing me the hint of uncertainty that lurked inside him, making him wonder if he was a consolation prize.

"It felt like you'd died," I said, willing him to do what he was best at, to look down into the heart of me and see the truth. "And I wanted to be dead too if I couldn't be with you."

"That's the . . . darkest thing I've ever heard you say," he said, searching my face. I met his eyes and raised him a soul-filled stare, showing him I had nothing left to hide.

"It was dark without you."

"And that's the sweetest thing I've ever heard you say." His arms wrapped around my waist and pulled me tight, hugging me like he knew what it felt like to be lost.

"So say it back," I whispered.

"I love you too, Katie Mottola. I love you so much," he said, his voice breaking. "I love you a sick, disgusting amount that is probably unhealthy."

I pressed my lips together again, trying not to cry any more. I didn't want to do anything to interrupt the words spilling from my best friend's mouth.

"The past two weeks have been the most miserable two weeks of my life. I've lost weight, my dad threatened to put me in therapy, and I actually went down to the Catholic school and got an application to transfer at the end of the semester."

"You did?" I asked, terrified at the thought of BHH without Mitch.

"I did, even though it about gave Bubbe a heart attack," he said, his lips easing that little bit closer. "But I couldn't stand the thought of looking at you for the rest of the year and knowing that you'd never be anything more than my friend. It made me want to go emo and paint black teardrops under my eyes and give up funny shirts forever."

I looked up at him, thrilled to see his lips only inches from mine. We were going to kiss. And this time it would be just him and me—no guilt, no shame, just two people doing what felt so, so right. "I love you."

"I love you too." Then he kissed me, *really* kissed me, kissed me until I couldn't see or smell or taste anything but Mitch, until my nerve endings were fried from the pure overload of awesome and my head spun in dizzy circles like the rain falling outside the garage door.

By the time he pulled away—breath coming as fast as my own—I was pretty sure Mitch was made of magic. Or maybe the two of us together was what made the magic. Real magic. The kind that came from loving someone, the kind that couldn't be wished into existence and wasn't always convenient but was worth every ounce of effort and every bit of pain.

"Come on, let's go find you some dry clothes and make a birthday pizza." Mitch slipped his hand into mine and pulled me toward the door.

"Dry clothes and birthday pizza sound amazing."

"You stick with me, kid. I'll show you all about living large."

"I don't need to live large. I just need you." I smiled and squeezed his hand. "And clothes, and pizza, and some dry socks."

He leaned down and kissed me, just once, a light brush of his lips against mine that warmed me all the way down to the tips of my sockless feet. "All that can definitely be arranged."

And it was.

Acknowledgements

First up, a big shout out to Mel Francis for the *hours* of emergency brainstorming aid. Without her, this book would never have been born. (Thanks, Mel!) Also thanks to Caren Johnson, my agent, and the entire team at Razorbill. Much love to my amazing family, especially my adoration-worthy husband. And lastly, to my readers. You continue to amaze me every day with your pure awesome.